PENGUIN BOOKS
UNDYING AFFINITY

Sara Naveed is the author of *Our Story Ends Here*. Originally from
Pakistan, she spent her adolescent years in Sharjah, UAE. She has a
master's degree in banking and finance, and works as a content head
at a software firm. She lives with her family in Lahore.

You can follow Sara on Twitter (@SaraNaveed) and Instagram
(@sara_naveed) or get in touch with her through her Facebook page
(www.facebook.com/saranaveedwriter).

Undying Affinity

SARA NAVEED

[signature]

PENGUIN BOOKS

An imprint of Penguin Random House

PENGUIN BOOKS

USA | Canada | UK | Ireland | Australia
New Zealand | India | South Africa | China | Singapore

Penguin Books is part of the Penguin Random House group of companies
whose addresses can be found at global.penguinrandomhouse.com

Published by Penguin Random House India Pvt. Ltd
4th Floor, Capital Tower 1, MG Road,
Gurugram 122 002, Haryana, India

First published in Penguin Books by Penguin Random House India 2017

10 9 8 7 6 5 4 3 2

ISBN 9780143428183

Typeset in Sabon by Manipal Digital Systems, Manipal

Printed at Manipal Technologies Limited, India

www.penguin.co.in

*And, when you want something, all the universe
conspires in helping you to achieve it*
—Paulo Coelho, *The Alchemist*

A Message from Fawad Khan

Your undying support and affection makes me feel important. Something that many die for. I've done little in life to deserve this, but you've been too gracious and kind. May I and many others learn from people like you, to appreciate others with, if not such an extent of wholesomeness, just a nod or a smile. It's the least we can do to strive in the direction of positivity.

I am humbled and honoured to be the subject of your writing. I wish you the best and all the success with your future endeavours.

—Fawad Khan, actor

Prologue

Present
Washington DC, US

It was 6 a.m. when his phone started to buzz. He was sleeping on the couch next to the single bed in his daughter's room.

Still groggy, he almost decided to ignore it, but the buzzing was insistent, demanding.

He checked his cell phone, squinting his eyes against the light. He seemed unsurprised to see the name of the caller. It was his father, Muraad Hussain, calling from Pakistan.

There was a ten-hour time difference between Washington DC and Lahore, so it was 4 p.m. back in Lahore, he surmised.

'Hello?' he answered, his voice hoarse.

'Ahmar,' Muraad whispered.

'Dad . . . how are you?' He pushed the duvet aside, sat up and rubbed his eyes.

'Is everything okay?'

'No, son. I'm afraid not,' Muraad answered.

Ahmar stood up, a worried frown creased his features.

'Zia Munawwar is no more,' Muraad declared.

A long and disturbing silence ensued. Hearing Zia Munawwar's name, a chill swept down his spine. A blurred vision of *her* face came across his eyes.

'How . . . how did this . . . what happened?' Ahmar tried to gather his wits.

'He died of a heart attack. I want you to come to Pakistan immediately. The funeral is scheduled for tomorrow evening so you have enough time. There was something Mr Zia wanted to confess to you,' Muraad said.

Ahmar was traumatized for a minute, shocked.

'But Dad . . .' his voice trailed off.

'Ahmar,' Muraad interrupted him, 'Mrs Zia is very worried because *she* hasn't come yet.'

'What? Where is she?' Ahmar asked, surprised.

'Nobody knows. You have to come here. Zia wanted to talk to you but god did not give him enough time. He has left a message for you. Son, come back and resolve everything. I think it's time.'

Ahmar hung up abruptly, without answering. He was not sure what he was going to do. In Lahore, Muraad put down the receiver with satisfaction, unfazed by his son's behaviour. He knew he would do the right thing.

As Ahmar got up from the couch, his phone fell on the floor. The sound woke up the little girl lying on the bed.

'What happened, Papa? Why were you sleeping on the couch?' she whispered.

'Nothing, my love. I was tired. Just go back to sleep, okay? There's still time before school. I'll wake you up at 8 a.m.' He stroked her hair. She sighed and went back to sleep.

On his way to the university, where he worked, Ahmar called his agent to book a round-trip ticket to Lahore. Then he called his sister, Samira, who also lived in Washington. Ahmar wanted to drop his daughter at her place.

'You don't have to go, Ahmar. You've already suffered a lot,' Samira said.

'I have to. I want to know what is still left for me. Zia Munawwar wanted to say something to me,' he said.

'But he's no more,' Samira said.

'Yes, but he has left a message.'

Samira sighed heavily.

'Please take care of my daughter. I'll be back soon,' he said, hanging up the phone.

A Few Years Ago
Lahore, Pakistan

Summer had set in early that year, and mornings were already hot and humid. Zarish was in a hurry as it was her first day at the university, and she didn't want to be late. But by the time she got ready and left, Canal Road was already choked. The sidewalks were teeming with beggars, pedestrians and people hurrying to work. Sometimes, she wished the city was not so crowded. Lahore was culturally rich and was known for its Victorian and religious architecture, but rapid urbanization had spoilt it. She was glad she lived in a posh suburb, D.H.A. She had two brothers, Zohaib and Zahaan, and was the youngest of the three. Zohaib lived in Canada with his wife and two children. Zahaan lived with them and took care of the real estate business with their father, Zia Munawwar. Zarish's mother, Zarina, wanted to get her second son married, but Zahaan was not ready for such a commitment.

She sat in her car, lost in thought, beads of sweat forming on her forehead. She regretted wearing her new dark pink khadi kurta.

'What is wrong with the AC, Sikander?' she asked the driver.

Sikander shook his head and remained quiet.

'What do you mean?' she asked.

'It's not working. I have to get it repaired,' he said in a low, embarrassed voice.

'What? Did you know that it was not working before I got into the car?' she asked.

He did not respond.

'I am asking something, dammit! Answer me!' she screamed.

'Yes, Madam,' he answered.

'God, damn you!' she mumbled furiously.

She dialled a number, but no one answered.

'Why is he not taking my call?' she said loudly.

The car slowed down at a traffic signal, and she rolled down the window to get some fresh air.

Right then, her phone rang, breaking her reverie.

'Haroon, where the hell are you? Why didn't you answer my call earlier?' she asked.

'Ok, now tell me, which question should I answer first?' he asked, giggling.

'Shut up. I am serious. When are you reaching the university?'

'I am on my way. Can't you wait . . . you stubborn woman?'

'Ugh. I don't want to listen to your crap. See you at the university!'

Sometimes Haroon crossed the line with his silly jokes, but he was also loving and caring. Zarish and Haroon had been best friends since fifth standard. Their families had grown fond of each other too. They were always together; they had attended the same school and then the same college. After graduation, Haroon didn't want to continue studying. However, Zarish had changed his mind. She had forced him to apply for his master's degree at the university. It wouldn't be wrong to say that they could not live without each other. They shared every secret. She could never lie to him, and he could never lie to her. He was her sole male friend. He was the only person with whom she felt comfortable. She could express joy with him, cry along with him, and fight with him. Their friends and family members believed they were more than just friends. However, they always rubbished it as rumours. Haroon secretly loved her but never told her. However, Zarish had no such feelings.

After reaching the university, she tried Haroon's number again. He was always late.

'What's wrong now?' he answered.

'I have reached. Where are you?'

'I said I'm on my way.'

'Everyone is here, Haroon!'

Suddenly, someone grabbed her shoulder from behind. She turned around to find Haroon grinning at her.

'Woah! Why didn't you tell me you were here?' she said and pummelled him with her fists.

'You know I love teasing you,' he said, gently stroking her nose with his thumb.

'Can we go now, please?' she asked.

He nodded joyfully.

On their way to the seminar hall, she looked at Haroon. He was extremely good-looking, with caramel brown hair and light brown eyes. 'The girls will go bananas over him,' she thought.

Her friends always teased her about their relationship. They often wondered how she could not fall in love with someone as perfect as Haroon. Zarish didn't know either. She had never fallen in love. For her, love only existed in movies and books.

Half the seats were already taken when Zarish and Haroon entered the seminar room. They somehow managed to find two chairs, and settled down.

The dean of the university, Faris Ahmed, stepped on to the stage. One by one, he introduced the faculty members. In the end, one more person was requested to come to the stage—Muraad Hussain—the trustee of the university. With exceptional experience in the education sector, he had devoted himself to the betterment of the institute. He was deeply respected by everyone, teachers and students alike. He had a great sense of humour, and his speech had the audience in stitches.

Haroon was not interested in listening to the speech. He held Zarish's hand and led her out of the room.

'What's wrong with you, Haroon? This orientation ceremony is really important for us.'

Haroon rolled his eyes, showing disinterest.

'Fine . . . not for us. But at least for me!'

'No, I don't think this speech is important.' He held her arm tightly. 'Let's go! I'm hungry!'

'Fine, let's go!' Zarish said irritably.

Haroon gave her a crooked smile as they walked towards the cafeteria.

The rest of the day was uneventful. Zarish got back home in the evening. She took off her heels as soon as she entered her room. She was just getting ready to sleep when her mother came in.

'How was your first day at the university?' her mother asked.

'It was okay. A bit tiring,' Zarish answered and yawned.

'Do you want something to eat?'

'No, I'm not hungry. I just want to get some sleep,' Zarish said.

'Okay, I'll let you rest then.' She kissed her forehead, put the quilt over her and switched off the light.

Right then, Zarish's cell phone vibrated. It was her friend Ameena.

'Hello?'

'Hey Zarish, Ameena here. What's up?'

'Oh, hi. Nothing much. What's up with you?'

'I have planned something for tomorrow. Do you want to join us?' Ameena asked.

'Umm, yeah sure. I'm in. When and where? And who else is going?'

'Our entire girl clan. We are planning to watch a movie and get some dinner.'

'Okay, I'm in,' Zarish said excitedly. 'It will be really nice to see you guys.'

The next day, Zarish woke up to the smell of halwa puri. By the time she reached the dining room, the family was already at the breakfast table.

'So, what have you planned for today?' her father asked.

'Well,' she answered, taking a bite of the puri. 'I'm going out with my friends.'

'When you say your friends, you mean . . .' Zahaan asked.

'No, not Haroon. I'm going out with my school friends,' Zarish interrupted her brother.

'Hmm. Interesting,' Zahaan said and took a sip of his coffee.

'Be careful, *beta*. Stay safe. Our city is not politically stable,' her father said.

He was right. A lot had happened in 2013. Genocides and suicide bombings had become common occurrences across the country. However, unlike the other cities, Lahore was considered safe.

Zarish's parents had always been very protective towards her; her brothers treated her like a kid too. They took care of all her needs and bought her whatever she wished for, irrespective of the cost. Zarish loved being cosseted by her family. She was a spendthrift and could not imagine living frugally or marrying someone who didn't earn well.

Hers was a liberal family. Her father never imposed religion on his wife or daughter. He did not force them to wear a burka. In fact, they were free to dress as they liked. They had the freedom to live life on their own terms. Zarish could wear whatever she wanted. There were no restrictions.

Even though her family offered prayers occasionally, fasted in the holy month of Ramadan, paid zakat, had performed hajj once when she was little, they did not follow the rules of Islam very strictly. For Zia Munawwar and his sons, offering the Friday prayer was enough to be called good Muslims.

For the evening, she picked out a stylish orange top and wore it with her favourite denims. Zarish had a strikingly beautiful face, with big, round, almond-coloured eyes and full, luscious lips. She left her straight, long hair open and put on some light make-up.

Her friends, Ameena, Fatima, Saniya and Tooba, came to pick her up. She had been eagerly waiting for them. All her friends came from rich families and loved spending money.

At the restaurant, the girls ordered ice-cream shakes after their dinner.

'Hey, I think that guy is staring at me,' Fatima said.

'Who?' Zarish asked and turned her head to catch a glimpse of the person.

'The guy in the white shirt. He's sitting on your left,' Fatima said.

All the girls turned to check him out. He was a bit bulky and not very good-looking.

'Eww. I don't like him; he looks like a chimp,' Zarish said and made a face.

'Oh, c'mon, Zarru. He's hot,' Ameena said.

'First, he's not hot. Second, I'm afraid he is not even looking at you,' Zarish said sarcastically as she sipped her ice-cream milkshake.

'How can you say that?' Ameena asked.

'Because he is checking me out,' she replied with a wink.

'Oh yes. Zarish, the most beautiful girl on the planet,' Ameena declared, making air quotes with her hands.

'Of course. I am the prettiest girl, and I know it,' Zarish said and shrugged nonchalantly.

'You are obsessed with yourself, Zarish,' Saniya joined in.

Tooba giggled.

'Why not? I know I'm beautiful and I'm proud of it. There is not a single man on this planet who can deny it. I can get anyone to woo me.'

'Really?' Saniya asked.

Zarish nodded triumphantly.

'Fine. Then let's find out how good you are at getting a man,' Saniya said.

'What do you mean?' Zarish asked as a small frown creased her forehead.

'You have to prove what you said right now,' Saniya said. 'You have to make a man fall in love with you.'

'What?' Zarish said, shock writ large on her face.

'Wait,' Saniya said. The girls exchanged confused glances. After scanning the entire restaurant, Saniya finally found a person. She asked Zarish to go and talk to the man who was sitting across from their table with his friends and convince him that he was in love with her.

'What?' Zarish's mouth dropped open. 'Are you crazy? I don't even know him.'

'Oh c'mon, Zarish. It shouldn't be difficult for you. Let's see if he falls for you. It's a dare now,' Saniya said.

'You can do it,' Fatima said encouragingly.

'Wow. This is getting exciting,' Tooba said, rubbing her hands together.

'No way. It's not fair!' Zarish shook her head.

'Oh dear,' Saniya said, 'when will you understand that life is not fair?' She winked at Fatima and everyone started laughing.

Zarish felt pressured. It became 'a do or die' situation.

'We don't have time Zarish, hurry up,' Fatima said.

'Or just say you give up. Just say you don't have it in you,' Ameena said and smiled wickedly.

Zarish wasn't a loser. After all, she had said that she could get any man to fall for her.

'Get a life, girls! I don't need to prove myself. You all know how it was in school. Boys used to fantasize about me!' she said.

'Yeah, yeah,' Fatima replied with sarcasm.

'And Miss Saniya,' Zarish turned towards her, 'don't forget that your ex-boyfriend left you because he was in love with me.'

Saniya swore under her breath and the girls became quiet.

'So, girls, better get over this crap. I'm going to get some fresh bean salad for myself,' Zarish said and got up.

She reverted her gaze to the table where the person in question was sitting with his friends. Wearing a dark blue polo T-shirt, he looked quite boyish. He seemed absorbed in a serious conversation.

'Hey, look at that girl. She is pretty, and seems like she is staring at you,' one of his friends commented.

'I don't think so,' *he* said.

Again, Zarish found herself looking at him. The whole situation was unnerving.

'Why don't you go and talk to her?' one of the men suggested.

'Oh. C'mon, guys!' *he* rolled his eyes.

'Yeah, why not give it a try?'

'God,' *he* sighed. 'Are you serious?'

Zarish heaped her plate with roasted beans. To her surprise, the man in the blue T-shirt walked up to the salad bar and stood next to her. She moved a little to maintain some distance but could not stop blushing. He smelt amazing, like citrus and wood. He came forward to help himself to some salad. Her body tensed up.

Zarish kept looking at him but he did not look at her even once, which made her uncomfortable.

'How can a man ignore my good looks?' she wondered.

As he turned to leave, Zarish also turned in panic and bumped into him.

'Woah!' he exclaimed.

Zarish gasped loudly. His salad plate fell from his hands and ruined her top completely.

'What the f***!' she said loudly.

'Oh, damn. I'm sorry,' he blurted out.

'Sorry?' she scowled. 'You've ruined my top. Do you think apologizing will make any difference?'

'Woah. Hold on. Hold on. What else do you want me to say?' he asked. 'It wasn't my fault anyway. You suddenly turned and that's why we collided.'

As he spoke, she observed his dark brown, mesmerizing eyes and his thick black brows. He had a perfectly shaped nose and firm full lips. His perfectly styled hair covered the nape of his neck.

'Do you understand what I am trying to say?' he said, interrupting her reverie.

'What? Are you blaming me?'

'I'm not blaming anyone. Simply stating the facts,' he answered in a casual tone, folding his arms.

'Huh?' she frowned.

'Sorry once again. You can get your clothes washed,' he said and walked towards his table.

'What the hell?' she whispered. She turned to see that he was laughing with his friends. They seemed to be making fun of her. Just then, Fatima came up to her.

'Damn, Zarish. Your top is ruined,' she said.

'I know. Damn him!' she screamed and hurried towards the washroom.

'I don't understand these girls,' the man said to his friends. 'They never accept their mistake. Did you see what she did? She spun around and bumped into me.'

'C'mon, mate. Don't worry. Girls are crazy, and I'm sure she did it on purpose,' one of his friends said.

'Why?'

'Because she wanted your attention. Simple.'

Zarish's friends followed her to the washroom and found her standing near the sink.

'Hey, are you okay?' Saniya asked.

'I can't believe what that guy did to my top,' Zarish grimaced as she tried to wash off the stain.

'It was your fault, Zarish. Don't blame him.'

'What?' Zarish scowled.

'Let's go back. It's getting late,' Fatima suggested.

They all walked to the parking lot. Zarish was about to get into the car but she stopped.

'Wait,' she said.

'What happened now?' Saniya asked.

'Let me teach him a lesson first.'

'How?' Fatima asked.

'He ruined my clothes. I'm going to ruin his,' Zarish replied.

'C'mon, Zarish. This is not a game of revenge. We're leaving anyway,' Saniya said.

'No. We're not done here. Not yet,' Zarish hissed.

Just then, the man and his friends came out of the restaurant. He bid them goodbye and walked towards his car. Zarish asked Saniya to drive up to where his car was parked. They did not like the idea, but Zarish insisted. Saniya did as she was told and skidded her car to a stop right next to him, splattering him with mud.

They sped off quickly, and did not get a chance to see his reaction.

'What the . . .' he said, shocked.

The incident didn't let her sleep. She stayed awake all night, thinking about what she'd done. She felt embarrassed and remorseful. After all, she could not solely blame him for ruining her clothes. It was her fault too.

'I hate myself right now. I should not have done that. I wish I could meet him and apologize for my stupidity,' she thought.

'C'mon honey, wake up. It is almost 10 a.m. You should not sleep till so late. You will be late for your classes. Hurry up,' her mother said as she drew open the curtains.

'Let me sleep for a while, Mom. I slept quite late last night,' Zarish mumbled in a drowsy voice.

'Darling, you have to attend your classes today,' she said and sat on the bed. Zarish yawned and made a face.

'Get up, darling. Get ready,' Zarina said as she got up and walked towards the door.

'And by the way,' she said, 'Haroon has been calling since morning. He says you are not answering his calls.'

At the university, Zarish told Haroon the entire story from last night. He collapsed in fits of laughter.

'How could you be so stupid? I feel bad for him,' Haroon said.

'I know. Me too,' she said as she bit her lower lip.

Haroon met Shehryar, also known as Sherry, one of his friends from school, on the way to class. He introduced his other friends, Maha, Danish and Saleha, to Haroon and Zarish. Everyone settled down and became quiet as a female professor entered the classroom. Dressed in a white and blue cotton salwar kameez with her hair flowing down to her waist, she looked quite young. The boys could not stop gawking at her. She put her files on the lectern and stood facing the class.

'Hello everyone. I am Maleeha Ejaz. I will be teaching "communication for managers".'

Haroon and Zarish exchanged looks.

'I have done my master's in linguistics in England and currently I'm doing my MPhil at this university. I have been teaching here for the last two years.' She paused for a second and then spoke again, 'So, this was my introduction, now I would like you to introduce yourselves.'

'Guys, I found Miss Maleeha quite hot,' Sherry said. They had gathered at the cafeteria for lunch after their class.

'She was just okay,' Maha said, making a face.

'Actually, I agree with Sherry. Miss Maleeha is really pretty,' Haroon said, taking a sip of his coffee.

'She looks really young. I wonder if she's married,' Saleha said thoughtfully.

'We have to find out,' Sherry said and winked at Haroon.

'She's our teacher, guys. Let's not get involved in her personal life,' Zarish said irritably. 'Plus, you guys can't hook up with a teacher. Gross. C'mon.'

'Zarish, you really shouldn't be concerned. We know better,' Haroon said and put his arm around her but she pushed him away.

After a while, Haroon and Sherry got busy exchanging notes on girls. Zarish felt left out.

'Haroon, did you see that girl in the pink dress?' Sherry asked.

'No, which one are you talking about?' Haroon asked as he stuffed his mouth with samosas.

'I don't know her name. I just saw her today morning. She is so hot. I think we should go talk to her.'

Zarish felt irritated with their conversation. They didn't have anything to discuss other than women.

'Let's see who gets to her first,' Sherry said.

'Hey, hey, hey, are you trying to challenge me, dude?' Haroon raised his eyebrow.

'Whatever you want, Haroon,' Sherry said with a smile.

'Nobody can outrun me in this matter. I'm *that* good with girls. Ask Zarish,' Haroon said and pointed at her.

'I don't know,' she mumbled.

'Let's see, man,' Sherry said, taking a sip of his drink.

The first thing Zarish did after getting home in the evening was check her Facebook and Twitter accounts. Suddenly, her phone beeped. It was a message from Haroon.

Hey Zarish,
I'm really sorry for my behaviour today. Please don't be angry because you don't look cute when you are angry. I was just kidding. Nobody can replace you, darling.
Love you,
Haroon

The message made her smile. He surely knew how to make her feel better. He knew how to fix her bad mood. Only Haroon could do this. Only him. However, she could not make herself fall in love with him. He had all the qualities she wanted in a man: he was good-looking, filthy rich and fun-loving. But he had failed to win her heart. She'd always believed in the phrase 'opposites attract', and wanted her partner to be unique; someone who was completely opposite to her. Haroon was a show-off, a spendthrift, just like she was. He lived in the moment. She wanted someone who was mature enough to understand her. Haroon was childish and immature, and she knew he would never grow up. Zarish wanted a man, not a boy.

However, her father was of a different opinion. He felt Haroon was the perfect match for his daughter. He and Haroon's father had a mutual understanding that their children would get married someday. They were just waiting for them to make up their minds.

The next day Zarish went to the university rather early. She wanted a book regarding her course from the library. On her way to the class, she called Haroon but he was still on his way. She decided to go to the class all by herself.

Their first lecture was on 'investment analysis', to be taken by Wahab. The class started on a slow note and soon put the students to sleep. All of a sudden, the dean of the university, Faris Ahmed, came in.

'Class, how are you all?' he asked.

The students responded positively.

'I hope Sir Wahab is teaching you well,' he said and looked in the professor's direction. Wahab looked a little uncomfortable about this intrusion.

'I have some news for you. The teacher we had hired for the "financial statements analysis" class has gone abroad to complete his PhD. Ahmar Hussain Muraad will be taking this course now. He is also one of our trustee's sons.'

'Like we care,' Zarish thought and rolled her eyes.

After their classes, Haroon, Zarish and the rest of the gang went to the cafeteria.

'Sir Wahab's lectures are so boring. I simply can't stand him,' Maha complained.

'Yeah, same here,' Danish added.

'Why don't we talk to the authorities and get him replaced?' Haroon suggested.

Zarish collected her books from the table and put them in her bag.

'I don't think that's a good idea, Haroon. Plus, it's impossible,' Zarish snapped back.

'Everything is possible, Madam,' Haroon said.

'How?' she asked.

'We can go and talk to Sir Faris about this,' Haroon suggested.

'Do what you want, guys,' Zarish replied.

Just then, the girl Haroon and Sherry had a crush on, crossed their table. Haroon became alert and his eyes followed her. He suddenly stood up, combed his hair with his fingers and adjusted his clothes.

'What? Where are you going?' Zarish inquired.

'I'll be right back.'

All of them looked at Haroon with confused expressions as he walked off. Zarish's eyes followed him and she soon realized what he was up to. She glared at him furiously.

'Oh. Haroon is back on his mission,' Danish said with a grin.

The gang talked excitedly about Haroon and his love interest, giggling and high-fiving each other, but Zarish was infuriated. She got up and walked towards the corridor.

'Why the hell am I getting angry with Haroon? After all, it is his life and he has the right to live it on his own terms. He is handsome and can get any girl. He is my best friend, and I should be happy for him. But I am not. I don't like him talking to other girls. It makes me jealous. I thought I was the only one in his life; that he liked spending all his time with me. But this is not the case. So why am I sulking here alone? Even I should talk to other guys. Nobody has the right to tell me how I should live my life,' with these thoughts clouding her mind, she walked all the way to the parking lot. Suddenly, she froze. She got a sense of déjà vu as she spotted *his* car.

'No. This cannot be *his* car. No way,' she thought in dismay. The night she went out with her friends flashed across her mind. Just then a man wearing a dark blue linen shirt and black pants got out of the car.

Zarish gasped in horror. It was him; the guy they had splattered with mud. She felt ashamed again and started trembling as beads of sweat rolled down her forehead. She saw him coming in her direction and quickly turned her face. He did not see her and walked down the corridor, towards the main block of the university.

'What on earth is *he* doing here? I should find out,' Zarish thought as she bit her lower lip.

Zarish had to find out why he had come to the university. She followed him as he walked towards the south block of the main building. He stopped in front of the dean's office, knocked at the door and then entered. She tried to eavesdrop but all she could hear was murmuring. She wondered why he had come to meet the dean. Did he know she studied here? Had he come to file a complaint against her? Of course, he looked young enough to be a student. Maybe he was enrolling late.

The door of the dean's office flew open and they both stepped out. He shook hands with the dean and then started walking towards the parking lot. As their paths crossed, Zarish caught a whiff of his perfume. It was similar to what she had smelt the other night: citrus and wood. She loved the fragrance.

Haroon splashed some water on her face.

'What the . . .' she screamed.

He burst into hysterical laughter. They were sitting inside the cafeteria.

'What the hell, Haroon?' Zarish fumed.

'C'mon. I was just kidding; trying to cheer you up,' he said and tried to hug her but she pushed her. She wiped the water droplets from her face with the back of her hand and looked away.

'Is something wrong? Is it something I did?' Haroon said and put his hand on top of hers.

'Look. It's not you. It's me. So, don't bother about it,' Zarish said and pulled her hand away.

'Will you please tell me what is the matter,' he asked calmly.

'It's not important. I have to go now. I'm really exhausted.' Zarish stood up and started walking.

'Hey, wait!' he called out, but she didn't stop. However, he did not give up.

'Come. I'll drop you home,' he offered.

'My driver is waiting for me outside. See you later,' she said and quickened her pace, leaving Haroon behind.

Zarish reached home and went straight to her room. She threw her bag on the floor and lay down on her bed.

'I guess I should tell Saniya about him,' she thought and picked up her phone to call her.

'Hey, Zarish! How are you doing, darling?'

'Hey, I'm good. What's up?' Zarish said, sitting cross-legged on the bed.

'All good, buddy. What's going on?'

'Guess whom I saw at the university today,' Zarish said.

'Who?'

'Gosh . . . you won't believe it, Saniya. It was *him*; the guy from the restaurant!'

'What? Oh my god. That's unbelievable. What was he doing there? Does he study there or what?'

'I don't know but I will figure it out. I was just wondering if he knew I studied there . . .' Zarish's voice trailed off.

'Hey, no. That is not possible,' Saniya assured her.

'I hope so,' Zarish said thoughtfully.

Zarish entered her first class, communication theory, fresh and happy the next morning. Their teacher, Jamal, looked quite strict and sombre, but possessed a benign personality. His voice had a fine quality to it. The students adored him. Recently the students had found out that Jamal was engaged to Maleeha. They made an adorable couple, but she looked quite young compared to him.

'I guess it's a love marriage. What do you think, Zarish?' Sherry asked her later that day. Both of them were sitting at the juice corner.

Zarish took a long sip of her mango shake before replying, 'Yeah, right. Both of them are so beautiful, obviously they had to fall in love.'

Zarish's answer made him a bit curious. He turned towards her.

'So, is it necessary for two people to be good-looking to fall in love?' he asked and moved closer to her.

Zarish felt uneasy.

'No. It's not necessary,' Zarish said.

'Hmm.' Sherry sighed.

'Listen, I need to go to the computer lab. I have to take some printouts. I'll see you around later then?' she said and stood up.

'Okay. Sure, Zarish,' Sherry said casually.

'I hate it when he flirts with me. I hate it when any guy flirts with me,' she thought as she walked towards the lab. She crumpled the disposable juice box angrily and threw it in the other direction. It hit the windshield of a car, covering it with the sticky liquid.

'Gosh . . . this car looks familiar,' Zarish thought. She didn't want to face the music if the car belonged to *him*. With this thought, she hurried towards the lab.

'Hope you've understood all the details,' Faris Ahmed said in a solemn voice.

'Yes, Sir. I've got it,' the man replied.

'I am happy you stepped in. We were desperately looking for a teacher,' Faris said.

'That's why I'm here, Sir. Right at your service.'

'I appreciate that, Ahmar,' Faris said. 'Welcome to our university.'

Ahmar smiled and nodded as they shook hands.

He casually walked towards the parking area. On his way, he saw students hanging out together at the cafeteria. He felt nostalgic and wished he could go back to those carefree days.

Someone honked from behind, making him come back to reality. As he unlocked his car, he noticed his windshield covered with mango shake.

'What the hell? Who did this to my car?' he gasped.

At home, he was greeted by his servant, Bashir.

'Bashir Chacha . . . Please get me a cup of tea immediately,' Ahmar ordered.

His father, Hussain Muraad, one of the trustees of the university, was sitting on the couch, watching TV. He went and sat beside him.

'What happened, Ahmar?' Muraad asked, breaking his gaze from the TV screen.

'Nothing, Dad. I am just a little tired,' he said as he rested his head on a cushion.

'How was your meeting with Faris?' Muraad inquired.

Bashir Chacha brought two cups of tea on a tray and put it on the table near them.

'It went well, fortunately,' Ahmar replied, picking up a cup of tea.

'So, all set to join the campus?' Muraad asked.

'I guess,' he murmured.

'Terrific. Make your father proud.'

Ahmar had just returned from the US after completing his MPhil degree from a renowned university. Muraad wanted his son to come back and work in his own country. Ahmar's mother had died right after giving birth to his sister, Samira. Muraad had brought up the two kids all by himself. His friends and relatives, including his children, had tried hard to convince him to remarry but he never agreed.

The next day, Zarish and Haroon were sitting in the university cafe with the rest of the gang.

'Why are your eyes baggy?' Zarish asked, concerned.

'I am overworked,' Haroon said as he leaned back in his chair.

'Why don't you quit work for a while? I mean, you can complete your degree first and then think about the business.'

'No, Zarish. That's not so easy. I have to look after the business. Dad can't handle it any more. Plus, I'm the only heir.'

'Fine. I don't want to get into an argument,' Zarish said and looked away.

'Because you always lose,' he teased her.

'Whatever,' she said and rolled her eyes.

Wahab started the class on how to invest in the stock market. Zarish yawned after hearing the topic. This was the only subject she wasn't interested in.

Saleha, seated right next to her, was also not enjoying the lecture. In fact, she seemed upset. Zarish wanted to ask her the reason but she felt a bit hesitant as they rarely talked to each other.

'Is everything okay?' Zarish finally asked in a low voice.

'Yes. No. Not really,' Saleha said dejectedly.

'Why, what happened?'

'I'll tell you after the class.'

After the class, Zarish confronted Saleha again.

'Will you tell me now what's bothering you?'

Saleha hesitated a bit at first, but then blurted it out.

'How would you feel if the one you like rejects you?'

Zarish turned to look at her and burst out laughing.

Saleha narrowed her eyes in confusion.

'I don't know that feeling. No one has rejected me yet,' she said proudly.

Saleha seemed surprised.

'Yes. Really. Nobody has ever refused me. In fact, I'm the one who rejects!' she added.

'That's so cool, Zarish.'

'Hey. Now tell me what is the matter. Who rejected you?' Zarish asked.

'I don't know if rejection is the right word, but I feel dejected.'

'Who is he?'

'He seems happy in his own world. He never notices me.'

'Is he from our batch?'

'I'm talking about Sherry, Zarish,' Saleha finally admitted.

'Oh. Okay. Right,' Zarish said.

'Yeah,' Saleha said in a feeble voice.

'What if he starts liking you?' Zarish said.

'How on earth is that possible?' Saleha asked.

'Everything is possible. It just needs some time and patience, honey.'

'Oh, Zarish,' Saleha said as she hugged her tightly.

Suddenly Zarish felt that she had a female friend in the university; a friend with whom she could hang out and share her secrets.

Later, in class, Jamal announced that he had planned a surprise quiz. Though Zarish had revised the previous lectures, she found the quiz quite difficult.

'What's the answer for question number three?' Danish asked Zarish.

'I don't know,' she whispered.

'I can't believe you haven't studied for this quiz,' Danish said with a frown.

'If I find someone cheating . . .' Jamal declared when he noticed Danish moving his head. 'I will not cancel his or her quiz.'

Everyone heaved a sigh of relief.

'All right, now stop it. Carry on with your quiz,' Jamal said.

Right then Faris Ahmed knocked on the door.

'Good morning, everyone!' he said.

'I wonder what bad news he's got today,' Haroon told Sherry.

'I want you to meet your new professor. Please come in, Ahmar Muraad.'

Just then, a man wearing a black suit walked in.

Zarish froze.

'No. No. No. Damn it! It's the same person I had met at the restaurant,' she mumbled under her breath.

'What's wrong, Zarish?' Saleha asked.

'Err. Nothing. I'm feeling dizzy.'

'Gosh . . . he is so handsome. Doesn't he resemble Fawad Khan, the actor?' Maha asked excitedly.

'Yeah, a bit,' Saleha replied, staring at the new teacher.

'So, Jamal, when is Ahmar's first lecture?' Faris asked.

'Sir, it's right after mine,' Jamal said with a smile.

'I think I need to go to the washroom,' Zarish whispered.

She splashed cold water on her face. 'I can't believe he's here. I can't believe he has come to teach us! He looks so young. What if he knows I study here? What if he wants revenge?' she said out loud to herself.

She knew it was time to apologize. She couldn't keep running from him forever. He was here to teach them and that incident could really spoil her reputation. It could affect her grades. With these thoughts, she walked out of the washroom.

Ahmar sat in his office, lost in thought. He knew it would be difficult to adjust here. He didn't even know if he really wanted to be here in the first place. What other options did he have? He was doing exceptionally well in the US. He had the life he had always dreamed of. But his father wanted him to come back. He was only twenty-nine and his whole life was ahead of him, but now he had no other option but to teach in a private institute in Pakistan. Someone knocked on the door, breaking his reverie.

'Come in,' he said.

It was the peon.

'Sir, it's time for your class.'

'All right, where is it?' Ahmar asked.

'Room No. 202. Second floor.'

He picked up his files and laptop and walked out of his office.

Zarish calmed herself down and tied her hair into a loose bun. Right then her phone buzzed inside her purse. It was Haroon.

'Hey,' she answered.

'Where are you, Zarish?' he asked.

'Hey, I'm all right. I had gone to the washroom. Didn't Saleha tell you?'

'No. I can't find her either.'

'It's okay. I'm coming back. Wait for me at the cafe,' she said and hung up.

Her phone beeped again. It was a message from Haroon; he was going to the class directly and would meet her there. She was busy typing a reply when someone bumped into her.

Her cell phone fell from her hands. The other person was holding a bundle of files and a laptop, which also came crashing down.

'Damn! My MacBook!' Ahmar cried out.

Zarish was shocked to see him. He picked it up without noticing her.

'It hasn't broken. Don't worry,' Zarish said. He looked up.

'You?' he said, pointing at her in utter confusion.

'Yes. Me,' she said.

'I've seen you somewhere.' He narrowed his eyes.

'I guess you have,' she mumbled, handing him his files. She was too embarrassed to look him in the eye.

Right then, Saleha came out of the classroom.

'Hey, Zarish. Let's go inside,' she said and then turned to look at the professor. 'Excuse me, Sir. The entire class is waiting for you.'

'Yeah. I am coming,' he said in a low, husky voice.

Ahmar stood there for a while, perplexed.

'Oh yes, I think she's the one, the rich spoilt brat,' he mumbled as he remembered the incident.

She quietly went and sat down next to Haroon in the class.

'Hey, you look nervous. What happened?' he inquired.

'I have to tell you something.'

'What?'

'Sir Ahmar is the same . . .' She could not complete her sentence as Ahmar entered the class.

'Good afternoon, everyone!' Ahmar announced, standing close to the lectern. He cleared his throat before speaking again, 'I am Ahmar Muraad, as you already know. I've done my MBA and MPhil in strategic management. I have a bachelor's degree in structural engineering from a university in the US.'

Maha and Saleha were whispering into each other's ears. Obviously, they were gushing about the new teacher.

'I wanted to complete my PhD, but my father called me here,' Ahmar said slowly, his eyes pensive and distant. 'Anyway,' he said, coming back to the present. 'Do you have any questions for me?' he asked the students.

'Let's play with him,' Haroon whispered.

'What? No!' Zarish said inaudibly.

'Sir, I have a question,' Haroon raised his hand.

'Yes sure. Go ahead.'

'What subject will you be teaching us?'

'Didn't Faris Ahmed tell you?' He cocked a questioning eyebrow.

'Yes Sir, he did,' Saleha interjected.

Haroon glared at her, but she ignored him.

'I suppose this young guy doesn't know about it then,' Ahmar said with a smirk.

'The name is Haroon, Sir.'

'All right, Haroon, I will be teaching you the financial statement analysis course.'

'If you have a major in strategic management, then how can you teach us FSA?' Haroon pointed out.

The class broke into excited murmurs.

'Hold on, class,' Ahmar said and tapped lightly on the lectern. 'Let me clear his doubts.'

A frown creased Haroon's face.

'FSA is part of the MBA degree. I was quite good at the subject but I didn't take it as a major. I have an in-depth understanding of the subject, that's why I opted for it.'

Haroon nodded in agreement, embarrassed for asking a stupid question.

'Anything else you guys want to know?' he asked again, but this time no one answered.

'All right. Good. Now please introduce yourselves. Let's start from the left.'

'Shit . . . what am I going to say to him now?' Zarish shuddered at the thought.

One by one, the students introduced themselves, telling him their names, education, hobbies, etc. Finally, it was Zarish's turn. She could not bring herself to stand up and talk. She felt terrible about what had happened the other night and regretted her actions. Ahmar leaned against the lectern and looked straight at her. She hesitated, words stuck in her throat.

Haroon and Sherry chuckled.

'There is no need to laugh,' Ahmar said. 'Give her some time.'

Zarish took a deep breath and said in a thick voice, 'My name is Zarish Munawwar, and I have a bachelor's degree in economics. I don't have any hobbies or interests. Thank you.' She quickly sat down after finishing her sentence.

Ahmar raised his eyebrows in astonishment. He clearly remembered her now. She was the same girl who had sprayed him with mud. He had been furious that day and wanted to call her out for her incivility and idiocy. But today, her behaviour amused him.

'Well, no hobbies or interests . . . hmm . . . are you sure about that?' he asked with a raised brow.

'Is he going to narrate the whole incident in front of the class? Shit!' she thought.

'That can't be possible. I'm sure you *do* have some. Maybe you don't want to share it with the class or *me*,' he said, emphasizing the last word. Ahmar knew that she knew what he was hinting at. He wanted to tell her that probably her hobbies included insulting people at restaurants. But instead he moved on to the next student.

'What is wrong, Zarish? You look worried,' Saleha asked.

They were both sitting in the library.

'Nothing,' Zarish mumbled.

'Oh c'mon. Look, I'm not blind. I could see the stress on your face. What's wrong? You can tell me.'

Zarish's face reddened with embarrassment yet again and it became impossible to hide the truth from her friend.

'Oh Saleha!' Zarish cried out. 'I don't know what to do.'

'Will you tell me what happened?'

Zarish narrated the whole episode.

'I think you should apologize to him, Zarish,' Saleha suggested.

'Do you think he will listen to me?' Zarish asked.

'Of course, he has to. He doesn't look mean. He seems to be a decent person. He is just a little arrogant. Just talk to him.'

'Yeah, I should,' Zarish muttered.

Just then, Haroon came in and sat down beside them.

'What's up, girls?' he asked.

'Zarish has to apologize to Sir Ahmar,' Saleha said.

'What for?' Haroon asked, looking puzzled.

'Haroon, please calm down,' Zarish pleaded. 'Sir Ahmar is the guy from the restaurant.'

Haroon's jaw dropped.

'Yeah, it's him,' Zarish said with a sigh. 'And now I have to apologize. Otherwise . . .'

'He can't do anything,' Haroon interrupted her. 'Trust me. I won't let him hurt you.'

'That's not the damn point!' she snapped back.

'Then what's the point?' he asked.

The librarian gave them a cold stare and she had to lower her voice.

'It might affect my grades,' Zarish whispered agitatedly.

'He won't do that,' Haroon assured her. 'We won't let him.'

'Haroon, why don't you understand?' Zarish raised her voice again and got another stern look from the librarian.

'We'd better get going. I don't want the librarian to kick us out.'

After his first lecture, Ahmar sat in his office, sipping tea; somewhat relieved. But his mind kept going back to Zarish Munawwar. He snapped back to reality as Jamal and Wahab entered the room.

'So how was your first day, Ahmar?' Jamal asked.

'It went well.'

'I hope the students are not bratty.'

He again thought of Zarish.

'No,' Ahmar lied. 'Not at all. Everyone seems nice.'

'That's good,' Wahab joined in. 'I think the students don't enjoy my subject.'

'That's because it's a bit dry,' Jamal joked.

'That's not true. I think it is the teacher's responsibility to make the subject interesting. So, we shouldn't blame the subject,' Ahmar said.

'I agree with you,' Jamal said but Wahab remained silent.

Zarish walked purposefully towards Ahmar's office. She didn't know what she was going to tell him; she just wanted to come clean.

'Don't lose your confidence; don't break down; stay strong,' she told herself. Before she could knock on the door, it flew open, and she found herself face to face with Jamal.

'Miss Zarish, are you all right?' he asked.

Zarish realized that she was covered in sweat. 'Uh . . . yes. I'm fine, Sir,' she stammered. 'I . . . uh . . . just wanted to talk to Sir . . . Ahmar . . .'

'Oh, okay, sure. Come in,' he said and stepped aside. Ahmar was busy on the laptop, totally unaware of the visitor.

'Let's go, Wahab,' Jamal said and they both left the room. Zarish stood near the door, feeling uncomfortable. She couldn't decide what to do. Should she go in? Should she wait outside? Should she just leave? Just then someone patted her on the shoulder.

'Gosh . . . Danish! It's you. I got scared,' she said looking relieved.

'What are you doing here?' he asked.

'I could ask you the same question,' she said.

'I wanted to ask Sir Ahmar a few questions regarding the course.'

'Oh. I am here for the same reason,' she lied.

'Great. Let's go inside then.'

'Sure,' she agreed.

'Good afternoon, Sir,' Danish greeted him.

'Please sit,' Ahmar said, pointing at the chairs.

Zarish sat down gingerly.

'Any queries regarding the course?' he asked politely.

While Danish and Ahmar discussed the upcoming project, Zarish stared blankly at the wall; still battling her inner turmoil and uncertainties. Ahmar shifted his gaze to her.

'Do you have any questions, Miss Zarish?' he asked.

Zarish snapped back into reality.

'What does he want? Why does he always look at me so intensely?' she wondered.

Ahmar cocked a questioning brow.

'Uh. No. I don't have any questions,' she muttered.

They thanked him and got up to leave.

'Miss Zarish Munawwar?' Ahmar called out. Her heart skipped a million beats when she heard her name again. She felt weak in her knees, devoid of all energy.

'Yes, Sir?' is all she managed.

'I think this belongs to you?' he said.

She turned around to see that he was pointing at her notebook on the table.

'Oh. That's mine,' she murmured. He pushed the notebook in her direction with a lopsided smile on his face. She could not understand why he was in such a good mood. In fact, she'd never seen him smile before. She picked up her notebook and almost ran towards the door.

Ahmar found her behaviour rather peculiar. 'I guess she is still embarrassed because of that incident. She thinks I'm still mad at her,' he thought as he packed his stuff and exited the office.

Zarish ran down the corridor and made her way to the parking lot. She called her driver so that he could come and pick her up.

As Ahmar walked towards his car in the parking lot, he spotted Zarish's car exiting the university gate.

'Miss Zarish,' he muttered under his breath and smirked.

Zarish came home feeling exhausted. She greeted her parents and hurried towards her room. She threw her bag on the floor and picked up her laptop to check her Facebook account. While going through her newsfeed, she came across a post from her university's page where Ahmar had commented.

Without thinking much, she sent him a friend request.

'I don't think he will add me back,' she muttered to herself.

Just then her mother came into the room.

'Zarru, how was your day? Are you hungry?' she asked and sat beside her on the bed.

'Yeah, Mom. I am,' she said.

'I'll bring you something to eat,' she said and stroked her cheek.

'What were you doing?' Zarish asked.

'Nothing much. I was watching this new soap on TV.'

'Which one?'

'*Humsafar.*'

'Oh. I want to watch it too. My friends were discussing it the other day,' Zarish said and got up from the bed.

The protagonist, played by Fawad Khan, again reminded her of Ahmar Muraad.

'Mom,' Zarish said.

'Yes, honey?' Zarina turned to look at her.

'Umm,' she murmured, 'there is something I need to tell you.'

After hearing the story, her mother advised her to apologize. Zarish agreed.

'How was your first day?' Muraad asked his son.

'Good,' Ahmar replied, his eyes glued to the laptop screen.

Ahmar always checked his social media profiles before going to bed. He was shocked to see that Zarish had sent him a friend request.

'Why would she want to add me?' he thought and shut down his laptop without adding her.

The next day Zarish felt lighter and happier for no particular reason. She wanted to believe that Ahmar had forgotten what had happened and forgiven her.

'Your assignment will be uploaded on the main server. You may download it from there,' Ahmar announced in the class.

He was dressed in a pair of beige pants and a maroon pullover. She noticed his fiery eyes as he delivered the lecture. A strand of hair had fallen over his brows and it made him look sexy.

'I wonder if he responded to my friend request,' Zarish thought, trying hard not to let his good looks drive her crazy.

'So, if you have any doubts . . .' Ahmar said to the class, 'please feel free to ask me. Are we clear?'

The students nodded.

'Hey Zarish, up for a cricket match?' Haroon asked her after the class.

'You know I don't play cricket.'

'Who's asking you to play?' Sherry joined in.

'Uh, then?' she asked.

'Just come and watch the match,' Haroon said.

'It's going to start in fifteen minutes. Do you want to come?' Sherry asked.

'You want to go?' Zarish turned towards Saleha.

'Uh, okay. Sure,' Saleha said.

By the time they reached the playground, the match had begun.

Zarish was happy that Haroon was taking an interest in sports again. At least he was not chasing after those stupid girls. Zarish spotted Ahmar and Jamal on the other side of the playground.

'Zarish, look who's here,' Saleha said.

'Of course, I know. Your Sherry is going to bowl.'

'No, stupid. I'm talking about someone else,' Saleha said and giggled.

'Sir Jamal?' Zarish asked innocently; she knew what Saleha was getting at.

Saleha tapped her lightly on her head.

'Ouch!' Zarish squealed.

'I'm talking about your nemesis, Sir Ahmar,' Saleha whispered in her ear.

'As if I care,' Zarish said and shrugged her shoulders.

'Are you sure you don't care?' Saleha asked.

Zarish found herself staring at Ahmar. She observed his every move and facial expression.

'Why is he so intimidating and extraordinarily sexy?' she thought.

Ahmar and Jamal were enjoying the match. Later, Maleeha joined them too.

'How's the match going?' Maleeha asked.

'It has just started. Our boys are doing really well,' Jamal said with a grin.

'Ahmar, do you like cricket too?' Maleeha asked him.

Ahmar turned to look at Maleeha.

'Yeah, I do, but not more than football.'

'Right, right,' she said and rolled her eyes.

'Do you want to drink something?' Jamal asked her.

'I wouldn't mind a Diet Coke.'

'Sure. Do you want anything, Ahmar?'

'No, I'm fine, man. Thanks,' he replied.

Jamal went in to get the drinks.

'It's good to see you here, Ahmar,' Maleeha said and patted him gently on his hand.

'It's good to see you here too,' he replied.

Ahmar, Jamal and Maleeha had attended college together and had been friends ever since.

'How's Samira?' she asked.

'She's good. Busy with her married life.'

'That's lovely. I'm so happy for her.'

Ahmar nodded.

'Muraad Uncle must be happy that you're here,' she said.

He nodded with a smile.

Later that day, Zarish called Saniya to tell her that the same guy had joined their university as a professor. Saniya gasped in horror.

'So, what are you going to do?' she asked

'Nothing,' she said. 'He hasn't confronted me yet.'

'That's good. Maybe he has forgotten about it.'

'Yeah. Right.'

'As far as I remember, he was very handsome,' Saniya said with a chuckle.

'Yeah, just like Fawad Khan?' Zarish said with a smile.

'Yes. Why don't you ask him out!' Saniya exclaimed.

'Hey, c'mon. He is my teacher, I can't date him.'

'So, what, Zarish? Don't behave like a weirdo. This is the twenty-first century. There is nothing wrong with dating a teacher.'

'I don't know. No, this can't happen,' Zarish finally said. 'It's not right.'

'But you want this to happen, right?' Saniya probed.

Zarish didn't say anything. She changed the topic and quickly hung up. Later, she again checked her Facebook profile to see if he had accepted her request. It was still pending.

'Damn. When are you going to add me back?' she wondered.

A feeling of emptiness filled Zarish as she sat with Maha and Saleha in the cafeteria. She felt like something was missing. But she could not put her finger on it. Perhaps it was because she had not seen Ahmar yet. Why did she think about him all the time? Her stomach twisted into a thousand knots at this thought.

'Why don't we girls plan a shopping spree?' Maha asked Saleha and Zarish.

'Sounds like a good plan,' Saleha said excitedly.

'Later we can also catch a movie,' Maha suggested.

'Guys, please. No romantic movies. I would love to see some action,' Zarish said as she dipped a French fry into ketchup before putting it into her mouth.

'Err. Okay. As you wish,' Maha said.

'Thank you,' Zarish replied.

'But why do you hate romantic movies?' Saleha asked.

'Because she doesn't have a boyfriend yet,' Maha said with a giggle.

Zarish gave her a dirty look.

'Am I right?' Maha inquired.

Zarish nodded with her mouth full of fries. She wanted to change the topic.

'Then what about Haroon?' Maha asked.

'What about him?' Zarish asked innocently.

'Aren't you a couple?' she wondered.

Zarish's brows lifted in surprise.

'Aren't you guys in love or something?' Maha asked.

'Well . . .' is all Zarish managed.

'Hmm?' Maha looked at her with curious eyes.

Saleha listened to their conversation cautiously.

'Okay, hold on. What do you want me to say, Maha? Just tell me. I swear to god I will say it,' Zarish snapped.

'I want to know the truth,' Maha declared.

'Ok. What do you think the truth is?' Zarish asked, smiling artificially.

'I don't know. It just seems like you are attracted to each other. He appears to be very affectionate and protective towards you.'

'That is true. We are best friends, but we're not in love with each other. I love him but only as a friend,' Zarish answered, hoping to put an end to the volley of questions.

'Just as a friend?' Maha asked again.

'Yes,' Zarish said in a firm voice.

'Fine. I believe you.'

'You should,' Zarish said curtly.

'Are you both done here?' Saleha finally broke her silence.

Maha nodded.

'Shall we go to the library? We have to finish an assignment, right?' Saleha reminded them.

'Are you talking about Sir Ahmar's assignment?' Zarish asked.

Zarish could not wait to attend Ahmar's class. She wanted to ignore the storm inside her as she was not sure what she felt for him. As soon as he stepped into the class, Zarish felt relieved.

'Done with your assignments?' Ahmar asked.

Zarish did not want to, but she could not stop herself from gawking at him. He was dressed informally in a white shirt and blue jeans. He scanned the room through his thick-rimmed glasses, his eyes intense as usual. His hair perfectly framed his face, with strands falling on his forehead. A pair of loafers completed the look. 'This guy surely has a sense of style,' she thought.

Danish, who had been assigned the task of collecting assignment papers, tapped her shoulder.

'Your assignment?' he asked, interrupting her daydream.

'Here you go,' she said absent-mindedly as she handed him the paper.

'What about yours, Haroon?' Danish asked.

'Mine is with Zarish,' he told him.

'What is it doing with Zarish?' Danish asked. 'Did she write yours too?'

'That's not your concern,' Haroon spat.

'What's going on here?' Ahmar asked, folding his arms.

Haroon gave Danish a cold stare.

'Nothing, Sir. Danish and I were just discussing the assignment,' Haroon lied.

'May I see your assignment, please?' Ahmar asked politely.

Haroon took the assignment from Zarish's hands and gave it to Ahmar, who flipped through it quickly.

Both Zarish and Haroon exchanged a quick nervous glance.

'Have you written this?' Ahmar asked.

'Uh. Yes. Why?' Haroon asked nervously.

'Hmm. So, Haroon, can you please name the five companies that you've selected for your project?' Ahmar inquired.

Haroon went totally blank. Obviously, Zarish had written the assignment, and he had no idea about the details.

'Yes?' Ahmar probed.

Haroon remained silent.

'Okay. So, Zarish has written this paper for you. Get ready to face the consequences. Especially you, Zarish,' Ahmar said, pointing at her.

'But, I . . .' she blurted.

'No ifs or buts!' Ahmar interrupted her. 'I won't tolerate this sort of behaviour in my class.'

'But he is my friend, Sir!' Zarish said out loud. Everyone turned to look at her, including Ahmar. 'I just wanted to help him. This is what friends are for,' she said assertively. Ahmar crossed his arms and looked at her disapprovingly.

'Sir, it was just an assignment. He was busy so he asked me to do it. It won't happen again. Don't make a fuss over it, please,' she boomed.

Saleha, Sherry and Maha were stunned to see her confidence.

'Still, if you want to deduct my marks, go ahead. The decision is solely yours. Nobody can change that,' she said.

'Done with your melodramatic speech, Miss Zarish?' Ahmar asked briskly.

She nodded.

'Good. Thank you. Let's proceed with our lecture now.'

Zarish could not believe that he just snubbed her.

'How can he treat me like that?' she asked herself.

'I need to ask him what his damn problem is!' Zarish told Saleha after the class.

'Zarish, he is just doing his job,' she told her.

Zarish's face turned red with anger.

'You need to calm down,' Saleha said as she caressed her shoulder.

'Does he want revenge?' Zarish asked.

'I don't think so. He's mature enough not to think that way,' Saleha said.

Zarish leaned against the wall and moaned. 'This day is getting worse by the minute. First, Maha pissed me off and now him,' Zarish whined.

The weekend passed quickly. Zarish went out shopping with her friends but could not stop thinking about Ahmar. She longed to see his face. On Monday, Zarish could not hide her enthusiasm. She wanted to talk to Ahmar and clear the air between them.

Her eyes lit up as Ahmar walked into the classroom. Dressed in a white shirt and grey pants, he looked breathtakingly handsome. Zarish noticed that he'd not brushed his hair like he usually did. His messy hair made him look even sexier.

'He looks sexy as hell,' Maha commented.

'What? No way. He can't be called sexy,' Zarish protested.

'Of course, he can be called sexy. Just look at him. You can see his sexy chest hair beneath that white shirt.'

'Stop it, Maha. Please. You're disgusting!' Zarish bellowed as Maha burst out laughing.

'What's your problem anyway? Can't I admire his sexiness?' Maha asked.

'Keep your dirty thoughts to yourself, please,' Zarish snapped back. She hated Maha for putting this image in her mind. She could not stop staring at his chest now.

'Damn . . . he's sexy,' she thought and then abruptly lowered her gaze. She could feel her cheeks burning up.

Ahmar greeted everybody in the class and began the lecture. After the class, he distributed the assignment papers and left the room. Most of the students had scored well. Zarish was astonished to see her marks. She had got only six out of ten.

'How much did you get?' Haroon asked her.

'I got six. Only six,' Zarish cried.

'You scored better than me. I got four,' he said with a chuckle.

'This isn't funny, Haroon. I can't digest such low marks.'

'I know, I know, you've always been a good student,' he said with a hint of humour in his voice.

Zarish rose from her chair and ran outside after Ahmar.

She stormed into his office without knocking. He was busy reading a file.

'This is not fair, Sir!' she said.

Amazed by her sudden appearance, Ahmar tilted his head to look at her. Her cheeks were red with anger, and hands closed tightly into fists.

'You know you didn't ask for permission before entering my office,' he said brusquely.

'I know, but what *you* don't know is that I don't deserve such low marks,' she said with a frown.

He shut his file and placed it on the table.

'I have scrutinized your assignment and given the marks it actually deserves.

'No, Sir. I know I deserve more marks. If this is about helping Haroon then . . .'

'No. It's not about that,' he said before she could complete her sentence.

'I know it is, Sir. Or maybe you still want to take revenge,' she said accusingly.

'What?' he gasped in shock.

She nodded.

'What revenge?'

'You still haven't forgotten what happened that night, have you?' she asked him at last.

'What are you talking about? Which night?'

'Don't pretend. You know what I am talking about: the night when my friends and I insulted you. This isn't our first meeting and you know that.'

Ahmar sighed and leaned back in his chair.

'Well, Miss Zarish . . .' he said. 'This is surely not about that night. In fact, I had completely forgotten about that. I know it was not my fault. You suddenly bumped into me. Later, you and your friends played a really stupid game. But trust me, I still did not take it seriously. I forgot about it the very next day.'

She studied his face and realized he was telling the truth.

'I'm not a kid who would come and seek revenge. C'mon. Mature people don't do that,' he said and smiled.

'That smile . . . oh my!' Zarish thought.

'Oh, really?' she said, acting innocent.

He nodded slightly.

'What about my assignment then? I worked really hard on it,' she said with a sad face.

'Keep it on my table. I will look at it again.'

'I was just trying to help my friend and . . .' she explained.

'It's okay. I understand. But don't do such things in the future; it might affect your grades.'

'Okay,' she muttered.

'Anything else?' he asked as he picked up his file again.

'Are you still angry with me?' she asked.

He looked at her again, his expression softening.

'I was never angry with you, Miss Zarish,' he put down his file and looked at her intently.

Zarish could feel his eyes on her and that made her blush. His seductive stare made her go weak. She looked away as colour filled her cheeks.

She felt a sudden urge to leave, but her legs refused to move. Her body stiffened and her hands began to tremble. Her heart thudded against her chest.

'Are you okay?' he asked in a concerned voice.

'I've never felt this good before,' she thought and then smiled at him.

Zarish could not sleep that night. She kept tossing and turning in bed. She could not get his burning and sensual stare out of her mind. The way he stared at her, the way he talked to her, everything was so mesmerizing. And how could she forget his smile? Around him she was caught in a vortex of emotions. She was a different person with him. She wanted to look good for him, wear pretty clothes.

Zarish sat up, tied her hair into a bun, and turned on her laptop. She checked her Facebook profile and was pleasantly surprised to see that Ahmar had accepted her request. She could not believe it. She opened his profile page and clicked on his pictures. He looked really handsome in all of them. After minutes of contemplating, she decided to write him a personal message.

Hello Sir,
I am glad you accepted my request. Looking forward to your lecture tomorrow.
P.S. Thank you for forgiving me.
Take care,
Zarish Munawwar

She smiled as she read the message again and hit send. She folded her arms and hugged herself tight. She was in a state of bliss and wanted to remain there forever.

She waited for his response for a while, but he did not reply. Finally, she switched off her laptop and lay down on her bed, falling asleep within seconds.

Ahmar was watching TV with his father.

'How's it going at the university?' Muraad asked his son.

'So far, so good.'

'Do you like any girl there?' Muraad asked teasingly.

Ahmar laughed half-heartedly.

'Dad. I've not come here to check out girls. C'mon,' he said.

'I know, son. I was just generally asking. Do you like anyone?' he asked, not giving up easily.

'I don't think so.'

'Sure?'

Ahmar gave his father a questioning look.

'I have seen so many pretty girls there.'

'Then why don't you find one for yourself?' Ahmar said and chuckled.

'It's your age to get married, not mine,' Muraad said and patted him on his thigh.

'I don't want to get married, Dad. I've told you numerous times,' Ahmar said in a grave voice.

'How long are you going to stay alone? One day you have to settle down,' Muraad said calmly.

Without replying, Ahmar got up and went to the other room. He opened his laptop to check his Facebook profile. He was surprised to see Zarish's message. He sent a quick reply:

You are welcome.

He tried to work on his project but his mind kept going back to Zarish.

The next day, Zarish emptied her closet and threw all her clothes on the bed. She couldn't decide what to wear. She finally picked out a yellow plaid top with a pair of high-waisted denims.

Haroon was waiting for her outside in his car.

As soon as she sat in the car, Haroon hit the accelerator and the engine roared to life.

'What's the rush?' Zarish asked, irritated.

'I like driving fast,' he said and grinned.

'Whatever. You didn't even notice my new clothes,' she complained and looked out of the window.

In actual fact, Haroon did notice how pretty she looked when she sat in the car but didn't say anything.

'It is useless to expect something from you,' she told him.

'You are right, Zarish,' he said sarcastically.

She felt hurt. She wanted him to compliment her but he seemed lost in his own world.

In the cafeteria, she ordered a mango milkshake and settled down to check her notifications on Facebook. She was flabbergasted to see Ahmar's message in her inbox.

Just then, Saleha and Maha joined her.

'Hey Zarish, what's up?' Maha said as she pulled a chair to sit down.

'Nothing much,' she said absent-mindedly, her eyes glued to her mobile phone.

'Anyway, how much did you score in Sir Ahmar's assignment?' Saleha asked.

'Damn! I just remembered something. Thanks for reminding me, Saleha. I have to go and meet him right now!' Zarish said and rushed towards the main building.

Maha and Saleha exchanged confused looks.

'Come in,' Ahmar said when someone knocked on his door.

'Good afternoon, Sir,' Zarish greeted him.

Ahmar looked up and seemed a bit surprised to see her in his office.

'Good afternoon, Miss Zarish,' he said.

She took a few steps forward and stood near the chair. He quickly looked at her from head to toe which made Zarish uncomfortable.

'A-a-actually . . . I . . .' she stammered.

He kept looking at her, without blinking his eyes. She could feel the growing tension in her body.

'I . . . I am here . . .' she stammered once again.

'I know why you're here,' Ahmar said, interrupting her thoughts. Zarish got confused. She herself did not know why she was in his office

'Why?' she said in a confused tone.

'There can only be one reason, Miss Zarish,' he said.

Every time he said her name, her heart skipped a beat and butterflies fluttered in her stomach. Zarish could see that he was amused.

'And what is that?' she croaked.

'You're here for your assignment,' he finally said.

She felt disappointed with his reply.

'Oh,' is all she managed.

'Here,' he said and gave her the assignment. 'You may check it now. I hope I didn't disappoint you this time.'

She took the file from his hand and looked at her marks.

'Eight out of ten. That's all?' she complained.

He nodded in amusement.

'Thanks for being so generous,' she said sarcastically and closed the file.

'Still not happy with your marks?' he said, narrowing his eyes.

She shook her head.

'Well, then I should tell you that I am not happy with your work either.' He shrugged.

'What do you mean?' she cried.

He nodded.

'I rechecked it just for your satisfaction. I think you can do better than this,' he said as he leaned back in his seat.

Words froze in her throat. She just stared at him, surprised by his remarks.

'One of the students from your class scored ten out of ten. I think her name is Fariha. You should go and check her assignment. See what mistakes you have made and then discuss them with me,' he told her.

'Fine, Sir. Next time I will prove that I can do better than this,' she said bitterly.

'Please don't feel bad, Miss Zarish. My intention was not to offend you. Please take my comments as constructive criticism. It will help you in the future.'

Her body tensed up and tears rolled down her cheeks. Ahmar noticed them too.

'I should go . . .' she murmured and turned to leave.

Ahmar could comfort her but he felt helpless. Zarish wiped her tears with the back of her hand and left his office hurriedly.

Ahmar clenched his fists and banged them against the table.

'Why does she have to be so shallow and melodramatic all the time?' he asked himself.

Zarish ran into Haroon in the corridor.

'Hey, Zarish, where are you going?' he asked. Zarish wiped her tears and managed to smile. Haroon noticed the tension on her face.

'What's wrong, Zarish?' he asked as he caressed her cheeks. 'Why are you crying?'

'Nothing, Haroon. Let me go.' She tried to free herself.

'I won't let you go unless you tell me what's wrong,' he said.

She looked at him for a moment and then burst out crying. He pulled her close and put his arms around her. Passers-by looked at them suspiciously.

'Let's go out and talk. People are looking at us,' he said and led her out.

'Now tell me, why are you crying?'

Zarish sighed.

'I asked Sir Ahmar to recheck my assignment, but he gave me only eight out of ten.'

Haroon looked at her quizzically.

'I thought I deserved more and complained, but he sort of insulted me.' She shrugged.

'So, you started crying? Really?' he asked, surprised.

She simply nodded. She did not tell him the real reason behind those tears. She cried because she liked him and couldn't bear his sarcasm. She felt hurt when he spoke to her rudely.

Haroon started laughing.

'God. Zarish! You're such a cry baby. Grow up,' he said and burst into laughter again.

Zarish got irritated.

'I worked really hard on the assignment.'

'C'mon. Stop acting like a nerd! You are blaming that poor guy for nothing. You got what you deserved. Try to be happy. Don't freak out unnecessarily. I got lower marks than you, but I'm not complaining,' he said with a wide toothy grin

'You got what you deserved too! You don't study, that's why you don't have any expectations. But I do.

You waste your time partying with those stupid girls,'
she quipped.

'Whoa! Where are you going with this?' he asked,
amused.

'This is the truth. You'd better accept it,' she said.

'Fine. You first grow up and stop acting like a kid,'
he teased.

'Whatever,' she said.

It was late at night when Zarish opened her laptop to
check Ahmar's profile. She wondered if she should send
him a message. But then she remembered what he'd said
in the afternoon and stopped herself. Why did his words
affect her like this? This was not the first time a teacher
had scolded her. Why was he different? Not wanting to
get distracted, she closed Facebook and went back to her
assignment. Just then a chat window popped up on her
screen; it was Ahmar.

> Hello. Hope you're fine. I'm really sorry if I offended
> you in the afternoon. My intention was not to hurt
> you; I just want you to do better. Don't take my advice
> negatively.

All the hatred she'd felt for him in the afternoon vanished
and she started giggling like a little girl. She tucked her
hair behind her ear and started typing her reply:

> I think I overreacted today. I will not disappoint you
> again.

She hit the send button and sighed heavily. He was quick to reply:

> You did not disappoint me this time either. It is just that I expect more from you.

She replied:

> I am more than willing to try my best.

She sent him the message and waited for his reply.

> Cool. Take care then.

She wrote:

> You too. ☺

When they reached the university the next day, Zarish and her friends found out that the faculty members had organized a field trip to Badshahi Mosque, one of the most popular historic monuments in Lahore.

As the students were getting inside the bus, Zarish's eyes met Ahmar's. Dressed in a cool blue shirt with grey pants, he stood with Wahab and Jamal. She did not know if he was looking at her as he was wearing a pair of sunglasses. 'He is stunningly handsome,' she thought.

She was reminded of her conversation with him last night. She blushed when she realized that he had initiated it. Her body trembled just thinking about it.

Her heart skipped a beat when Ahmar took off his sunglasses and shot her a look. She instantly looked away, feeling embarrassed. Perhaps he had caught her staring at him.

As they neared Badshahi Mosque, Wahab started his live commentary: 'Badshahi Mosque was built in 1671 by Mughal Emperor Aurangzeb towards the end of the Mughal rule. For your information, Aurangzeb was the son of Mughal emperor Shah Jahan, the builder of the Taj Mahal in Agra.'

It was uncomfortably hot that day. Despite wearing a lawn salwar kameez, Zarish was sweating profusely.

'Damn,' she cried.

'Are you okay?' Saleha asked.

'I shouldn't have worn high heels today. They're hurting my feet. Stupid heels.'

'Let's get you a pair of chappals from one of the shops outside the mosque.'

'Okay,' Zarish muttered.

Ahmar noticed the uneasiness in her stride but did not say anything. Wahab, who knew a lot about Pakistan's cultural history, led the group inside the mosque.

Everyone had to take off their shoes before entering the main prayer hall, but Zarish was not aware of this. Ahmar stopped her midway.

'What's wrong?' she asked.

'You cannot go inside with your shoes on. Please take them off.'

'Oh. Gladly.'

He watched her as she took off her heels. He noticed how her long, black hair fell over her shoulders as she bent down.

'Ouch,' she cried out in pain.

'Do they hurt?' he asked.

'Yeah. A bit,' she said as she looked down at her swollen feet.

'You can sit here for a while and then take the rest of the tour.'

She nodded.

They locked eyes for a moment before Ahmar joined the other students for the afternoon prayer in the main hall. Zarish was awestruck to see Ahmar praying so ardently on a weekday as her family members only prayed on Fridays. Some of the female students also prayed but Zarish remained reluctant.

Later, when they were exiting the mosque, Zarish saw Ahmar distributing sweets to poor children sitting on the pavement outside the mosque.

He had a contented smile on his face. She had never seen him so happy.

'This man is something else,' she murmured.

Posters about the upcoming carnival were put up all over the campus.

'Guys! The carnival is coming up! What's the plan?' Sherry asked everyone in the class.

'I've heard students will get a chance to put up food stalls,' Maha joined in.

'I overheard the teachers talking. They said each group will be assigned a mentor,' Saleha said.

'I think I will ask Sir Jamal to be our mentor,' Sherry said.

'It's not up to us. The head of the department will decide that,' Saleha told him.

'I wish Sir Ahmar is my mentor,' Zarish thought.

Ahmar was chit-chatting with Jamal and Wahab over samosas and tea.

'Did the HOD assign you a group?' Jamal asked Wahab.

'Not yet,' he replied.

'I've heard the carnival is quite boring. Is it true?' Ahmar asked as he took a bite of his samosa.

'No, that's not true. The university plans this carnival every year so that the students can have fun; make memories that last a lifetime,' Jamal said.

Ahmar nodded.

'So, Jamal, when is your wedding?' Wahab teased.

Jamal blushed like a teenager. Both Wahab and Ahmar burst out laughing.

'I'm ready for it. Maleeha has to agree,' he said coyly.

'Do you want us to talk to her?' Ahmar asked.

'Oh c'mon. I'll wait for her answer,' he replied.

'Why don't you propose to her?' Ahmar asked.

'We are already engaged. I don't need to propose to her again,' he said.

'Of course, you have to. Girls become very emotional and sensitive when it comes to marriage. They want their partners to express their feelings again and again,' Wahab said.

'Hmm,' Jamal seemed lost in thought.

Zarish, Haroon, Sherry, Maha and Saleha were on the way to their next class when Zarish spotted the elevators in the main hall.

'Guys, guys, guys . . . I'm too tired to climb the stairs,' Zarish said, making a face.

'Shall I carry you?' Sherry said flirtatiously.

'Oh please,' Zarish muttered.

'Back off!' Haroon snarled.

'You guys go ahead; I'm going to take the elevator,' she said, winking at them.

'That's only for faculty members. In case you didn't know,' Sherry said with a smirk.

'I don't care,' she said.

Zarish stepped inside the elevator and pressed the button for the fourth floor. Suddenly, the lift stopped and its metallic doors opened.

Someone wearing a familiar pair of shoes stepped in. Shoes she often noticed: loafers. Flabbergasted, she banged her head against the wall of the elevator.

'Ouch!' she cried.

'Are you okay?' Ahmar asked.

She realized she was alone in the lift with him.

'I guess,' she said as she gently massaged her head.

'Shall I have a look?' he said, stepping closer.

'Uh . . .' Zarish took a step back nervously.

Ahmar hesitated.

'I . . . I am fine,' she stammered.

Embarrassed, Ahmar looked away, but she couldn't take her eyes off him.

'By the way, I can complain about you to the management,' he told her.

'What for?'

'For using this elevator. Students are not allowed to use it. It's only for . . .'

'I know it's only for faculty members,' she completed his sentence. 'I was tired, so I took it.'

'You're impossible,' he hissed.

The lift stopped on the fourth floor and the doors opened.

'I know you won't complain about this . . .' she paused, 'Because . . . I trust you,' she said as she looked fixedly at him.

He felt a strange sensation when she said she trusted him. He saw something magical in her eyes. Something unusual. Something dark and unknown. An unspoken emotion.

'Why does she trust me?' he wondered.

She walked out, leaving him alone in the lift. Zarish did not know why she had said those words. Did she really trust him?

The HOD announced the final list of the groups the next day. Zarish had Sherry and another classmate, Zoya, in her group. To Zarish's surprise, Ahmar was their mentor. The mere thought of spending more time with him sent a shiver down her spine.

The next few days passed in the blink of an eye. Everyone was busy preparing for the carnival. Students cheered and enjoyed themselves, but Zarish was stuck with Sherry and the newbie, Zoya.

Just a day before the carnival, Zarish was busy putting up flyers for their food stall.

'I need more Scotch tape,' Zarish told Zoya and Sherry who were helping her out.

Ahmar stopped by to see their progress.

'So what food item did you guys select?' he asked.

'Sir, we will be selling cheese balls,' Sherry told him.

'Great. Who will get them?' he asked.

'Zarish will make them,' Sherry said.

Ahmar turned to look at her, but she looked away.

'I would really like to taste them,' he said in a low voice.

Zarish blushed.

'Okay then. See you tomorrow at the carnival. May the best group win. Uh, Miss Zarish Munawwar,' he turned towards her.

'Yes, Sir?' she stammered.

'I want you to lead this group. I hope that's okay with you.'

She nodded slowly.

The university grounds were beautifully decorated for the carnival. The food stalls were draped in fairy lights of different colours.

Zarish's cheese balls were much appreciated, and they earned good money. The proceeds of the sale would go to charity.

'Hey, I need two cheese balls,' one of the students called out.

'Yeah, sure! Zoya, will you please help him out?' Zarish asked.

Zoya nodded, placed two cheese balls on a plate and gave it to him.

'How much?' he asked.

'Rs 200, please,' Zarish said politely.

'What? That's too much for two cheese balls,' he yelled.

'No, it's not,' Zarish said, frowning.

'Yes, it is. They shouldn't be more than Rs 50 each.'

'I think you should just get the hell out of here,' Zarish said furiously.

'This is no way to talk to someone, Miss Zarish,' Ahmar interrupted.

Zarish looked at Ahmar hysterically.

'You can leave if you don't want to eat them,' Ahmar told the boy.

'Sir, these cheese balls are really not worth Rs 200,' the boy said persuasively.

'I said leave,' Ahmar hissed.

'But Sir . . .'

Ahmar shot him an annoyed look.

'May I taste one, please?' Ahmar asked Zarish after the boy left.

'Sure Sir,' she said and handed him a plate.

'They're delicious. Really worth the price,' he said, taking a bite.

Zarish smiled back nervously.

Haroon and the rest of the gang seemed to be having the time of their lives. He was not bothered about his stall. He just drank energy drinks and goofed around with girls. Zarish chose to ignore him.

Soon it was time to declare the results. Zarish's stall earned the maximum money and was declared the winner. The entire team was called on stage and Faris Ahmed presented them with the prize. Hussain Muraad came up to congratulate them.

'I'm really proud of all of you,' Muraad said and patted them on their backs.

'They are all my dear students,' Ahmar said proudly.

Zarish's face fell. She did not like being called his student.

Later that night, Ahmar walked into his bedroom and switched on the lights. He changed his clothes and settled on his bed with his laptop. There were eight new messages in his inbox. He clicked on the one from Zarish Munawwar.

Thank you for supporting my team. We did it.
P.S. Your dad is adorable. Take good care of him.
Goodnight.

He hit the reply button and typed a message:

It's my duty to help you. Don't thank me.
You also take care of yourself.

He promptly checked his other messages and then got back to his project. But Zarish could not sleep as she was waiting for his reply. She switched on her laptop again and checked her inbox.

After reading his message, she sent him a reply:

Are you still awake?

She waited for his message anxiously. Ahmar was stunned to see her message. 'Why is she still up?' he wondered.

Yes. What are you doing up so late?

Zarish smiled at his reply and typed her message:

I can't sleep.

Ahmar: Are you an insomniac?

Zarish: Well, maybe. Can we chat for a while?

Ahmar: I am busy right now. Have to work. You go to sleep.

Zarish: Fine. Goodnight.

She felt disappointed and switched off her laptop.

'Why is he up so late? What could be more important than me?' she wondered. 'I am sure he has more important things to do than talk to me. I am just his student. Nothing more. Nothing less,' she told herself bitterly.

'Wake up, Dad!' Ahmar said as he knocked on his father's bedroom door at 6 a.m.

'Get ready in fifteen minutes. I'm waiting for you at the dining table,' he ordered.

It took Muraad half an hour to come to the dining table. Bashir Chacha had made cheese omelettes for them.

'The carnival went really well yesterday. I am proud of the students,' Muraad said, taking a bite of the omelette.

Ahmar smiled at him.

'The cheese balls were delicious,' Muraad said.

'Indeed,' Ahmar nodded.

'By the way, what's the name of the girl who made them?' Muraad asked.

'Zarish,' Ahmar told him. 'Zarish Munawwar.'

'Hmm. She seems to be a nice person. I really liked her.'

Ahmar sipped his tea pensively.

'What do you think?' Muraad asked.

'Hmm?' Ahmar remained indifferent.

'Do you like Zarish?'

'Dad, I'm going to be late for my class. I have to go,' Ahmar said, ignoring his father's question.

Muraad looked at his son intently.

He gave his father a quick hug and started collecting his laptop and files.

'Son . . .' Muraad said.

'Hmm?'

'I really meant what I said about Zarish. I like her,' Muraad said sincerely.

'Good for you, Dad. See you.'

While driving to the university, his father's words echoed in his ears. Ahmar tightened his grip on the steering wheel.

'Why does he like Zarish? Doesn't he understand that she is just my student?' he murmured under his breath.

Zarish wanted to meet Ahmar before going to class. She knocked on his office door but there was no answer. With a lunchbox in hand, she stood there for a minute. Finally, she put the box on the floor, next to the door, and turned to walk away, but accidentally bumped into Ahmar.

'Woah!' Ahmar exclaimed.

'Sorry, Sir,' she gulped.

'Why do you always bump into me? Huh? And, what are you doing outside my office?' he asked, sounding a bit irritated.

'I . . . uh . . . I came here to give you this,' she said as she picked up the lunchbox from the floor.

'What's this?' he asked and cocked his brow.

'I made cookies for uncle . . . I mean Sir Muraad,' she said embarrassedly.

'Miss Zarish, I think I forgot to tell you. My father is diabetic.'

'Oh, don't worry. They are sugar free,' she replied.

'Are you sure?' he asked, not sure if he could trust her.

She nodded.

'Well, then you can give them to him yourself. He will be in his office in an hour or so,' he said casually and then turned to unlock his cabin.

'You don't want to taste them?' she asked promptly.

'Later,' he said as he entered his office.

Zarish looked glum.

It was late afternoon when Zarish decided to give the cookies to Muraad. She had been carrying the lunchbox in her bag the whole day. Why was she being so nice to Muraad? Because he was Ahmar's father? Or because she liked him as a person? She knocked on the door before entering his office. It was classier than Ahmar's office. The walls, painted in dark hues, gave the room a royal look.

'Pleased to see you,' Muraad said.

Zarish smiled at him but then realized that he seemed rather tired and unwell.

'Are you feeling okay, Sir?' Zarish asked in a concerned voice.

'Yes, just a bit worn out, I guess,' he said as he picked up a glass of water. Zarish nodded. The lunchbox was still in her hands.

'Can you please pass me those spectacles? They are kept on that shelf,' he said, pointing at the wooden shelf.

'Sure, Sir,' Zarish said obediently.

All of a sudden, Muraad felt a severe pain in his chest. He fell from his chair, breaking the glass in his hands.

Zarish quickly turned around after hearing the sound. She was stunned to see him on the floor, writhing in pain.

'Sir!' she cried.

Zarish quickly called an ambulance. The news spread across the campus and more students and teachers gathered around the scene. Zarish wanted to call Ahmar but she did not have his cell number. She asked one of the students to tell him about his father's critical condition.

At the hospital, Muraad was rushed to the ICU. Zarish waited outside the emergency room in the corridor, worried.

'I hope you come here soon, Ahmar,' she prayed in despair.

After about fifteen minutes, Ahmar walked in in a huff.

'Where is Dad?' he asked the nurse impatiently, sweat dripping down his brow.

'He's in the ICU,' she told him.

'Can I see him, please?'

'No, not without the doctor's permission. You can wait here. They are still examining him.'

'Who brought him here?'

'The young lady standing over there,' the nurse said, pointing at Zarish.

Ahmar took a deep breath, ran his hands through his hair and walked towards her.

'Why didn't you tell me about my father?' he yelled.

Zarish could see that he was very upset. The veins on his forehead were visible and it seemed they would burst any minute. She'd never seen him this angry before.

'Sir, please try to understand . . .' she stammered.

'No! You try to understand. That man lying inside the ICU is my father. Do you get that?'

'I know, but there was no time to inform you,' she said calmly, unfazed by his temper.

'You could have called me right then! How could you get my father here without telling me?' he shouted.

The nurse warned him to lower his pitch.

'You have no idea what you've done,' he hissed.

Zarish could not believe that he was accusing her. Instead of thanking her, he was getting angry for nothing.

'Listen to me! I helped your father. I was there in his office when this happened,' she snapped.

He looked at her furiously.

'Instead of thanking me, you are blaming me? Do you think that's right?' she said as a tear rolled down her cheek.

Ahmar took a long, deep breath. Zarish sniffed. Just then a doctor escorted by a nurse stepped out of the ICU.

'What's the matter, doctor?' Ahmar asked. His voice was heavy, almost on the verge of breaking down.

'Are you his son?' the doctor inquired.

'Yes. How is he doing now? Is he going to be okay?' he asked worriedly.

'It was a minor heart attack. We have conducted all our tests. He is unconscious but will recover soon. Don't worry.' The doctor patted him on his shoulder.

'How long are you going to keep him here?' Ahmar asked.

'Just a day or two,' the doctor affirmed.

'Thank you.' He shook hands with him.

'Don't thank me. Thank this young lady who brought your father here just in time. Otherwise, his condition would have deteriorated.'

Ahmar nodded, feeling guilty for yelling at her.

'Here is the prescription for the medicines. You should get them right away,' the doctor said.

Ahmar turned around to apologize to Zarish, but she had disappeared.

The next morning, Zarish came in early to check on Muraad. She found both of them asleep. Ahmar lay sprawled on the couch, snoring. She could not help but smile. She put the lunch bag on the table and sat beside him.

'He looks so innocent while sleeping, so young,' she thought. She observed his thick, black lashes, the upturned nose and pink lips . . .

He suddenly woke up, surprised to find Zarish sitting beside him. He rubbed his eyes with his fingers and looked at her groggily. She noticed that his shirt was completely crumpled.

'Good morning,' she said, smiling.

He just nodded, a little uncomfortable in her presence. He was looking for the right moment to apologize to her.

'What did the doctor say? How is he doing now?' she asked.

'The doctor said he will be fine. No need to worry,' he whispered.

'Phew. That's a relief.'

'I'll go and call the nurse,' he said. 'Will you stay here for a while, please?' he asked.

'I'm here for as long as you want me. Don't worry,' she said.

Later, when he went back to the room, he could not find Zarish. Maybe she had left or maybe she was still angry with him. He came and sat beside his father on the bed. Muraad was still unconscious, wrapped up in needles, tubes and an oxygen mask. The machines in the room beeped continuously. Ahmar held Muraad's hand and pressed it firmly.

'You will be fine, Dad. I love you,' he whispered and cried quietly.

After a while, Ahmar stepped out of the room and found Zarish sitting on a bench in the corridor. He was surprised to see her, but also relieved. She looked up at him and smiled.

He sat down beside her. It made Zarish uncomfortable and she look down at her hands nervously.

'I'm sorry about what I said yesterday,' he said.

Zarish turned to look at him.

'You saved my father's life, and I blamed you. I'm sorry,' he murmured.

'You were upset.'

'I should have thanked you but instead I yelled at you,' he said and sighed regretfully.

'It's okay,' she said. 'I understand. Don't think about it.'

Both of them sat silently for a while.

'I am really close to my father,' Ahmar broke the silence. 'Ever since my mother died, he has taken care of my sister and me. I am what I am because of him.'

'How did your mother die?'

He winced after hearing the question and she noticed it.

'I was only four when she passed away. She was suffering from anaemia. She lost a lot of blood during my younger sister's delivery,' he whispered.

Zarish listened to him intently.

'My father had to raise two children all alone. It was the hardest task ever . . .' his voice trailed off.

'Why didn't he remarry?'

'I wish I knew. Maybe he did not want to share his love with any other woman. Or maybe he knew that no other woman would love his kids the way my mother did.'

'So, you have lived with your father since your mother's death?' she asked.

'Not always. I shifted to the US after finishing my high school. It was a tough decision, leaving him, alone, but he wanted me to go. He wanted me to achieve something big in life.'

'And what about your . . .' she continued.

'Aren't you supposed to go home now?' he interrupted. 'It's quite late,' he said looking at his watch.

'No, I don't want to go back. I want to sit here all night and talk to you,' she thought.

'Yeah,' she said with a sigh.

'I'll drop you home. Come,' he offered.

'I will call my driver. You should stay with your dad.'

'I owe you. Let me drop you home. Please,' he insisted.

The thought of sitting beside him in his car made her heart jump. She thought about their first meeting; how she had hated him that night. The memory brought a smile to her face. All this seemed like a dream to her. A never-ending, pleasant dream.

'What are you thinking about?' he asked, interrupting her thoughts.

'I am thinking that you need to slow down. You're driving like a maniac,' she lied.

'Are you lying?' he asked with a wicked smile.

'What? No. Why?' she lied again. 'You can read minds or what?'

'No, I can't. Your words didn't match your eyes,' he said as he looked at her intently.

Zarish looked outside the window and smiled.

The next day Zarish was busy preparing boiled chicken and corn soup, and vegetable sandwiches for Muraad.

The maid, Nusrat, was amazed to see her working in the kitchen.

'Nusrat, pass me the cabbage,' Zarish ordered.

'Yes, Baaji,' Nusrat said and did as she was told.

Zarina stepped into the kitchen and was stunned to see her daughter busy at work, covered in sweat.

'What's going on here? What are you doing here, Zarru?' her mother asked.

'Mom, I'm cooking some food for Sir Muraad,' she said, wiping the sweat.

'But why are you doing it? Doesn't he have his own children to look after him?'

'He has a son. Do you remember my FSA professor I told you about?'

'Yeah. I think so.'

'Anyway, I wanted to cook something for him because he's a nice person,' Zarish tried to reason it out.

'Really? Have you ever thought of cooking something for your own father?' Zarina said, folding her arms.

'Mom! Please don't start now. I'm running late so please let me finish what I am doing,' Zarish said irritably. Her mother left the kitchen shaking her head. She made a mental note to tell her husband about this.

Ahmar was busy talking to the doctor when Zarish reached the hospital. She sat down on one of the benches and decided to wait for him. After a while, he joined her.

'Good morning, Sir,' she greeted him with a coy smile.

'Good morning. What are you doing here?' he asked, looking amused.

'Well, I brought home-made lunch for Sir Muraad and you,' she replied. 'I prepared it myself,' she added.

Ahmar felt a bit odd.

'You shouldn't be here, Miss Zarish. You should be at the university, attending classes.'

'I know what I'm doing. Now will you please let me meet your father?' she insisted.

'You are so stubborn.'

She ignored his comment and followed him into Muraad's room.

'Good morning, Sir! How are you feeling now?' she asked.

Muraad was resting on his bed. He looked better and happier than yesterday.

'Doing great, Zarish. How about you?' He was glad to see her.

'I'm fine. Thank you,' she said as she sat beside him. 'Look what I brought for you,' she said, taking out the lunchbox from her bag.

'Home-made chicken and corn soup, and vegetable sandwiches,' she announced as she removed the lid.

'Hmm,' he sniffed. 'Smells delicious.'

She put the food on a plate and gave it to him.

Ahmar walked into the room and shut the door behind him. He leaned against the wall and observed them talking. 'My father really seems to like her,' he wondered.

'I can take you home tomorrow. I just spoke to the doctor,' Ahmar declared.

They both turned to look at him, unaware of his presence.

'Thank god!' Muraad said cheerfully. 'I don't have to stay in this hell any more.'

'Relax, Dad,' Ahmar said, standing beside the bed.

'I think I should get back to the university now,' Zarish said as she stood up.

'Why don't you go with Ahmar? He is leaving as well,' Muraad said.

'I don't think I can leave you alone here,' Ahmar said.

'C'mon, kid. I'm doing fine now. There are so many pretty nurses to take care of me,' he said, giggling naughtily.

Zarish realized that Muraad had the same smile as Ahmar.

'You shouldn't miss your lectures. You can check on me later,' Muraad said.

'Are you sure, Dad?' Ahmar asked.

Muraad nodded.

'Take care of yourself,' Zarish said.

'You too, honey.'

Ahmar and Zarish shared a quick hesitant glance and then walked out of the room.

Ahmar got a call from his father as soon as he sat in the car.

'Yes, Dad?'

'I really like her,' he said.

A warm smile spread across Ahmar's face.

'You don't have anything to say today?' Ahmar asked her on their way to the university.

Zarish was lost in thought and did not hear his question.

'Hello?' he asked again.

'Sorry, are you talking to me?' she asked dazedly.

'Of course. Unless there is someone else in the car with us,' he said, looking around.

'As if you talk non-stop.'

'Okay. Let's get started then,' he said, relaxing his shoulder muscles. 'What were you thinking about earlier?'

'Uh. Nothing,' she replied instinctively.

'It seems you don't want to talk.'

'No. It was nothing,' she said with a frown.

'Fine. It's better to stay quiet then.'

As he pulled into the parking lot of the university, Zarish gasped in fear.

'What's wrong?' he asked.

'My friends are here.'

'So?' he asked.

'So, I don't want them to get the wrong idea,' she said. He shrugged.

'I don't want them to think I'm dating my finance teacher,' she said sarcastically.

'Oh,' he said and cocked his brow. 'You're right, actually.'

Ahmar drove the car around the parking lot until he reached a spot where there was no one.

'You can get off here,' he said.

'Thanks. See you in the class, Sir.' She left the car reluctantly.

Haroon and Sherry were standing with the rest of the students near the parking lot.

Zarish waved at Haroon from a distance and walked towards the library.

Hey!' he called after her.

'Hey,' she turned to greet him.

'Where have you been? No calls or messages?' he said. She shrugged. She didn't want him to know where she had been for the last two days.

'Do you know Mr Hussain Muraad had a heart attack two days ago?' he asked her.

'Um. Yeah.'

'By the way, I called you so many times but you didn't answer,' he said.

'I . . . uh . . . I was busy. Anyway, I have to complete my presentation. So, see you later,' she said, leaving Haroon behind.

'OMG! Really? Are you dating him?' Saleha asked after hearing Zarish's story. They were sitting in the cafeteria. Zarish covered her face with her hands.

'Tell me!' Saleha asked impatiently.

'Saleha, it doesn't mean anything! He just drove me home twice; it doesn't mean he likes me,' Zarish clarified. 'Or maybe it does,' she thought.

'He told you so much about his life,' Saleha added.

'That doesn't make any difference, Saleha,' Zarish said with a sigh. 'It was a difficult time for him. He just wanted someone to talk to.'

'It does matter! C'mon. He hasn't shared his personal stories with any other student apart from you!' Saleha exclaimed.

'I helped his father. He is just being nice to me. That's it.'

'Or maybe he likes you.'

Zarish gave her a stunned look. 'Are you insane?' she asked.

'I'm just telling you one of the possibilities.'

'Keep this one out of the list please!' Zarish exclaimed.

After class, Zarish and Saleha walked towards the parking lot. It was a lovely evening. A cool breeze blew in Zarish's face, refreshing her instantly.

'I guess it is going to rain today,' Saleha said, looking at the sky.

'I hope so.'

'Somebody is waiting for you,' Saleha said, nudging her.

Zarish immediately thought of Ahmar but then saw Haroon leaning against his car.

'I'm going home. You take care of yourself,' Saleha patted her on her back and left.

Zarish sighed and walked towards him.

'Hey,' Zarish said.

'Hey,' Haroon replied immediately.

'How are you doing?' she asked.

'Come, I'll drive you home.'

'I can go with my driver. He is already here.'

'Send him back. I'll drop you,' Haroon said in a demanding voice.

'Err . . . okay.' She did not want to argue with Haroon on this matter because she knew it was useless.

Ahmar and Wahab headed towards the parking lot too. Wahab's car had gone for repair, so Ahmar was dropping him home.

Ahmar was about to get into the car when he saw Zarish and Haroon.

'Hey, what's the matter?' Wahab followed his gaze.

'Nothing,' Ahmar said.

'They make a cute couple, don't they?' Wahab said casually.

'Why are we talking about them? It is their private matter,' Ahmar said scornfully.

'It's just an observation,' he said.

Ahmar hit the accelerator and drove off.

'Times have changed. These days, girls and boys go out together. I remember during our time it was quite difficult to take a girl out on a date. Wasn't it?' Wahab asked.

'Yeah,' Ahmar whispered.

For some reason, he did not like Wahab calling them a couple. He didn't know why.

The evening was slowly turning into night. Zarish rolled down her window and the cool wind struck her face, sending a chill down her spine. She missed Ahmar terribly.

'Is there something you want to say?' Haroon broke the silence.

Zarish looked at him.

'Not really,' she said, looking outside again.

'Where were you the last two days?'

'I was at the hospital with Sir Muraad,' she told him.

'What?'

She nodded.

'I know he had a heart attack, but what were you doing there with him?' he asked.

'I was the one who took him to the hospital,' she mumbled.

'Seriously?' he exclaimed.

'Yeah.'

'You could have called me.'

'It all happened in a rush. I had no time to inform anyone. Not even Sir Ahmar. He was angry with me for the same reason.'

'That's rude. He should have thanked you.'

'He did. He just freaked out initially. I guess it is normal. I apologized for my mistake,' she said.

'I didn't expect you to be on his side. You have changed.'

'What are you talking about?'

'You are not the Zarish I have known my entire life.'

She looked at him unbelievingly.

'The old Zarish would have been angry if someone spoke to her rudely. I know how you usually react, but you apologized in this case. I can't believe it,' he said.

Zarish thought about what he'd said.

'Don't say I'm wrong here. I know you too well. Even you can't deny it. What's with this sudden change?'

'There is no change! Stop humiliating me,' she yelled.

Haroon fixed his gaze on the road.

'I was just being nice to him and his dad. He is our mentor and it is our duty to respect him. Get it?'

'Since when have you started respecting that douche bag?' he asked sarcastically.

'Shut up, Haroon. Just shut up!'

Haroon's face distorted with rage and he pressed the accelerator harder.

'Drop me home right now!' she said, hiding her tears.

Later that day, Ahmar's mind went back to Zarish. After this incident, his opinion of her had slightly changed.

He no longer considered her a rich brat. Though she was melodramatic and emotional at times, he believed there was also a good side to her. And then he thought of her and Haroon. He had seen them leaving the university together. Not just that day, they were together most of the time. Probably they were just good friends. Or maybe they were lovers. He could not figure out their relationship. His shoulder muscles tensed up as he lay on the bed and switched off the lamp.

'Why am I bothered about her relationship with Haroon? Why am I even thinking about this right now?' he wondered.

Zarish was still angry with Haroon. She did not respond to any of his calls or text messages. She ignored him all night. He came to meet her at her house in the morning. Soon both of them resolved their issues. He got flowers, chocolates and stuffed toys to cheer her up.

Earlier things were different. Whenever they had a fight, Haroon would buy her things and that would make her happy. But now she did not want to argue with him so she forgave him easily. She only cared about Ahmar as he was becoming the centre of her world. She had breakfast with Haroon at her place and then they left for the university together.

It was time for Ahmar's lecture. Zarish, Saleha and Maha sauntered into the class. Zarish wanted to see him and ask him about his father's health. She was surprised to see him in the class, setting up the projector for the lecture.

Zarish tried to get his attention, but he ignored her. She had specially worn a cream-coloured jumpsuit to impress him. She felt disappointed when he did not look at her and went about his business.

'He looks so handsome today!' Maha whispered in Zarish's ear.

She did not like it when Maha or any other girl praised him. She *never* liked it.

Slowly the class filled with students. Haroon decided to sit right behind Zarish.

'Aren't you going to sit beside me?' Zarish asked him.

'I'm fine here, Zarish,' he said with a smile.

Zarish just shrugged. She turned her attention towards Ahmar who had begun the lecture.

He walked to the whiteboard and wrote 'cash flow statement' on it.

'Have you heard about this term before? I assume you all have,' he said out loud.

Most of the students just nodded but nobody spoke. Ahmar's eyes scanned the classroom and his gaze stopped at Zarish. Her cheeks flushed.

'Miss Zarish,' he said.

She just nodded.

'Would you like to enlighten the class?' he said, folding his arms.

'Yes, Sir,' she said confidently.

'Please go ahead,' he said.

'A cash flow statement is a report that gives out details about the cash inflows and outflows of an organization,' she beamed as she knew her answer was correct. An uncomfortable silence ensued.

'Are you sure?' he asked finally.

She nodded assuredly.

'See. This is where you people go wrong. You become overconfident and think you know everything. This foolish attitude ultimately leads you to your failure!' he bellowed.

Zarish gasped in shock. She didn't understand why he was so angry all of a sudden.

Saleha tried to comfort her by holding her hand tightly. Haroon's entire body got stiff.

'That's not fair, Sir,' Haroon interjected.

Ahmar glanced at him.

'This is not how you talk to a student, especially a female student. I am sure she is offended,' Haroon said.

Ahmar grinned mockingly.

'Okay. So now Mr Haroon will speak on behalf of Miss Zarish,' Ahmar said sarcastically.

Haroon felt like punching him and breaking his jaw. He clenched his fists tightly. Zarish stared at Ahmar in disbelief.

'Friends speak for friends here. What an interesting class. Very nice,' Ahmar said, his voice dripping with sarcasm.

Zarish felt helpless. She wanted to run away from the class. She could not understand the reason for this sudden change in his behaviour.

'Sir, please. You can tell me my mistake,' she said.

'No,' he said sternly. 'I want all of you to go through this topic and come back thoroughly prepared for the next class. I'm leaving now,' he said as he gathered his stuff and left the class in a hurry.

Zarish ran after him.

'Zarish! Wait!' Haroon called after her, but it was too late.

She tried to catch up with him but he was already in his car. She saw him drive away like a maniac.

'What's wrong with him? Am I responsible for his rude behaviour? He seemed annoyed at something. Was he worried about his father's health? I have to know the truth,' she thought.

On his way back home, Ahmar thought about Zarish. 'Though she gave the correct answer, I was rude to her.

What's wrong with me? I shouldn't have a damn problem with her friendship with Haroon,' he thought.

The weekend was here. Zarish could not meet Ahmar till Monday, so she decided to pay him a visit. His house was at the end of the road, covered in ivy. It looked really old and imposing from outside but had a warm and cosy feel to it. The gate was open so she parked her car in the driveway. The garden was gigantic, mostly covered with neem trees. Surely, someone was fond of gardening.

She observed her surroundings for a minute and then walked towards the heavy door made of carved timber. She inhaled deeply and knocked on the door twice. Ahmar opened the door after a few seconds. He looked damn cute in a baby pink T-shirt and beige pants. He was not wearing his glasses. His eyebrows shot up with surprise when he saw her.

'Hey,' she said enthusiastically.

'What are you doing here?' he scowled.

'Won't you invite me in? It's really hot outside,' she said, smiling cutely.

'Come in,' he said and moved aside.

'Wow. Your house is so . . . beautiful,' she said, looking around.

Beautiful lampshades with yellow lights glowed in every corner, giving the house a cosy, lived-in feel. The warm colours of the wooden furniture complimented the dark hues of the walls.

'Did you come here to tell me this?'

'Of course not,' she said with a grin. 'Can't you be nice to your guest?'

'An unwanted guest,' he hissed.

She rolled her eyes at him.

'Now, may I know why you're here?' he asked.

'I came to see Sir Muraad.'

'He's fine now,' he said curtly.

'You didn't tell me he got discharged from the hospital. I think I had the right to know.'

'Just because you saved his life?' he asked sarcastically.

'Yeah. Uh. No. I mean,' she whispered, feeling confused.

'Fine, Miss Zarish. I'm sorry about that. He is in his room. You can go and see him if you want,' he said and walked away.

Zarish felt the bitterness in his tone and attitude. She ignored him and entered Muraad's room.

He was lying on his bed, absorbed in a book.

'Good afternoon, Sir,' she greeted him cordially.

'Oh, Zarish!' he exclaimed as he tried to sit up.

'Please don't get up. I will come and sit next to you,' she said.

Muraad smiled and nodded.

'How are you doing, Sir?' she asked, caressing his hand.

'Feeling fantastic. As usual.' He grinned.

She smiled.

'I'm really happy to see you here.'

'So am I.'

Ahmar came into the room bearing a tray of glasses filled with orange juice. He gave one to her.

'Thank you,' she said.

She seemed amused by the fact that her teacher was doing household chores. She chuckled. Ahmar caught her smiling and flinched.

'What happened, Zarish? What's so amusing?' Muraad said as he took the glass from Ahmar's hand.

'Err . . . nothing, Sir. I just find it funny to see Sir Ahmar working around the house,' she said and giggled again.

Ahmar rolled his eyes and put the tray on the side table.

'Ahmar does all the work. He is a really good cook too,' Muraad told her.

'Really?' she asked as she took a sip of the orange juice.

'Yes. He has many sides to his personality. Don't just see him as a boring teacher,' he said, smiling.

'I would actually like to try it someday,' she said, teasing Ahmar.

'Why not? We won't let you go hungry. Ahmar will cook something for you,' Muraad said.

Ahmar opened his mouth to protest but then stopped. He couldn't say no to his dad.

'What would you like to eat, Miss Zarish?' Ahmar hissed.

'Anything you want, Sir.'

'Good,' he said coldly and left the room.

She followed him into the kitchen. Everything seemed to be in order and the kitchen seemed well maintained even in the absence of a woman. Ahmar stood near the kitchen stove chopping vegetables. She stood beside him, and folded her arms casually. He remained indifferent.

'Sir Ahmar Muraad. You never fail to impress me. Today, I've come across another thing about you that has left me completely awestruck,' she broke the silence.

'What was the first thing?' he said and looked at her.

'Some things cannot be told.'

'Your wish,' he said, tossing the vegetables into a pan.

'So, besides cooking and torturing your students, what else do you like to do?' she teased him.

'Are you an interviewer? Or have you joined the university journal?'

Zarish chuckled at his question.

'No, your unwanted guest slash interviewer is just curious,' she told him.

'You don't have to be curious about me.'

'So that means you are not going to answer my question?' she asked.

'And what was your question?'

'What else do you like to do besides cooking and teaching?' she repeated her question.

'I have always been interested in music . . .' he began.

Zarish took the stirrer from his hand. For a moment, their fingers touched and eyes met.

'I was the lead singer of a local underground band during my college days,' he continued. He seemed lost in thought.

'Band? Wow!' Zarish exclaimed.

'We used to perform quite often, mostly for fun.'

She stirred the vegetables, still astounded.

He nodded and took the stirrer from her hand.

'I can't believe this. Why doesn't anyone know about this at the university?'

'Because I'm not a show-off, you know. I don't feel the need to discuss my personal life.'

'Can I ask you a favour?'

'Don't even think about it, Miss Zarish,' he said sternly.

'Wait, what?' she asked, surprised.

'Don't ask me to sing for you here.'

'No. Not here,' she said, grinning.

'Then where?' he asked lifting his brow.

'The summer festival is coming up. Why don't you perform?'

'Are you crazy?'

'Maybe. But it's a humble request. Please, Sir. Don't say no. Please, please, please,' she begged.

'No!' he said.

'Please, Sir.'

'I can't and I won't,' he said and walked to the fridge to get cheese and tomatoes.

Zarish felt irritated.

'Why not?' she asked, sounding helpless.

'Because I don't like showing off. The students should participate, not me.'

'Students will appreciate it. Trust me,' she said, looking into his eyes.

He looked up at her and shook his head.

'I just want to see you sing. Please.'

He ignored her and continued cooking.

'Is that a yes?' she asked, her face lighting up.

'Yes and no. The food is ready,' he declared.

Ahmar had cooked chicken and vegetable pasta, and it turned out to be delicious.

'I enjoyed the lunch,' she said, wiping her mouth with a tissue paper.

'Now you know you're not the only one that makes good food,' Ahmar said with a grin.

Zarish blushed because she knew it was a compliment.

'I think I should leave now,' she said as she stood up.

'Shall I drop you?'

'Thanks, but I've got my car today.'

'Great. Come, I'll walk you to your car,' he said thoughtfully.

She took her leave and walked to the main door.

'Why did you behave so rudely with Haroon and me in the last class?' she suddenly asked.

'Uh. I was just having a bad day. Sorry about that.'

'You hurt my feelings,' she said, unlocking her car.

'Zarish,' he said.

She turned around to look at him.

'Thanks for coming today. Dad was really happy.'

'The pleasure is mine, Sir.'

'And about the summer festival, I will discuss it with Sir Faris, and let you know,' he said with a smile.

'Great!' She nodded cheerfully. 'I had a really good time. Thank you for the lunch,' she said.

'The pleasure is mine,' he said, still smiling.

All the faculty members had gathered in the conference room for a meeting with Faris Ahmed. The dean discussed the upcoming events, which included the summer festival. He also discussed the schedule for the upcoming examinations.

After the meeting, Ahmar stayed back to talk to Faris.

'Yes, Ahmar?' Faris said.

'Sir, I wanted to talk to you about the summer festival,' Ahmar said.

Faris nodded and continued to read the file in his hand.

Ahmar was not sure if it was appropriate to talk about his performance at the event.

'What have you thought about the concert?' Ahmar finally asked.

'Well, we will have to select the best among those who are interested,' Faris answered.

Ahmar didn't know if he was required to be a part of the selection process, so he kept quiet.

'I know you are good at music, and I want you to help me select the students,' Faris said, grinning.

'Sure, Sir,' Ahmar finally smiled.

There was a real buzz around the festival in the university. Students queued up outside audition halls. Maleeha and Ahmar were in charge of the singing try-outs, while Jamal and Wahab had to select actors for the plays.

Haroon participated in the singing auditions, but both the teachers rejected him.

'Better luck next time, Haroon,' Maleeha told him.

Haroon felt dejected.

'Your voice has a good texture but you need to practise more. You can try again next year,' Ahmar said.

Haroon controlled his anger and thanked them before leaving the hall. He asked Zarish to meet him in the football ground.

'Hey. It's okay. Never mind,' Zarish consoled him.

He rested his head on her shoulder.

'Music is your passion. Moreover, this is just a university concert. Don't feel dejected, Haroon,' she said and caressed his cheek.

He held her hand and pressed it against his chest.

'I know you're right. I didn't like how they told me I was not good enough. Those teachers were telling me how to sing. Can you believe it?' he said irritably as he freed himself from her grasp.

'Hey.' She held his hand again. 'It's okay. Calm down, please.'

Perhaps it was just bad timing, but right then Ahmar happened to pass by. He was on his way to the parking lot when he saw them together. He was consumed with jealousy. He could not understand why this was happening. He wanted to snatch her hand and take her away forcefully.

He wanted to confront her for being so intimate with her male friend. But he knew he didn't have the right to stop her or control her life. Therefore, he quickly opened the door of his car, roared the engine to life so that she could notice his aggression, and drove off. It happened exactly how he had planned it. She saw his car heading towards the exit gate. Perhaps she understood his feelings or heard his thoughts.

Ahmar could not ignore the thoughts that clouded his mind. Why did it bother him? It was her life and she had the right to spend it as she wanted. He knew they were good friends, but he still felt anxious.

He took a decision right then. He would ignore her from now on. After all, she was a mere student. Nothing more and nothing less. He decided to stay away as much as possible. She was trying to get involved in his life and he was aware of that.

She and Haroon were meant for each other, he thought. They were close friends and had known each other since they were kids. Ahmar knew he had to break away, maintain some distance. It was the right decision, for both of them. He really regretted introducing her to his father and letting her into their lives.

On the other hand, Zarish felt something entirely different. She could sense from his attitude that he had issues with Haroon. Perhaps he did not like the intimacy they shared. However, she could not change this. She could only change his thinking. She had to tell him the truth about her relationship with Haroon; they were just friends and nothing more.

Later that day, she sent him a message:

> Hey. I want to talk to you. It is important. Sometime tomorrow, please?

'I hope I can tell him easily,' she thought as she chewed her lip.

Ironically, Ahmar didn't check his messages that night. He got up early the next morning, had breakfast with his dad and drove off to the university.

Bad news awaited him. The band they'd selected for the festival had backed out as the lead vocalist was unwell. He felt distressed. He spoke to Faris but nothing came out of it. He was asked to arrange for a new band immediately.

'We can look for some other singers. Don't lose hope,' Jamal assured him. Ahmar sighed.

'How about Haroon?' Jamal asked.

'He needs a great deal of practice,' Ahmar said sarcastically.

'Ahmar's right. We need to get someone who sings well,' Maleeha interjected.

Zarish and Sherry were drinking cold coffee in the cafe when Saleha and Maha joined them.

'Guess what? The lead vocalist is unwell, so his group is not performing now,' Maha said.

'Really?' Zarish exclaimed.

'Yes. We just got the news,' Saleha said.

'So, who is going to perform now?' Sherry asked.

'We have no idea. The faculty members are discussing it,' Maha said.

'I think I know someone who can,' Zarish said.

Zarish went to Faris with her idea.

'I know he is passionate about music. He sings exceptionally well,' Faris said thoughtfully.

'Then please let him perform. I don't think we will get anyone else at such a short notice.'

He looked convinced.

'Will you ask him to perform?'

'Certainly, I will. You don't need to worry about that.'

'Thank you, Sir,' she said and turned around to leave.

'Miss Munawwar?' he called out.

'Yes Sir?'

'I'm glad Ahmar has such loyal and obedient students,' he said with a smile.

'He's a great teacher.'

'Undoubtedly,' he said.

'Thank you for introducing him to our lives,' Zarish said. 'My life,' she thought.

'Oh. C'mon,' Faris said, a little embarrassed.

'Sir, I have another request.'

'Sure. Go ahead.'

'Please don't tell him it was my idea.'

'Oh, don't worry about that,' he assured her.

Zarish smiled gratefully.

'What?!' Ahmar said when Faris asked him to perform at the concert.

'But Sir, don't you think it would be unfair to the students?'

'Not at all. I know you are an incredible singer and nobody can match up to your talent. I want my festival to be a success. So, you will perform. Clear?'

Ahmar nodded.

Even though his problem had been solved, something still bothered Ahmar. He sat in his office, thinking about his next step. It had been a while since he had performed in front of an audience. He could not just go on the stage and start singing; he needed practice. Ahmar had to see if his voice still had the same spark it had a long time ago.

He entered the auditorium and walked to the stage in a backdrop of silence. He picked up the guitar that lay lifeless on a chair and strummed the strings. The music broke the silence and his face cracked into a smile. A few minutes with the guitar and he realized that he had regained familiarity with the instrument. He carried on the process as he played the chords. There was a time in his life when he could not imagine himself away from the world of music. His life had changed drastically in the last few years.

Each chord on the guitar took him back in time to the playground of the university as his friends surrounded him; all of them praising his voice and prowess with the guitar. A song hit his lips and he started humming it.

An unusual voice hit Zarish's ears as she walked past the auditorium. It was warm and comforting. Sparked with curiosity, she gently pushed open the door of the auditorium hall to peek in, and saw Ahmar sitting on the stage, playing the guitar and singing. He was lost in the tune but Zarish's footsteps on the wooden floor brought him back from his trance.

'Hey!' she said.

For a moment, Ahmar felt like ignoring her and wanted her to leave but he did not say anything. He did not forget that he was still her mentor and could not be rude to her. Whenever he thought of her, Haroon invaded his mind. It made Ahmar envious that Haroon and Zarish were together. Ahmar failed to understand why he felt this way.

'Yes?'

'I hope I didn't interrupt your singing session.'

'You already did,' he replied curtly.

'I'm sorry about that.' She walked to the stage as she spoke. 'You have an amazing voice.'

'Thank you,' he replied.

'I wanted to speak to you,' she said.

'About what?'

'Congratulations for getting the opportunity to sing at the festival.'

She tried to sound happy.

'How do you know about that?' he asked, frowning.

'Does that make a difference?'

'Of course, it does. Tell me how you know about it.'

'I asked Sir Faris to give you a chance,' she said.

'You . . . what?'

Zarish saw his eyes burning. He abruptly got off the chair.

'Yes, I knew that you wouldn't volunteer by yourself so I decided to give you a little push.' She tried to chuckle.

Ahmar's cold stare forced the smile to retreat.

'Look . . . I really wanted to see you sing,' she said sheepishly.

He inhaled deeply, trying to rid himself of the anger.

'I know you might think this is stupid, but actually it's not,' she tried to explain her actions. 'I wanted to bring your passion for music back to life.'

'Thanks for showing your generosity, but it was certainly not required.'

'Don't be nervous. You can do it. I trust you.'

'Your trust doesn't matter to me anyway,' he hissed.

Zarish felt the coldness in his tone but tried to ignore it.

'Is something wrong? You seem a little worried,' she asked.

He gazed at her intently.

'Can I be of some help?' she offered.

No. Actually, yes.'

'What is it?'

'Leave this hall, please,' he said.

His harsh words hit her hard, and though she tried to ignore them as much as possible, tears welled up in her eyes. She turned and walked out of the auditorium.

'He makes me cry all the time, as if my feelings mean nothing to him,' she thought as she walked out.

Ahmar rapped the chair hard with his knuckles.

'No. I can't be rude to this girl. I can't treat her like this just because I don't like Haroon,' he thought. Almost on an impulse, he rushed outside to catch up with her.

'Zarish!' he called after her.

Zarish stopped when she heard him call out her name but did not turn lest he see the tears.

He walked towards her to make her stop but lowered his gaze to the ground.

'I'm sorry. My mind was preoccupied with something.' His gaze remained lowered with embarrassment.

'It's okay, Sir,' she said without turning back, wiping the tears brushing past her cheeks. She did not want to cry in front of him. But her emotions betrayed her.

Ahmar heard her trying to choke down her sobs.

'It's not the first time that you've spoken to me like that. I am used to it,' she sniffed.

'Don't say that please,' he whispered.

'I have to go home, Sir.'

Zarish stepped ahead but he held her hand. She could not believe it. It was the first time he had touched her. She could feel the electrifying sensation run through her entire body. His touch brought a warmth and excitement. She felt butterflies dance in her stomach, and it aroused her. Her heart fluttered. It was a strange feeling for her. She had not felt the same excitement, warmth and arousal when Haroon held her hand or touched her.

Ahmar was amazed at his own audacity. He felt different whenever he was around her. She slowly turned around to face him and their eyes locked in an intense gaze; so deep, it felt like he was reaching into her soul.

It took only a couple of seconds for him to realize that they were standing in the corridor. He immediately let go of her hand and took a few steps back.

'Why did you leave my hand? I've never felt so good,' she thought.

He cleared his throat and broke the reverie.

'Uh, you okay?' he asked.

She nodded, pressing her lips into a fine line.

'This is not the end. You have to help me for my training sessions,' he declared.

'Me?' She raised her brows.

'Yes. You.'

'Okay. Sure,' she murmured shyly.

'Meet me after your classes tomorrow,' he said, looking into her eyes and observing her reaction.

She just nodded, moving her gaze downwards.

Zarish started her new mission in life. Every day, after her classes, she would help Ahmar with his practice sessions. She could not fathom the reason why he had chosen her, of all people, for this purpose. He had a beautiful voice, but his singing appeared to be slightly rusty. She had spent most of the sessions staring at him as he sang with his eyes closed. Now, the practice sessions had concluded and it was the last day before the summer festival. Ahmar was packing his stuff and was ready to leave for home.

'Will you do something for me?' he asked.

'Yes, Sir?' she said, shutting her book.

'I noticed Haroon's guitar skills. Will he play for me at the festival?'

Zarish thought for a few seconds.

'He plays the guitar really well,' he commented.

'I know. I have to ask him first.'

'Sure. Why don't you call him here? We can talk about it . . .' He zipped his bag.

'Um, sure.' Zarish called Haroon to check if he was at the university. Luckily for her, he was. She asked him to join her and Ahmar in the auditorium, to which he agreed.

'He's coming,' she told Ahmar.

'Great.' He nodded.

'Actually, he was really upset when you guys rejected him,' she said, feeling a pang of sympathy for her friend.

'I know,' he said with a sigh.

'But I believe you guys had your own criteria for the selection,' she said.

'Don't worry. I'll handle it,' he reassured her.

Just then, Haroon made an entry into the auditorium.

'Zarish?' he called out.

'Haroon, I'm here!' Zarish replied, gesturing him to join her on the stage.

Haroon stepped on the stage, passing a nonchalant look towards Ahmar. However, Ahmar remained indifferent.

'You're performing with Sir at the festival,' Zarish told him.

'Really? How? As a guitar player?' Haroon said sarcastically.

'Absolutely not, Haroon,' she said.

'You will sing with me as the other vocalist,' Ahmar declared.

Hearing this, Haroon's eyes gleamed with hope. 'Really?' he asked.

Ahmar nodded, smiling.

'But I was rejected,' he said, looking at Zarish.

'I'm giving you another chance. Join me tomorrow morning for the practice session. We don't have much time.'

'All right.' He shook his head.

'Make me proud!' Ahmar told him.

'I will, thanks.'

Zarish was smiling all the way. For her, it was a win-win situation.

'Zarish, I have to go. I have to meet Sherry at the cafe. You want to come?' Haroon turned to look at Zarish.

'I'm leaving for home, Haroon. My driver is waiting for me outside,' she told him.

'All right, no problem. I'll see you at the practice session tomorrow.' He shot a quick smile at Ahmar and then left.

'We should also leave now,' Ahmar said.

Zarish nodded.

'Come. I'll walk with you till the gate.'

'I'm glad that you considered Haroon,' she said.

'I admire his skills,' he said.

'Thank you for that.'

'And thank you for believing in me and my vocals,' he said, smirking.

Zarish smiled but wondered about his mood swings. One instant he would appear arrogant and intimidating and the next moment he would be exceedingly sweet, polite and supportive. How could a man have two sides? Perhaps he suffered from a split personality disorder.

'What happened?' he asked, interrupting her thoughts.

'Err. Nothing,' she gulped.

'Are you sure?'

'Actually, there is something I want to tell you, in case you might have a different opinion about it now.' She hesitated.

Ahmar narrowed his brows.

She felt that this was the right time to clarify to him about her relationship with Haroon.

'Haroon and I are just good friends. I hope you are not getting a wrong picture about the two of us.' She tried to chuckle at the end of her statement.

'Well.' He folded his arms. 'I didn't need to know that.'

'It might help you understand a few things.'

'I have no complaints and no demands, Miss Zarish.' He raised his hands in surrender.

Zarish smiled.

'Goodbye,' he said, heading towards his car that was parked in the lot.

All night, he thought about what Zarish had told him. She and Haroon were just good friends. He felt relieved to some extent but could not ignore the intimacy in that friendship. From the way Zarish had suddenly clarified about her friendship with Haroon, Ahmar realized that she wanted him to believe her story. He wanted to believe her. Though he did not know the actual reason behind that feeling, he still felt at ease.

'What if Haroon considers her to be more than a friend?' he wondered.

The much-discussed summer festival had arrived. All the arrangements were in place and there was excitement in the air. The students were scattered around the grounds chirping enthusiastically about the event.

The festival turned out to be a huge hit. Sherry and Saleha enacted Shakespeare's *Romeo and Juliet*. Their excitement continued offstage after the play. Zarish saw them chatting and they looked good together.

Everyone from the university contributed to making the festival a successful event. Faris won accolades for organizing it. Last, but not least, Ahmar's spellbinding performance could not be missed.

Ahmar's level of energy drove the audience crazy. He was an exceptional singer and everyone lauded his talent. During the performance, Ahmar ensured that Haroon had enough opportunities to sing as well. The audience was thrilled to see the two of them perform together on stage. Zarish made a silent wish that the conflict between the two of them would end now.

The dean announced the date for the final term semester exams. Every student got busy preparing. Haroon and Sherry had promised themselves that they would study hard in order to pass this semester. Zarish helped them in their efforts.

She found excuses to take counselling sessions with Ahmar in his office along with the other students. Sometimes she would also go to his office alone. She tried to analyse the reason behind this every time. She felt as if she needed to spend more time with Ahmar, as if that would help her to comprehend what lay behind her feelings.

Zarish wanted to know whether it was just a mere crush or something deeper. She did not want a simple infatuation to take over her feelings. She bugged him every now and then till the exams began.

'How long are you going to sit here?' Ahmar asked her one day.

'Um. I'm just left with one question,' she answered innocently.

'Go ahead,' he said.

'Do you have other plans?'

'Yeah. Actually, I had to go out with Jamal and Wahab today,' he said, looking at his wristwatch.

'Oh.'

'But not before you get cleared with this question,' he assured her.

'I got it now, Sir. I'm done.'

'Let me check.' He took the paper from her hands, their fingers brushing.

She noticed his hands were warm. Zarish drew back her hand with a flushed face. Ahmar pretended like nothing had happened and started reading the paper. Zarish exhaled but continued to stare at him.

'What is so special about this person? He is good-looking but not extraordinarily good-looking. He looks a lot older than me. He is probably twenty-nine or thirty and I am just twenty-two—a difference of around eight years. That's too much. Isn't it? Oh god. And, he doesn't even seem interested in me. Then why am I wasting my time on this person? Why?' she wondered.

'You're good. Well done. Now we're done here,' he said, pulling her out of her trance.

'Oh! That's it?' She came back to reality.

He nodded instantly.

'So?' she said.

'So what?'

'Is that all? No more practice questions for me?' She did not want to leave.

'That's it for now. Practise the ones we've already done.' He got up from his seat and shut his laptop.

'It seems that you are in a hurry,' she murmured.

'Kind of.'

'I guess I should leave then,' she said grumpily.

'Hmm.' He nodded as he packed his things.

She got up from her seat and walked out of his office in a huff, slamming the door behind her.

Ahmar heaved a sigh of relief and smirked when she left without bidding him goodbye. He knew that she wanted to practise some more questions, or to be precise, spend more time with him; but he did not want to give her much space.

The exam week passed uneventfully. The credit went to Zarish as she helped most of her classmates with their doubts. The students who were earlier about to fail now found themselves better prepared for the examinations. Even Haroon could proudly predict that he'd pass with good grades. It was now time to relax as the results were to be declared a week later.

One afternoon, on the way to the cafeteria, Zarish noticed a pamphlet stuck on the noticeboard.

The Masquerade Ball
All participants have to strictly follow the ball's dress code i.e. black and red, along with masks. Otherwise entry will not be allowed.
P.S. Entry for couples only. Singles not allowed.
Thanks,
Admin

Zarish frowned upon reading the notice.

'Did you read about the masquerade ball on the noticeboard?'

Zarish asked Saleha at the cafeteria.

'Yeah, I did,' Saleha said, sipping her mixed-fruit juice.

Zarish sighed, rested her elbow on the table, leaned her head forward and glumly placed a knuckle on her cheek.

'What's wrong?' Saleha asked, observing Zarish's gloomy expression.

'I'm worried about the ball,' Zarish confessed.

'Why?'

Zarish sat up straight.

'The ball requires a date,' Zarish said, squinting her eyes.

'So, why is that a big deal?' Saleha shrugged.

'I don't know!' Zarish exclaimed and quickly hid her face behind her hands. Of course, she could not tell Saleha what her heart desired at that moment.

'Who else could be the best date for you apart from Haroon?' Saleha said, pinching Zarish's arm playfully.

'Stop teasing me.' Zarish felt irritated.

'I'm not teasing. I'm stating a fact.'

'Yeah, yeah.' Zarish rolled her eyes.

'Or do you want someone else to escort you to the ball?' Saleha asked.

Zarish blushed all of a sudden.

'No. No way. That's not what I meant.' Zarish hid her face again.

'You shouldn't have a problem in selecting your date. I'm the one who has a dilemma,' Saleha sounded glum.

'Hey. Don't say that.' Zarish caressed Saleha's hand. 'Have you asked Sherry yet?'

'He should ask me first,' Saleha hissed.

'Maybe he is mustering the courage to ask you.' Zarish tried to lighten the mood.

'Maybe. Yeah.' Saleha sighed.

Zarish walked all alone down the hall towards her class, several thoughts jumbled in her mind. She was still unsure if she really wanted to go to the masquerade ball with Haroon. Her heart wished that she could pair up with Ahmar somehow. She cursed her heart. It wished for something that was impossible. Even if she asked him as her date, she knew he'd never agree. He would not want anybody to think of them as a couple. It would have been easier if Zarish was a teacher or Ahmar was a student.

As she reached for the doorknob, Ahmar popped up at her side.

'Morning, Miss Zarish.' He smiled unusually.

'Good morning, Sir,' she said. He looked quite dashing. His strange and intimidating smile melted her heart.

'Come into the classroom.' He stood aside to let her enter.

Hesitating slightly, she walked past him.

Zarish smelt the citrus and wood cologne. He kept enough distance to ensure that their bodies did not touch.

Ahmar started his lecture, drawing everybody's attention except Zarish, who kept staring at him. In the beginning, she had had a different approach. She had been keen on learning more about his subject. Now, things had changed. She let her concentration slip during the lecture because she knew she could take extra classes from him later. It would mean another opportunity to be with him, one she did not want to miss. She knew that she was getting more obsessed with him each day.

During class, Zarish saw Saleha using her phone to text someone with an animated expression. After the class ended, Saleha came up to Zarish and hugged her tightly.

'Hey.' Zarish sounded surprised.

'Guess what?' Saleha let go of her and grabbed her arms.

'What?'

'Sherry asked me to the dance!' Saleha whispered in her ear.

After her classes, Zarish headed toward Ahmar's office. She made an excuse to get away from Haroon and her other friends. It was around 9 p.m. and almost all faculty members and students had left the university except for those who had stayed back for their extra classes.

'Why does he always work till so late?' she wondered.

The door creaked when she opened it.

Ahmar's desk was stacked with files and papers. He was so absorbed in his work that he did not even notice her.

'Busy bee.' Her voice made him look up.

'Hey. What are you doing here so late?' he asked, glancing at his wristwatch.

'I had an extra class today,' she said, stepping closer to his desk.

'Do you want to sit?' he asked.

She shook her head.

'Don't you have to go home? It's quite late,' she said.

'Yeah, Dad is waiting for me. I'm just rechecking these exam papers,' he said looking at the papers.

'When will the results come out?'

'Before the masquerade ball,' he said still looking at the papers.

'He doesn't seem interested. He is not even looking at me,' she thought, wallowing in self-pity.

Ahmar was busy stapling the papers together.

'Err. I think I should leave now. Pay my regards to Uncle,' she said quickly. She felt unwanted.

Ahmar noticed her discomfort.

'What's wrong?' he asked suddenly, unconsciously stapling his hand in the process.

'Damn,' he said exasperatedly.

Zarish turned around to look at him.

'What happened?' she rushed towards him.

Ahmar looked at her intently. She bent down, sat on the carpet and observed his index finger closely.

'It's fine,' he whispered.

'It's not fine. Your finger is bleeding.'

'It's all right, Zarish.' He tried to release his hand from her grasp.

She caught his stare and held his hand for some time. He looked at her quizzically and felt his heart thumping against his chest.

'Let me fix this.' She took out a tissue paper and neatly wrapped it around his injured finger. He just looked at her with unblinking eyes.

It seemed like everything around him came to a standstill: he could not hear the ticking of the clock; he could not hear anything apart from their heartbeats and breathing.

He felt her warm and delicate skin on his hands. He noticed her for the first time: her long, black hair; her thick, dark lashes. He observed her nose, which seemed perfect on her face. Her skin was noticeably fair and her cheeks rosy. He felt like caressing them. And then he noticed her lips. He wanted to kiss her. He felt disgusted at his wild thoughts but also felt happy. He did not want to break his gaze but had to.

'It's okay. Thanks, I'll do it myself,' he said in a low voice.

The trance broke and she quickly drew herself back.

'I guess I should leave now,' she murmured. She stood up, her body stiff.

'Wait,' he hissed.

Zarish looked at him, embarrassed. Her cheeks turned red.

'It's too late for you to go home alone,' he said still looking at his finger, avoiding her eyes.

'I can call my driver. It's not too late,' she murmured.

She could sense that he was keen to drop her home. Maybe he wanted to talk about what had happened or he wanted to express his feelings for her.

He finally looked into her eyes and asked her not to call her driver.

'Is that an order or a request?' she asked, folding her arms.

'Whatever you want to think,' he said.

She followed him to his car in the parking lot. Thankfully, there was no one there.

Sometimes the thought of getting caught with her mentor crossed her mind, but she knew she was not doing anything wrong. 'Or am I?' she thought, confused. But she was sure of one thing. As long as Ahmar was there to protect her, she did not have to worry.

'How do you feel now?' Zarish asked him in the car. She did not feel shy any more which was quite surprising, even for her.

'About what?' he asked. He held the steering wheel firmly, eyes fixed on the road.

She pointed at his finger.

'Feeling a little dizzy,' he admitted.

'Please get it dressed as soon as you get home,' she said, leaning against the headrest.

'What do you tell your family when I drop you home?' he asked.

'Nothing,' she said as she bit her lower lip. 'Just that a friend dropped me home.'

'Am I your friend?' he asked.

She looked at him quizzically.

'Why are you looking at me like that? Does the thought of being my friend worry you?' he asked after observing her reaction.

'No. I'm not worried about that,' she said yawning.

'Then what?'

'First tell me. Are you my friend or just my teacher?' she asked.

He avoided her question and continued to focus on the road.

'Hmm?' She was waiting for his answer.

'Stop cross-questioning me.'

'Well . . . I am not. I just want to know what you feel because it really doesn't matter what I feel,' she said grumpily and looked out of the window again, rubbing her eyes.

'Well, it does matter, Zarish. You just won't understand,' he said, shaking his head.

'Then make me understand, please.'

'This is not the right time.'

'Why not?'

'Because you seem sleepy.'

Zarish woke up with a start. She rubbed her eyes and looked around. They were still in his car. He had parked his car right outside her house, not wanting to wake her up. She looked at Ahmar, who was looking at her intently.

'Don't worry. You're not far away from your home. I've parked the car outside your place,' he said.

Zarish could not see him properly in the dim light, but she could make out the outline of his features.

'How long have you been staring at me like this?' she said and turned to face him.

He wrapped his fingers around the steering wheel, rested his head on it and continued looking at her.

'I asked something,' she said, squinting her eyes.

He did not reply and remained in the same position.

'Okay. If you're not going to answer this, then I have another question for you. Why have you been staring at me at all, Ahmar?' she asked.

This was the first time that she had addressed him only by his first name. Ahmar blinked with surprise after hearing his name.

'You forgot to add sir before my name,' he said with a confused expression on his face.

'No, I didn't,' she said calmly.

'Are you sure?'

'I thought we were friends!' She shrugged casually.

'When did this happen?' he asked.

'Right now. Will you be my friend?' she said and held out her hand. Ahmar could see the enthusiasm in her gesture.

'Hmm,' he said animatedly and held his chin.

'You don't have to think so much. People die to become my friends,' she said, rolling her eyes.

He burst out laughing.

'What makes you think that? What's so special about you? To be honest, I don't find you different from any other girl in the university. There has to be a distinctive factor to stand out from the rest; something worth praising. For me, you are not unusual at all. And, in this case, I'm not dying to become your friend, Miss Zarish,' he said.

For a second Zarish thought she had not heard right. She looked down at her hands, her cheeks growing hot with embarrassment.

'Feeling bad now?' he asked, almost teasing her.

She gave him an awkward look, which made him laugh again. She had never seen him laugh like that before. She did not know whether to feel happy or remorseful.

'You should think about it seriously. I'm sure you'll get my point,' he said, smiling.

'If you don't want to be friends with me, then what, Ahmar?' she asked, ignoring his comments.

Her tone and her facial expression turned serious. Ahmar stopped laughing after hearing her question. She looked at him closely, waiting for a response. However, he did not know what to say. He switched his gaze to the other side. The magic was lost.

'Is it 11:30 p.m.?' she gasped, looking at the clock inside the car.

Ahmar looked at her, glad that she had changed the topic.

'I'm going to get grounded tonight. It's really late,' she said, shaking her head.

'Yes. You should go,' he whispered.

'You should go home too. Sir Muraad will be worried.'

'He knows I will come late.'

She bit her lower lip and nodded.

'So . . . see you tomorrow then?' he asked.

'Yeah . . . sure. Take care,' she said as she opened the door and got out of the car.

'Best of luck for your results.'

'Goodbye, Sir Ahmar,' she said and walked away.

He smiled to himself.

Ahmar reached home around midnight. He made himself a cup of instant coffee and headed towards his study. He sat at his desk, switched on the laptop and started correcting the exam papers. Only two days were left to declare the results, and he still had a lot of papers to correct.

But he could not concentrate; his mind kept going back to Zarish. He looked at his finger and remembered how she had held it for a long time. It was as if he could smell her around him; her fragrance was everywhere. He felt happier than ever. This was the first time he had looked at her not as his student, but as a woman. He wondered if it was okay to think about her this way. The thought made him uncomfortable.

'I can't let myself get too close to her. She is my student and it should stay like that. I shouldn't think too much about what I felt for her tonight. These feelings might be temporary and she can never know about them. I have to keep a distance from her but how am I going to stop her? I think she has gone too far,' he thought.

Zarish lay in bed, lost in thought. Though she held a book in her hands, she had not read a single page. All she could do was think about Ahmar.

'I may not be perfect but there is always room for improvement. Our relationship did not start off on a good note but I know he likes me, but he won't admit it just yet. If I change, I will only change for him,' she thought.

The loud sound of her mobile phone broke her reverie. It was Haroon. She did not feel like talking to him and listening to all his stories, so she decided to ignore his call. She switched of the bedside lamp and went to sleep.

The next two days passed at a snail's pace for the students, but not for the teachers. All the faculty members were busy checking papers. Their classes had been cancelled but Zarish and her friends still came to the university to pass time.

'Hey, why didn't you answer my call last night?' Haroon asked her. She was sitting alone on the steps with a novel in her hands.

'I was sleeping,' she answered nonchalantly.

'But you could have called later.' He sat beside her.

'I forgot.'

Haroon observed her for a minute.

'Why do you seem so indifferent today? What's going on?' He leaned against her arm.

'Sit up straight, Haroon. I don't want people to get the wrong idea,' she said, inching away.

'What?' he cried.

'Yes,' she said, not looking up.

'Do you hear yourself? I think you're not in your senses today. So, I'm just going to ignore what you said.'

'Whatever,' she said, adding, 'if we're friends, then we should act like friends. Don't try to get too cosy with me.'

Her statement made Haroon laugh.

'Well, you didn't mind it before,' he said and crept closer to her. 'What happened now?'

She looked at him unbelievingly and shook her head.

'I only want to be close to Ahmar,' she thought.

'I have to go, Haroon. I have to meet Sir . . .'

'Wait. What? Sir Ahmar? No way . . . not again!' he cried.

'Sir Wahab,' she corrected him and stood up.

He caught hold of her powder blue chiffon dupatta. 'What are you doing?' she yelled.

'Actually, I wanted to ask you to the dance,' he said, smiling sheepishly.

'Is this how you ask someone for a dance?'

'Yes. How else?'

'Fine, I'll think about it. Now leave my dupatta please. Stop acting like a jerk.'

He started laughing again. Zarish snatched her dupatta from his hand and walked away shaking her head in disbelief.

The parent-teacher meeting was scheduled for the next day. It was going to be a friendly interaction between teachers and students. All the parents had been invited to check their children's progress.

Haroon did not feel like inviting his parents, as he knew he had not performed well.

However, both Mr and Mrs Zia had come to attend the meeting. They were keen to know how Zarish had fared. All the teachers praised her for her confidence, intelligence and hard work. She had scored good marks in almost all the subjects.

She had deliberately kept Ahmar as the last teacher on the list. She wanted her parents to meet him at the end, as he was *special*.

'Where are we going now, Zarru?' Zia asked her.

'We're going to meet Sir Ahmar. He's my finance teacher,' she declared.

'Hmm.' Zia nodded.

'Is he the same teacher you're always talking about? Didn't his father have a heart attack? I remember you had made lunch for him,' Zarina said.

'Yes, Mom!' Zarish said jubilantly.

Zarish knocked on Ahmar's cabin door, but he was busy talking to other students and their parents.

'Uh-oh. I think there's a long queue,' Zia said after seeing the situation.

'We can come and meet him some other time.'

'No, Dad. Wait. I'll go and talk to him,' Zarish said and barged in.

'Why is she insisting on meeting him today? I'm tired; I want to go home,' Zia told Zarina.

'Let's just meet him for Zarish's sake,' Zarina said.

Ahmar continued to talk to the other parents, not paying any attention to Zarish. She felt helpless, but did not leave the room. She knew her parents would not wait for too long.

'Sir!' she interrupted his conversation.

He glanced at her.

'Yes, Miss Zarish?' he asked politely.

'I want you to meet my parents. They're waiting outside.'

'Yes, sure. I'll meet them. Give me some time,' he told her and resumed his conversation.

Zarish lost her temper.

'I want you to meet them right now,' she said loudly.

The two students and their parents turned around to look at her.

Ahmar felt embarrassed.

'They're important,' she said in a low voice.

'I'll be back in a minute. Please wait,' Ahmar excused himself and got up from his seat.

Zarish controlled her heightened emotions and took a deep breath. He looked at her furiously.

'Look. I know what I did right now was totally wrong and unethical, but I had no choice. They are getting impatient and won't wait any longer. Only I know how I convinced them to come here today. You can get angry later, but please meet them right now,' she said looking into his eyes.

'You're not worried about what I might tell them about you?' he asked.

'No. I am not,' she said boldly. 'I trust you.'

'That is not going to help you this time. I'm sorry,' his voice trailed off. He looked at her parents who were waiting outside the office. 'And . . . it is really rude to make your parents stand outside my office. You could have called them inside,' he said and walked towards the door.

'Hello Sir,' he said and held out his hand.

Zia unwillingly shook it.

'It is a pleasure to meet you,' Ahmar said.

Zia just nodded.

'Hello Ma'am,' Ahmar greeted Zarina.

She smiled at him.

'Please come inside,' Ahmar invited them into his office. They sat down on the two empty chairs kept in the corner. His cabin suddenly looked small and cramped.

'I apologize for making you wait outside for so long,' Ahmar said.

'That's not a problem. We're here because Zarish called us,' Zia said sarcastically.

'What's wrong with Dad?' Zarish thought.

'So, how are her grades?' Zia asked, changing the subject.

'And how is her performance?' Zarina asked eagerly.

Ahmar looked at Zarish and then at them.

'She's a hard-working student, but there are a few things that need to be improved,' Ahmar told them.

Zarish narrowed her eyes.

'Shit. He can't do this to me,' she thought bitterly.

'What sort of things?' Zarina asked in a concerned voice.

'You need not worry about that, Ma'am. We are here to take care of it,' Ahmar tried to lighten the mood. 'What I meant is, she sometimes acts a little careless about a few things. She's intelligent, but sometimes wastes her time on unimportant things. But we're trying to work on that. Aren't we, Zarish?' Ahmar looked at her.

'Uh. Yes,' Zarish gulped. She had no idea what on earth he was talking about.

'That's good then. I'm glad to know that our children are in dependable hands,' Zia said.

Ahmar nodded at him.

'We should leave now, Zia Sahib,' Zarina told him. 'Let's go Zarish.'

'You both go ahead. I will join you in a minute,' Zarish told them.

'Okay. It was nice meeting you, young man.' Zia shook hands with him again. Ahmar took a deep breath as her parents left.

'I need to talk to you,' Zarish told him.

'Not now. Can't you see other people are waiting?'

'Fine,' she exhaled. 'When will you be free then?'

'Go home, Zarish. There is nothing to discuss now. You should understand that,' he snapped at her.

Both of them stared at each other for a few seconds and then he walked away to meet the other parents.

Zarish left his office feeling dejected.

She tried hard but could not sleep as an eerie silence enveloped her room. She could hear the ticking of the clock and hum of the traffic from the main road. Whenever she tried to shut her eyes, Ahmar's face appeared in front of her. In fact, it had become a habit to think about him while going to sleep. It was stupid to deny that she had a crush on him. Maybe it was much more than a mere crush. She finally admitted to herself that she liked him. It could be more than that. She did not want to give the emotion a name though. She was afraid that it would remain unrequited. If it was love, then they both had to feel it. She could not bear the pain of loving him alone. Zarish wanted him to admit his feelings for her; she wanted him to take the initiative. But she had her doubts. She knew that they might never get involved romantically.

In the dark, she saw a figure near the door. It was her mother. She sat on the edge of the bed and stroked Zarish's leg.

Zarish removed the quilt and sat up.

'Mom, you're here.'

'Yes, I could see that you couldn't sleep,' Zarina said, caressing her daughter's cheek.

Zarish felt relaxed and suddenly forgot about her problems.

'So how did you find my friends and everyone at the university?' Zarish asked. Zarina could sense the enthusiasm in her voice.

'Everyone seemed nice and polite. I'm glad you have met such nice people,' Zarina said, smiling.

Zarish wanted to tell her mother about Ahmar.

'Do you want hot chocolate or something else?' Zarina asked.

'No, Mom. I'm fine. Err . . .' Zarish tried to initiate a conversation regarding him.

'What is it?'

'How did you . . . find Sir Ahmar?' her cheeks turned red as soon as she brought up his name.

Zarina gave her a questioning look.

'My finance teacher,' Zarish gave her a hint.

'Oh yes. He is a fine gentleman,' Zarina said nonchalantly.

Zarish observed her mother's reaction.

'I'm sure he teaches you all really well. That's one of the reasons you scored well in his subject,' Zarina said, getting up from the bed.

As an afterthought, Zarina added, 'Zarish, it would be better if you focused on your studies.'

Zarish noticed the sudden change in her mother's attitude, but she did not say anything. Zarina walked towards the door.

'I know, Mom. I was only saying that he's a really nice person,' Zarish murmured, feeling helpless.

Zarina had a feeling that Zarish had developed feelings for her professor. However, she did not want to talk about it with her daughter.

Zarish woke up late that morning. It was cool and windy outside. The morning breeze rattled against the glass panes. Zarish pushed open the window to feel the fresh air. She felt happy and calm. She picked up her cell phone to check her messages. There were six new ones: two from Saleha and four from Haroon. She quickly checked Haroon's first. They were all about the masquerade ball. She did not want to keep him waiting as that would irritate him even more. Besides, she knew asking Ahmar was a ridiculous idea. He would never attend the ball as her date. He would find it absurd.

She clicked on Saleha's messages. She wanted to go to the Mall of Lahore to buy accessories and clothes for the ball. She replied to her message and rushed to the washroom to get ready.

Zarish had already bought a dress for the ball. Saleha wanted Zarish's help to find something trendy for her, as she was not very good at shopping.

Saleha noticed that her friend had been quiet during the shopping trip. She decided to talk to her on their way back.

'So, what is the problem. Is it Sir Ahmar? Did he brainwash you?' Saleha popped an unusual question.

'No. He didn't do anything like that,' Zarish said, frowning.

'Then why is he different? Why does he mean so much to you?'

Zarish leaned back in her seat.

'I don't know. I actually do not know why I feel like that. Maybe the way he looks at me. There is something unusual about this guy. He never intrigued me before, but when I got to know him, I developed feelings for him and things changed,' Zarish explained.

'Do you realize the consequences of what you've got yourself into?'

'Like?' Zarish asked, sipping her Coke.

'Like he's our, I mean your teacher. He would never think of you in any other way. You are just his student like everyone else. He wouldn't put his job at stake for you,' Saleha said.

'I don't even want that!'

'Then?' Saleha raised her brow.

Zarish kept quiet.

'What do you want from him?' Saleha asked.

Zarish looked away, infuriated.

'See. I'll tell you what'll happen. If he doesn't have feelings for you, he will get angry when you tell him about yours. He might even complain to the dean, who might expel you. If he does have feelings for you, then his job is at stake. Someone from the university could complain about your affair and the poor guy could get expelled. Whatsoever the case might be, he will never jeopardize his career for you. Just forget about him. He is just your teacher,' Saleha lectured her.

Zarish cleared her throat and did not say anything. Both girls drove straight to Saleha's house. Zarish stopped the car in front of her gate.

'See you tomorrow at the ball,' Saleha said, stepping out of the car.

'I don't think I will be coming,' Zarish said.

'Why not?' Saleha asked her, annoyed.

Zarish just shrugged.

'Look, I know you felt bad about what I said earlier but that's the truth. Nobody can deny it. I would be happy if you behaved more maturely,' Saleha said, stroking her hand.

Zarish didn't look at her or say anything.

'I want you to come. Don't spoil your mood thinking about all this. It's temporary.'

'I'll see,' Zarish murmured.

Saleha's words echoed in Zarish's mind. Perhaps her friend was right. She should look at things maturely. Falling in love with a teacher was not a good idea. Perhaps it was just an infatuation. Zarish tried not to think about him despite knowing that her feelings would not change for him in an instant. She remembered the last time she'd seen him in his office during the PTM. He knew she wanted to talk to him, but he hadn't made any effort. Perhaps he was not interested. It was time for a change, for a break. It was time to know what he really felt.

As soon as she reached home, she replied to Haroon's messages. She asked him to pick her up from her house for the ball. She was going with him as his date.

Ahmar and Wahab had been given the responsibility to manage the masquerade ball. The dean trusted Ahmar a lot. Hence, he had asked him to take over.

Faris invited Ahmar to his office for a cup of coffee. 'I'm glad to see you working hard,' Faris said, smiling.

'Thank you, Sir,' Ahmar said.

'I have a surprise for you, Ahmar.'

Ahmar looked confused.

'We have decided to send you to Canada to manage one of our institutions there. We will take care of your visa and tickets. Your accommodation will be paid for by the university.'

This piece of news left him momentarily speechless.

'We have planned everything. Me and your dad,' Faris said, grinning.

'But Dad didn't say anything.'

'Like I said, it was a surprise for you.'

'Thank you, Sir,' Ahmar said and smiled, shaking his head in disbelief.

'Such an opportunity comes once in a lifetime. Don't let it slip away,' Faris said.

One by one, the students reached the venue for the masquerade ball. Everyone had to follow the dress code, which was red and black.

Zarish had asked Haroon to pick her up from her house. Haroon looked absolutely smashing in a black tuxedo. He reached Zarish's house on time and messaged her to come down. His mouth dropped open when he saw her walking towards his car. She was dressed in a maroon silk gown, her arms draped in a shimmery black stole. She looked gorgeous with her hair open.

'Hey,' Zarish said as she sat in the car.

'You look . . .' Haroon started.

'I know I look very pretty. My mom gave me the same compliment,' Zarish smiled.

'You should thank me, Zarish,' Haroon said.

'For what?'

'For asking you to be my date. No one else would have asked you,' he said, flashing his teeth.

'Shut up!' she frowned, hitting him hard on his shoulder.

He could not control his laughter.

Zarish knew they were quite late and most people were already at the venue. Haroon stepped out of the car and then opened the door for her like a true gentleman. Zarish felt quite amused by his gesture but she was more amazed when he held out his hand as soon as she stepped out. Zarish did exactly what he wanted and both of them walked towards the entrance hand in hand.

The hall was beautifully decorated. The entire credit went to Ahmar and Wahab for making it a memorable night for the students.

Maleeha entered the hall with Jamal. They looked stunning together. She looked gorgeous in a crimson chiffon saree, with her hair swept back into a low ponytail. The bright red lipstick looked sensational on her lips.

Everyone turned around when Danish and Maha walked in together. It was totally unexpected. Zarish looked around to catch a glimpse of Ahmar, but could not find him.

Saleha was very excited to see Zarish at the party.

'I can't believe you made it.' Saleha hugged her. 'You look lovely,' she said and then looked at Haroon, 'you look wonderful together.'

'Thanks. You look beautiful in this dress,' Zarish said and added, 'after all it was my choice.'

Saleha nodded and both of them hugged again.

'I can see the girls are quite excited,' Sherry joined them.

'Dude,' Haroon put his arm around Sherry's shoulder, 'and I can see that you and Saleha are together now. Amazing.'

Sherry blushed.

'Where are the rest of the people?' Zarish asked Saleha, quickly changing the subject.

'The one you're looking for is standing right there,' Saleha whispered in her ear, pointing at Ahmar.

Zarish's heart skipped a million beats as she turned around to look at him. He stood a few steps away with Wahab and Jamal. Could anyone be any more handsome? He was not dressed in a tuxedo like everyone else. He was instead wearing a sleek black suit, which looked very elegant on him. His neatly combed hair made him look smouldering hot, and Zarish's vulnerable heart melted.

'He looks so handsome tonight. Doesn't he?' Saleha asked her.

'He does,' Zarish murmured.

Jamal's voice echoed through the hall, breaking her reverie. Everyone stopped talking and looked in his direction. He was standing on the stage with a mic in his hand.

'Good evening, everyone! Welcome to the Masquerade Ball 2013!' Jamal screamed. The crowd cheered his enthusiasm.

Zarish and Saleha clapped gleefully as did the rest of the students. In the midst of the crowd, Ahmar caught a glimpse of Zarish. He wanted to keep looking at her, but the crowd wouldn't let him. Every now and then, someone stepped in between, disrupting his view.

'I don't want to bore you with a speech. I'm here to make a little announcement actually,' he said, smiling sheepishly.

Faris Ahmed and Hussain Muraad walked in right then and stood in a corner.

Maleeha was standing next to Ahmar, looking confused.

'What is he going to say?' Maleeha asked Ahmar.

'Perhaps he wants to add more fun to the evening,' Ahmar said with a wink to which Maleeha shrugged.

'I've completed five years in this university . . .' Jamal paused, 'it's a long time, huh?'

The crowd immediately cheered him on. Maleeha still looked confused.

'Why can't we just dance instead?' Haroon whispered in Zarish's ear. She shrugged in response.

'I have accomplished this because of one person,' Jamal continued, pointing in Maleeha's direction.

Maleeha's face turned red and she turned around to hide her embarrassment. Ahmar patted her on the shoulder, understanding her plight.

'Maleeha, please join me on the stage,' Jamal said.

Maleeha could not believe this was happening. She seemed hesitant; her face turning scarlet. Ahmar gave her a little push towards the stage.

'Please, Maleeha, I'm waiting for you,' Jamal said lovingly.

Maleeha finally gathered her courage and walked towards him. Jamal held her hand and made her stand next to him. The students cheered ecstatically.

'This will be discussed for years,' Wahab said as he came and stood next to Ahmar.

Ahmar nodded, his eyes gleaming. Suddenly the crowd parted and he saw Zarish standing in the middle of the hall. He looked at her intently but she seemed impervious to his presence.

Right then, Jamal, in front of the entire university, went down on one knee and proposed to Maleeha. The little love story unfolding on the stage distracted Ahmar and he again lost sight of Zarish.

'Miss Maleeha, would you like to spend the rest of your life with me?' he asked.

Maleeha's eyes became watery. She did not know how to respond. Instead of just nodding or saying yes, she started laughing.

'Please?' Jamal asked again.

'Yes, yes, yes. Now stop this drama,' Maleeha said.

The students whistled and applauded the beautiful couple.

Ahmar clapped absent-mindedly, his eyes searching for Zarish.

The dance floor was now open. The DJ spun a dance number, *Right Now* by Akon, and couples rushed to the floor to show off their moves. Zarish realized that she actually liked this song.

Taking full advantage of the fact that Zarish was standing alone in a corner, Ahmar walked up to her.

'I hope you're enjoying the evening, Miss Zarish.'

His urgent voice startled her.

'Oh,' she said sarcastically, 'like you care.'

Ahmar smiled at her response and folded his arms.

'What made you think that I don't?' He seemed amused.

She stared at him with an unfathomable expression for a few seconds and then looked away.

'I've noticed that you've been acting quite weird tonight,' he added, 'you didn't even come to meet me.'

'No, I am not acting weird,' she said curtly.

He narrowed his brows in confusion.

Soft, soothing music played in the background.

'Or maybe I am,' she added. 'I've learnt this from you. Unfortunately, your negative side is really influencing my behaviour.'

'I would never want any of my students to get affected by my behaviour. It will ultimately hurt me the most.' Ahmar's lips twitched.

'And what about the countless times you've hurt me?' she asked.

'What are you implying?'

'You have always called me your student. You've never distinguished me from the others,' she complained. 'Then why do you even expect me to come and greet you?' She looked away in fury.

He stared at her in silence.

'I wanted to talk to you the other day, but you ignored me. Fine, I understand you were busy but what about later? There was no response from your end. I kept waiting, but you didn't bother!'

Ahmar remained silent and lowered his gaze.

'I have finally realized that I hold no importance in your life. I was, I am and I will be just an ordinary student for you and nothing else,' she said, adding, 'even if I got a wrong signal from you, I would consider it my fault, not yours.' She paused, almost in tears.

Ahmar shifted his gaze towards her and looked at her intently.

'It was entirely my mistake. I'm sorry,' he said.

Ahmar wanted to hold her face in his hands and make her feel better. He wanted to console her by taking her in his arms, but he could not. He clenched his fists.

'I'm glad you've still not understood me. And you are never going to,' he said finally.

She looked at him questioningly and then sniffed. He stared at her for a while. Before he turned to walk away, she held his arm.

'Hey, wait. What do you mean?' She sniffed again. He glanced at her.

'Don't you ever cry again, Miss Zarish,' he said in a firm voice. 'I would rather die than see you in tears.'

Zarish stared at him in disbelief, her fingers still gripping his arm. He placed his hand over hers and squeezed it lightly. She gave him a weak smile. He smiled back.

'Come, let's dance, Zarish,' Haroon said.

'Uh,' Zarish hesitated, still thinking about Ahmar.

'What?' Haroon asked.

She didn't reply and he couldn't read her expression. Maha and Danish walked to the dance floor and the other couples followed. Ahmar stood near the bar counter and ordered a mocktail for himself. Wahab joined him, and both of them started talking. Zarish watched Ahmar's every move. He also kept staring at her. He noticed that she seemed hesitant to put her hand on Haroon's shoulder. When their eyes met, he signalled her to go ahead. She dithered, but then placed her hand on his shoulder. Haroon drew her closer and looked into her eyes. Zarish did not notice the emotion burning in his eyes as her attention was somewhere else.

Ahmar flinched after observing their closeness, but he controlled himself. He had to. He could not bare his soul in front of everyone. He swigged his drink.

'Are you okay?' Wahab asked in a concerned voice.

Ahmar nodded and then ordered another one.

'Would you like to have one?' he asked Wahab.

'No, thanks. I am fine. But . . . you don't seem okay,' Wahab said.

'I'm fine, mate. Don't worry.' He smiled at him and then looked at Zarish.

Haroon had wrapped one arm around her waist and held her hand in the other. Their bodies swayed with the slow rhythm of the song. But her eyes told a different story. She did not look into Haroon's eyes even once, and kept staring at Ahmar. Whenever Haroon pulled her closer, Ahmar felt a pang of jealousy.

The dance floor was filled with couples. Jamal and Maleeha seemed lost in each other. But Ahmar's eyes were locked on Zarish. He did not look away even once. His unusual and intimidating stare made her uncomfortable.

Suddenly, the music changed to a faster number. Haroon pulled her towards him and twirled her repeatedly. Zarish stared at him in surprise and breathed heavily. The room started spinning and she felt dizzy. He dropped her hand abruptly, and she lost her balance.

Ahmar rushed in her direction to prevent her from falling. He put his hand around her waist and pulled her, breaking her fall. Zarish opened her eyes slowly and saw him standing in front of her.

'Ahmar . . .' she whispered.

'Shh . . . just dance with me,' he whispered and drew her body closer, making her blush.

They were so lost in each other that they forgot the rest of the world.

He held her chin and lifted her face. They stared into each other's eyes for a long time.

Ahmar broke the gaze and pulled her by her waist. He brought his face closer to hers, their lips almost touching. He spun her again and dipped her, his hands wrapped tightly around her torso. They remained in that position for a few seconds, lost in the moment. He brought his face closer to hers and pressed his lips against her warm neck. His touch aroused her and she moaned.

He turned her around and held her from behind, his face in her hair. It smelt of fresh raspberries. She moved away, her eyes burning with passion. He held her face in his hands, tucked the loose strands of hair behind her ear and circled his thumb around her earlobe. Her body quivered and she tightly held his arm. He kissed her earlobe softly. Aroused, she put her arms around his neck and closed her eyes. He could not fight the urge and hugged her tightly. She ran her fingers through his hair.

Ahmar pulled himself back and gave her an intense look. Zarish traced her finger on his face and stopped when she reached his lips. He drew her closer again and pressed his body against hers. Their hearts thudded together; their heartbeats entwined.

Before he could reach out and kiss her lips, he heard someone calling his name.

'Ahmar?'

The magic was lost. Ahmar opened his eyes and looked around.

'Ahmar, where are you lost? I've called your name so many times,' Maleeha whined with her hands on her hips. He looked at her with a dazed expression. It had felt so real that he found it hard to believe that he was only dreaming.

'What's wrong with you?' Maleeha interrupted his thoughts.

'He's been drinking too much,' Wahab said.

'Beer?' Maleeha asked, raising a brow.

'No, it's only a mocktail,' Ahmar clarified.

'Whatever it is, I don't think you're okay.'

'No, I'm fine. Just a little dizzy,' Ahmar muttered.

'Do you want to go home?' Maleeha placed her hand on his shoulder.

'Yeah, maybe I should,' he replied and then glanced at Zarish.

She was standing with Haroon and her other friends about ten feet away. Her brows were narrowed and she looked upset about something. She glanced at Ahmar with a glum expression on her face.

Ahmar didn't know why she was upset. He smiled at her affectionately to make her feel better. His eyes spoke to hers and just like that he professed his love, without saying a single word.

She knew Ahmar Muraad had fallen in love with her. To hide the incredulity in her eyes, she looked away. She excused herself and walked towards the exit. He wanted to run after her, but then he thought it would be inappropriate. It was better to leave her alone.

'Does Ahmar Muraad love me?' she asked herself as she exited the hall.

Later that night, Zarish lay in bed thinking about the evening; how Ahmar had looked at her, his burning desire evident in his eyes; his smile that made her heart melt. The ringtone of her cell phone brought her back to reality. The screen flashed an unknown number.

'Who could it be at this time?' she wondered.

'Hello?' a familiar voice asked.

'Damn . . . it's Ahmar! Why is he calling me? Where did he get my number from?' she thought, panicking a little.

She took a long, deep breath before answering.

'Hello?'

There was a long pause. She could hear him breathing heavily.

'Why did he call me if he didn't want to talk? Maybe he dialled my number by mistake,' she wondered.

She remained silent too, waiting for him to say something but he didn't. Finally, she gathered her courage and initiated a conversation.

'Ahmar? Is that you?' she asked him.

'Yes,' he whispered.

'Where did you get my number from?' she inquired, sitting up on her bed.

'That's the silliest question to ask,' he said, sounding amused.

'Okay . . .' she paused. 'Why did you call me then?'

Ahmar hesitated.

'I saw you leave in a hurry. You looked unhappy. So, I just wanted to know if you were doing okay,' he said.

'Oh. Since when do you care?'

She heard him chuckle.

'Since now,' he murmured in a sexy voice.

'And what made you change your perspective?'

'What do you mean? I have always been a nice guy. I care for the ones I . . .' he stopped midway.

'For the ones you . . . what?' she asked.

'Nothing,' he said.

'You were about to say something, weren't you?'

'Say it, please!' she pleaded in her head.

'Not really,' he said.

'Are you sure?'

'Yes,' he murmured and paused.

An uncomfortable silence ensued.

'I wanna make up right now na na . . . I wanna make up right now na na . . .' he started humming in the most sensual and sexy voice.

'What?' Zarish screamed, her skin breaking out into goosebumps.

'It's a nice song, right? I heard it at the party tonight,' he said.

'Hey, are you drunk?' she asked abruptly. She was shocked to hear him in this state. He had never talked to her like this before.

'Uh. No.'

'There goes another lie. I saw you drinking at the party.'

'I just had a few mocktails.'

'Whatever. I don't think we should talk right now considering that you're not feeling normal. You won't even remember this conversation tomorrow,' she said.

'I will remember each and everything about this night, Zarish.'

She shifted nervously on her bed after hearing her name. It sounded even more beautiful when he said it.

'I don't believe you, Ahmar,' she said, well aware that she had called him by his first name.

'What should I do to make you believe?' he asked in a deep, throaty voice.

'I don't know,' she said with a sigh, still not able to believe that she was talking to him at this hour. Her entire body trembled.

'You can ask me whatever you want. I will answer every question. I promise,' he said.

'We could have a better relationship if you stopped lying to me constantly,' she snapped. 'Did that hurt? Anyway, I have to sleep now. I'm tired,' she added.

'I never lied to you, nor would I in the future,' he said, ignoring her comment.

'We'll see about that,' she said and yawned.

'Goodnight, sleepy head. You will be subjected to more interrogation tomorrow,' he said.

'Ahmar . . .' she said.

'Hmm?'

'I want to say something.'

'Yeah. Go on.'

'I think you're . . . you're growing on me.'

It was an entirely different morning for Zarish. She woke up to the sunlight streaming through the window. She rubbed her eyes softly, the mascara from last night staining her fingers. Her life had made a sudden shift. She had witnessed a prominent change in Ahmar's behaviour last night. Despite knowing he was not in his senses when he spoke to her, she still wanted to believe she had a chance with him.

The sudden buzz of her phone startled her. She turned around to pick it up from the side table. It was Ahmar again. She panicked for a second.

'Hello?' she said in a casual voice.

'Thank god you picked up my call,' he said, sounding amused.

Zarish flushed after hearing his voice.

'Good morning, Zarish. How are you?'

'Good morning. I'm fine. And you?'

'I hope I didn't disturb you,' he said, ignoring her question.

'You didn't disturb me, but yeah, I am a little surprised,' she whispered.

'I'm full of surprises, you know?' He laughed.

'He usually doesn't laugh so much. What's wrong with him?' Zarish wondered.

'Are you there?' he asked, breaking her reverie.

'Yeah, I'm here,' she said and tucked her hair behind her ear.

'So, what are your plans today? Do you have any classes?'

'No. Our classes will begin next week.'

'Oh.'

'I thought you knew that,' she said.

'Yeah, I do actually. I just wanted to know if you're free today or have some other plans?'

'Why do you care?' she asked. She sat on her bed and looked at herself in the mirror.

'God. I look pathetic,' she thought.

'You didn't answer my question,' he replied.

'But I want to know,' she insisted.

'Don't cross-question me, Miss Zarish.'

She sighed.

'Okay, would you like to go to the book exhibition at the EXPO Centre?' he asked.

'What?' she sounded shocked.

'Yes. Get ready quickly because I don't like people who do not value their time. I will pick you up in an hour. See you soon!' he said and hung up.

Zarish stared at the phone with a blank expression on her face.

Realizing that she had only an hour, she quickly undressed and rushed towards the washroom. After taking a quick shower, she stood in front of her wardrobe deciding what to wear.

After much contemplation, she picked out her favourite black harem pants with a printed, red chiffon blouse. She accessorized her outfit with a delicate wristwatch and a pendant.

Her cell phone rang when she was applying lip gloss. 'He's here. Oh shit,' she said excitedly.

Her father was out of town, which made it easier for her to escape. She told her mother that a friend of hers was going to pick her up, and she would be back in the evening.

She saw his car parked a few steps away from the main gate of her house. She opened the door and slid in swiftly. He was stunned by her beauty. He wanted to pay her a thousand compliments but words froze in his throat.

Without looking in her direction, he started the engine and drove off. The car smelt of fresh lavender and rosewood. She glanced sideways at him. He was wearing a light blue linen shirt with cream-coloured corduroy pants. Dark sunglasses covered his eyes and she couldn't make out his expression.

She intertwined her fingers nervously.

'Hello,' he said, breaking the silence.

'Hello,' she replied in a soft, musical voice.

'I know you were a little shocked after hearing about this plan,' he said and looked at her, his admiring eyes taking in every bit of her beauty.

'A little?' she asked, her cheeks flushing under his gaze.

He nodded, looking at her again.

'I still don't know why you're doing this,' she said, placing her hand on her forehead.

'A friend told me about this exhibition. So, I decided to check it out.'

'Yeah, but why did you ask me to come? I'm not a book lover.' She shrugged.

'I know, but I thought your perspective might change after this trip,' he said, grinning.

'Why are you so keen on changing my perspective anyway?'

'Why do you always ask so many questions?'

'Don't interrogate me. I have prepared a list of questions for you,' she said.

'Oh,' he said, 'great.'

'You always do this to me.' She looked away, feeling annoyed.

'Do what?' He seemed confused.

'Last night you said I could ask you anything,' she said.

He looked ahead, not meeting her eye.

Zarish tried to interpret his thoughts. She knew he would never answer her questions.

'See. I was right. Never trust a man who is drunk,' she said in a teasing voice.

He removed his sunglasses and looked into her eyes. Their eyes locked for a few seconds, but then he turned away.

'I knew you'd forget everything today,' she said glumly.

'First of all, I wasn't really drunk. And like I said, I haven't forgotten anything,' he said, trying to prove her wrong. 'I will answer all your questions when the time is right.'

'And when will that be?' she asked, folding her arms.

'Maybe now. Maybe later. Have you had breakfast?' he asked, changing the subject.

'No,' she said.

'Great. I haven't eaten either,' he said. 'After the exhibition, I'll take you to a nice place to eat. All right?'

'You don't have to,' she replied curtly.

Ahmar decided not to ruin her mood any further. He enjoyed teasing her. He turned up the volume of the stereo and drove the car in silence.

It took them almost half an hour to reach the exhibition. Since it was a Saturday, the centre had attracted a lot of book lovers. The place was bustling with activity. The sight of so many people packed in a small space nauseated Zarish. She felt a sudden irrational fear. He noticed the uneasiness on her face.

'Are you okay?' he asked, trying to comfort her.

'I'm fine,' she said, wiping the sweat off her face.

'I hope you're not claustrophobic. Are you?' he asked. 'I'll get you a glass of juice. Why don't you sit on that bench till then? I'll be right back.'

Zarish had to follow his order. What other choice did she have?

Within minutes, he was by her side again. He handed her a glass of orange juice, which she gulped down quickly.

'Feeling any better?' he asked.

'Yeah. I guess,' she said, feeling tired.

'Bringing you here was a bad idea,' he murmured.

She blinked her eyes mechanically at his words.

'Are you regretting it now?' she asked, looking at him.

'Your condition makes me feel like that, Zarish.' He lowered his gaze. 'You don't seem okay.'

'I'm completely fine now. Let's go check out the books,' she said, standing up.

Both of them checked out every bookstall that had been set up. A few renowned authors and editors had come from other countries to participate in the event. Zarish saw Ahmar talking to them animatedly and enjoying himself. She did not want to interrupt his conversation, so she decided to look around on her own. However, she was not into books and was soon bored, which Ahmar noticed. Zarish picked up a random book from a stall and shuffled through its pages.

'See, I told you it was a bad idea,' he said, startling her.

'Not at all. I'm enjoying myself,' she said, her heart beating faster when his arm brushed hers.

'Yeah. I can see that,' he murmured, inching closer.

He stood close to her, making her blush. She could feel his face in her hair. She moved away, shuddering at the thought of getting close to him.

'Did you like any book? Let me gift you one,' he said, scanning the shelves. She leaned over his shoulder, trying to get a glimpse of the titles. But her mind kept going back to the moment he touched her.

He picked a copy of *The Fountainhead* by Ayn Rand and *The Alchemist* by Paulo Coelho. Zarish was amazed by his choice.

'Here you go,' he said, handing her the books. 'I want you to read these books.'

'I don't read such books.'

'These books will help increase your intellect and might change your life too. I really want you to read these. I recommend them to all my students.'

'Students?' she asked sarcastically. 'Not again, Sir Ahmar,' she snapped.

Ahmar smiled as he walked up to one of the bookstalls.

'How's the exhibition going so far?' he asked one of the booksellers.

'It's going well,' he said.

'I would like to buy some books from your stall. Give me the total bill please,' Ahmar declared.

Zarish was astounded. She didn't understand why he had bought so many books.

'Why did you buy all these books? I can't read all of them,' Zarish said, nervously tucking her hair behind her ears.

'I have not bought these books for you, Miss Zarish,' he said in a calm tone.

'Then?' She narrowed her brows.

'Well.' He sighed. 'It's a long story.'

'I'm listening.'

'I will donate these books to an orphanage house located on Mall Road,' he said.

'Oh.'

'I help these children by either giving them money or buying them books.'

'That's . . . incredible,' she said.

'Not really,' he interjected. 'These children need our help,' he added, lost in thought.

'He is perfect in every way,' she thought and then remembered how generously he had distributed food among the poor children at the Badshahi Mosque.

'Hmm.' He sighed. 'Let me get these books to my car and then we can go for lunch.'

'Lunch is not necessary,' she said.

'I don't want you to faint this time. So lunch is a must.' He grinned as he walked towards the exit.

Ahmar took her to a fine dining Arabian restaurant, where every table was set in an enclosed cabin shaped like a Bedouin tent.

'I think you don't like the place,' he said, observing her reaction.

'No. Uh. What makes you say that?'

'The way you're looking at everything,' he said, smiling.

'Sorry, but this time your observation is wrong,' she said, playing with a fork. 'You can't always be right.'

'Hmm.' He folded his arms and rested them on the table. 'What do you want to eat?'

'Since you are the host, why don't you order for the table?'

'Yeah, but what if you don't like my taste?'

'You like. I like,' she said, smiling.

'All right, he said, signalling to the waiter.

Soon their food arrived; its mesmerizing aroma made Zarish even hungrier.

He had ordered hummus, a mixture of garbanzo beans, tahina, garlic and spices served with pita bread; fattoush, diced tomatoes, onions, chopped parsley and toasted pita bread tossed in a dressing of garlic, lemon, oil and salt; and shish tawook, made of barbequed chicken with fried vegetables and French fries.

Everything was delicious. Zarish gorged on it greedily.

'Wow,' she whispered, her eyes glowing with excitement.

After the meal, Zarish leaned back in her chair and crossed her legs. Ahmar noticed that she looked relaxed.

'Already tired?' he asked.

'Why? Do we have some other plans as well?'

'Hmm.' He thought for a while. 'Depends on your mood.'

'Hey, can I ask you something?'

Zarish's unexpected question made him a little nervous.

'Yes, sure. What is it?'

'What did you think about me when you met me for the first time?' she asked.

He took a deep breath.

'Well?'

'Do you really want me to get started?'

'Um, yes.'

'First impression is the last impression, do you believe in this?'

'Yeah, I guess so,' she said, sensing where this was going. She knew she had failed to make a good impression on him during their first meeting at the restaurant. The memory made her feel pathetic.

'I think I got my answer,' she said without waiting for his answer.

'But I haven't said anything,' he said, raising his hands.

'So, do you want to add more spice to make me feel worse? You embarrassed me the last time when we talked in your car.'

'Do you want an answer to your question or not?' he asked, sounding a bit annoyed.

'Fine.' She gave up. 'Please continue,' she said, pretending to listen.

'When I first met you, I thought you were irresponsible and ill-mannered.'

Zarish knew this was coming so she didn't seem surprised.

'You know why I formed this opinion,' he continued.

'It was a stupid thing to do. It was not intentional,' she interrupted.

'Yeah, I know. Maybe your intention was not bad but I was still hurt. I couldn't sleep that night.'

'Do you still feel angry when you remember that incident?' she asked sheepishly.

'No,' he answered. 'I don't sit back and think about the past again and again. I don't hold grudges or seek revenge.'

'Does that mean you've forgiven me?'

'I am not finished yet.'

Zarish heaved a long sigh.

'Bored already?' he asked, smiling mischievously. 'So, I was saying . . . Even though you played a dirty trick on me, I don't hate you.'

'What do you mean?' she inquired, sitting on the edge of the couch.

'That means you've kind of reversed the quote for me. In your case, the first impression is not the last impression,' he said, grinning.

Zarish lowered her gaze, her face flushed.

'I've seen you evolve over the months. You're quite good in academics, and you are not irresponsible, careless or ill-mannered any more.'

'Why does he talk about me only as his student? What does he think about me as a person, as a woman?' she thought.

'You are a good person, Zarish, but we all come with some flaws as well,' he said.

She looked at him with a confused expression.

'There are some flaws in you too, but those can be amended. I'll help you,' he said.

'Could you tell me now?' she asked.

'I'm sure this has something to do with Haroon,' she thought.

'Not today. I will tell you when the time is right,' he said.

'I'm sick of hearing the same thing again and again,' she said, looking away in disappointment.

He burst out laughing. She stared at him.

'Aren't you happy with the compliments I just paid you?' he asked.

'That was just general stuff. You didn't tell anything special. A lot of people have told me this before. This is not news for me.' She shrugged.

'There is something you haven't heard about yourself yet.'

'And what's that?' she asked.

'It's getting late. Let's go back.'

On their way home, Zarish remained quiet. Ahmar did not want this to happen. The silence was killing him. He wanted her to talk about her life, her experiences, her friends, her family and lastly the complicated subject of love. He wanted to know about her relationship with Haroon.

He stopped the car near her house. Both of them stared at each other for a while. Zarish did not feel like stepping out of the car. In fact, she wanted to spend more time with him.

'You seem lost, Zarish.' He broke the silence.

'I don't know. I've just been bitten by reality, I guess. I'd never thought so deeply about how poor people lead their lives. You've opened my mind.'

'Poverty is everywhere, Zarish. People should have the courage to get out of the vicious circle.'

'Do you think you can do it?'

'At least I can try. Next week we are having a fundraiser, a sort of charity event at the university. I want you to participate.'

'I will,' she promised.

'Take these books with you and read them,' he said, giving her the books he bought at the exhibition.

Later that night, as he sat at his desk, a lit cigarette dangling between his lips, his mind went back to Zarish. He remembered how she looked: her dress, how her hair hung over her shoulder, the make-up and jewellery she wore. He could not stop thinking about her soft smile, her glossy lips and her bright expressive eyes. Ahmar remembered how her cheeks flushed every time she caught him staring at her. The laptop flickered to life, diverting his attention.

His inbox was flooded with unread messages, but only the ones from Zarish caught his attention.

Hello, Sir Ahmar.
Hey wait, wasn't I supposed to call you just Ahmar? Right? ☺

He smiled after reading this and then scrolled down to
the next paragraph.

> I just wanted to let you know that I will donate money
> for the poor children at your orphanage. I've also
> convinced my friends to pool in funds. I will be waiting
> for your response.
> Yours forever,
> Zarish

For a few seconds, he stared at the laptop screen, unsure
what to reply.

> Thanks. I appreciate your efforts and we will discuss
> this topic more when we meet after the semester break.
> But before that I need to ask you something.

Zarish was lying on her bed when the message popped up
on her laptop screen. She wrote back nervously:

> Yes. Sure. What is it?

He was ready with his reply as Zarish received a message
within seconds.

> Why did you email me when you have my number?
> You could have texted me.

She gasped at his reply. Ahmar certainly wanted her to
message him on his cell phone. He wanted a personal bond
to develop between them. Her eyes scanned the message
and then she hit the reply button. There was a mischievous
grin on her face.

Texting seems somewhat personal. I did not want to do that before asking you.

He raised his brow as he read her message and then typed the answer:

It's all right. I won't mind if you text me, Miss Zarish.

Zarish could imagine the playful expression on his face. She could not stop smiling. Their conversation continued in the same fashion and they responded to each other's messages unceasingly.

Zarish: All right. Now can I ask you something?

Ahmar: Sure. Go ahead.

Zarish: Where did you get my number from?

Ahmar: Now that is something very personal. ☺

After their semester break ended, the university organized a fundraiser. With Saleha's support, Zarish was able to convince Sherry, Maha, Danish and the others to donate money for the event. She was happy because she was going to do something good for the first time in her life, and also because she was helping Ahmar.

Surprisingly, all of her friends, including Haroon, helped raise money. Ahmar was thankful to all his students, especially Zarish.

After the event, Haroon offered to drop Zarish home, but as usual she made an excuse. She hurried to meet Ahmar but to her surprise, he had already left. This made Zarish a little upset. He did not even give her any feedback regarding the event.

She doubted her own efforts. She didn't know if her help was welcomed or not. Did he appreciate it at all? With such thoughts clouding her mind, she walked to the parking lot. She felt even more upset when she did not find Haroon there. Feeling disappointed and completely dejected, she called her driver and asked him to pick her up.

'Ahmar could have informed me before leaving,' she thought bitterly. She took out her phone and sent him a text message.

> Good evening, Sir!
> You left abruptly from the event, and I did not get a chance to talk to you. I hope everything is okay.
> Yours, Zarish

Zarish was worried as Ahmar had not replied to her message the previous night. As Zarish crossed the university gate, she saw Saleha and Sherry. Zarish walked towards them.

'Hey,' Zarish said, giving Saleha a light hug.

'How are you doing, Zarish?' Sherry asked.

'I'm good. How about you?' she asked.

'Where is Haroon? I haven't seen him yet,' Saleha interrupted their conversation.

'He might have gone in already,' Zarish answered.

'Let's head to the class. It's time, girls,' Sherry said.

'Yeah, Sir Ahmar will be waiting for all of us,' Zarish said eagerly.

'He won't be taking our class today,' Saleha interjected.

'What do you mean?' Zarish asked.

'She's right,' Sherry added. 'We just found out that some other professor will be taking the finance class today.'

'It is just for today, right?' Zarish asked.

'I don't know.' He shrugged.

Zarish knew there was something wrong. He still hadn't responded to any of her messages.

'Where is he?' she wondered.

She decided to wait for another day. But the next day went by without any messages from Ahmar. He didn't even come to the university.

She dialled his number a zillion times, but he didn't answer. She refreshed her inbox to make sure the emails had not gone into the junk folder. She regretted not having Muraad's cell number.

She lay on her bed again, feeling hopeless and shattered.

'Why is he doing this to me? Is he angry with me? No, I don't think so. But why is he not taking his classes if he has issues with me? No . . . this can't be . . . I am not able to think clearly. Oh my . . . my head is spinning,' she thought with her eyes closed.

When she opened her eyes, she was on a pathway that passed through a forest and led to a meadow. She pushed away bushes that came in her way. The open meadow drew closer. It looked clear and beautiful from a distance. She soaked in the beauty of the scene in front of her with her eyes closed. As she walked ahead, she could see a man up ahead—wearing a black suit, his back towards her and his hair glossy from the sun. She was now only ten feet away from him. The man was not yet aware of her presence. When she reached out to touch him, he had already moved an inch from his position, but he still had his back towards her.

Zarish raised her hand and reached out to touch his hand. But, before she could touch it, he turned around to face her. When she saw that it was Ahmar, she smiled gently in relief. But, he did not return the smile. Instead, he stood there with agony writ large on his face, his brooding eyes poring back into the depths of hers. His pain worried Zarish. She caressed his cheek with her hand and stroked it gently to find that his skin was on fire.

'What's wrong?' she whispered.

He let her cup his cheek in her palm and shut his eyes. She could feel the heat of his skin against hers.

'What are you doing here? What place is this?' she asked, continuing to stroke his cheek but it elicited no response from him.

His eyes remained closed. She wondered if he was relishing her touch or the serenity of the moment.

'Ahmar?' she whispered.

He wrapped her in his arms, holding her tight against his body. She was dumbstruck at first but put her arms around his neck and rested her head on his chest. She wanted to decode his emotions but could not understand whether it was love, hurt, affection or lust that he felt for her at that moment. She tried to enjoy the warmth of his arms.

Ahmar brushed his fingers through her hair and then pulled her away from his chest. Gently, he touched her chin and lifted her face to bring it closer to his. Their noses almost touched, his eyes burning with sensual desire. She tried to read his gaze but failed. She wanted to hug him once again. She needed something more.

'Zarish,' he said, huskily.

'Yes?' she replied.

All of a sudden, he seemed to be weightless. The blood drained out of his face, leaving it pale. He wriggled out of her grasp and moved back a step. She stared at him in shock.

'Ahmar?' She tried to shriek out his name but her voice could not find the words.

He had transformed into a lifeless and emaciated form.

She took a step towards him to hold him again but as soon as she did so, he fell silently to the ground. She stood numb and speechless and could not help him up. He seemed to be dead. She couldn't believe it at first but soon grief overcame the shock. She crumpled on to the ground and sobbed uncontrollably.

'No!' she woke up screaming. Wiping the sweat off her face with the sleeve of her nightshirt, she sat up on the bed. Her screams had woken up her brother, who stood at the door, peering in.

'Are you all right?' he asked.

'Yes. It was just a stupid nightmare,' she mumbled, rubbing her head.

'Never mind. There is still time before daybreak. Get more sleep,' he said.

'What's the time?' she asked.

'It's 4 a.m.,' he replied, shutting the door behind him.

She thought about the awful dream. She had an uncomfortable sense of foreboding that it was a sign for something unpleasant. Did dreams turn into reality? She closed her eyes, her mind disturbed with such thoughts.

The next day, she went to meet Muraad in his office since he was the only person who could help her.

'May I come in, Sir?' she asked to which he nodded amiably.

Zarish sat quietly in his office for a few minutes since he was busy attending some important calls. Suddenly a tall bookshelf kept in the corner caught her attention, and she recalled their day together at the book fair.

'Everything seemed so perfect that day. He was so happy,' she recalled.

'So, what's new, young lady?' Muraad asked after finishing his call.

'Why have you changed our finance teacher?' she asked, coming to the point.

'Who told you so?' Muraad asked, smiling.

'Some other teacher took our finance class yesterday,' she told him.

'And you presumed that we have swapped your finance teacher?' he asked with a grin.

She looked at him confusedly.

'So . . . where is he then?' she asked.

'He is fine. Don't worry,' he said, sensing the concern in her tone.

'This was not my question, Sir. I want to know where he is.'

'Ahmar was right about his students, you all are very stubborn.'

'What? Did he say that about all of us or particularly me?' she thought.

'I want my answer, Sir. Please,' she said.

'Hmm.' He leaned in his chair. 'Since you're acting really stubborn right now, I will have to tell you everything, even though he told me not to.'

'What is it?' she asked, tensing up.

'He met with an accident on the day of the fundraiser.'

'A-acci-dent?' she stammered.

'Damn, damn, damn . . . I knew something was wrong,' she told herself.

'He just has an arm injury. That's it. His other medical reports are fine. The doctor has told him to rest for a couple of days. That's why he is not taking classes.'

'I need to see him. I need to see him,' she kept murmuring.

'Zarish?' he called out, but she hurried towards the door. Muraad looked at her in bewilderment.

'So my dream was an indication of his current state of health. I should have known,' she thought as she drove at breakneck speed to his house.

On reaching his house, she found the main door open. Without knocking, she pushed it and entered. Her eyes searched for him everywhere.

'Ahmar!' she called out his name. She tried hard not to cry but in vain.

'Zarish?'

She turned around on hearing her name.

'What are you doing here?' he asked in a concerned tone.

Without giving a reply, she ran into his arms and broke down into tears.

'Zarish?' he whispered, amazed by her action. She ignored him and hugged him tightly. This was the first time she had hugged him for real. The feeling was ecstatic. At first, he hesitated, but then the urge to hold her became too strong and he hugged her back. She had never thought such a moment would come in her life. She clutched his shirt, and felt every inch of his body. She felt his broad chest and rib muscles that moved every time he took a breath. He too found himself drowning in the intimacy they shared. His citrus and wood cologne filled her nostrils and she savoured it. Zarish closed her eyes and so did he. Perhaps this was the time to express her feelings for him. She knew she loved him and she was sure he felt the same. She clung to him, putting pressure on his fractured arm.

'Ah,' he moaned.

She stepped back, realizing he was in pain.

'I'm s-s-sorry,' she stammered.

'It's okay.' He cringed a little, feeling embarrassed.

Tears poured down her cheeks. Ahmar winced when he felt the wetness on his shirt. He pulled her back tenderly, coming back to his senses, and wiped the tears from her cheeks.

'Zarish,' he murmured. 'What's wrong?' he asked.

'Why didn't you tell me about your accident?' she asked.

'Because it wasn't important.' He shrugged.

'How can you say that?'

He knew she was annoyed with him. Really annoyed. He remained quiet and did not give any further explanations. He wanted to relieve her of the pain he had caused.

'Do you even know what I went through these last few days? Do you even care?'

He folded his arms and looked at her guiltily.

'I would have never come to know. It's thanks to your dad who thought it was important to tell me.'

'Damn . . . why Dad?' he thought.

'Don't you dare blame him now! He did the right thing. I knew something was not right. I had this terrible dream about you. I knew you were in trouble . . .' her voice trailed off.

'As long as I am standing alive in front of you, there is nothing to be worried about. C'mon yaar,' he said casually.

'Yaar . . . woah. Where did this come from?' she wondered but ignored it.

'What now?' He shrugged.

'Do you think this is funny?'

'No. Not at all,' he said, hiding his smile.

'Ahmar, you are seriously impossible!' she raised her hands in surrender. 'I was upset for the past two days. But you weren't even bothered.'

He looked away, smirking.

'You did not even bother to inform me. I have every reason to hate you right now. Do you understand?' she said, pointing a finger at him.

'Do you really hate me, Miss Zarish?' he said and held her finger, stepping closer.

'Do you?' he asked again.

'Yes,' she said, pretending to be confident.

Ahmar did not let her go; he wanted her to stay for dinner. He knew his father would come home quite late as he was supposed to attend a seminar that evening. There was nobody in his house except them. He did not let her enter the kitchen because he wanted to prepare dinner all by himself.

'This is so not fair,' she said, standing near the door. 'You're hurt. I can't let you cook all by yourself.'

'My right arm is fine,' he said as he gathered the ingredients for the meal. He did not even tell her what he was making.

'Do you cook often?' she asked, leaning against the kitchen counter.

'Not really. Just on weekends.'

'Then who cooks the rest of the meals?'

'We've a cook but he's on leave. He will be back soon.'

'Okay . . . what am I supposed to do? I am bored,' she asked, raising her arms.

'Maybe you can go check out the house.'

'Are you sure, Ahmar?'

'Yes,' he said, flashing her favourite smile.

She left the kitchen and wandered through the corridor. She walked around the house aimlessly. Suddenly, a dimly lit room caught her attention. The door was slightly open and she stepped in. It was Ahmar's study, covered entirely with bookshelves. There was a small wooden study table in the corner of the room; a MacBook and a few books were arranged neatly on it. Zarish touched the edge of the table, thinking about all the nights Ahmar had spent at it, chatting with her. A pair of spectacles caught her attention. She placed them back and diverted her attention towards the books.

In the kitchen Ahmar was giving the final touches to the Mexican dishes, tacos and burritos, he had prepared for dinner. He smiled as he thought about Zarish. How upset she got after hearing about his accident; how she ran into his arms after seeing him in the living room. She was special and held a strong place not only in his heart but also in his life. He realized it late, but eventually he did and that mattered the most.

They sat in the dining room, which was illuminated with candles. A soft glow enveloped the room, making it warm and cosy.

'Here are the tacos,' he said, putting the food on her plate.

'I'll take it myself, it's okay,' she said, trying to take the serving spoon from his hand.

Their fingers touched and eyes met. The intimacy made her blush. Suddenly a sound from the hall interrupted their moment. Ahmar and Zarish turned to see Muraad standing near the entrance.

'Dad, you're here,' he said, standing up.

'Hello, Sir,' she said, feeling embarrassed.

'I knew you would be here,' Muraad said pointing at Zarish. She nodded sheepishly.

'I told her about your accident. How are you now?' he asked his son.

'I'm fine now. Weren't you supposed to attend a seminar today?'

'I skipped it,' he said and chuckled.

Zarish smiled too.

'Are you happy to see him? He's not going anywhere, so stop worrying.'

'Yes, Sir,' she said.

'Did she think I was going to leave the university?' Ahmar interjected, looking at her in amazement.

'Yes, and she was very upset about it,' Muraad replied.

When Zarish looked at him from the corner of her eye, she saw him looking at her intently. She blushed.

'I can smell something heavenly. What's for dinner?' Muraad asked.

'I have made tacos. Want to eat?'

'Let's all eat together,' Muraad declared.

Ahmar put a plate full of tacos and salad on the table.

'My son is a great cook,' Muraad said proudly.

'Yes, he is. The tacos are delicious,' Zarish said, looking into Ahmar's eyes. He raised his head to look at her. She looked down at her plate, smiling.

'How will you go home, Zarish?' Muraad asked.

'I have my car,' she answered.

'Don't you think it's late for you to go home alone?'

'I will be fine, Sir.'

'I think it's too late for you to go alone. Ahmar, I want you to take your car and follow her till she safely reaches her house.'

Ahmar nodded, looking at Zarish.

'I don't want to trouble Sir Ahmar. He's not well, and I don't think he should drive,' she interjected.

Muraad and Ahmar exchanged a glance.

'I will be fine,' she said.

After bidding Muraad goodbye, she walked towards the main door. Ahmar followed her.

'Thanks for the delicious meal. The tacos were amazing.'

'My pleasure. I wish I could drop you home,' he said.

'It's okay. I can drive myself. You need to take care of yourself.'

'I will,' he said and folded his arms.

'When will I see you again?' she asked.

'At the university, of course.'

'Yeah, but when?'

'Soon.'

'I'll wait.'

'Take care, and inform me when you reach home. All right?' he ordered.

'Will do. I will text you or would an email be better?' she asked teasingly.

'Anything you like, Miss Zarish.' He chuckled softly.

When she returned home, her family members were sitting at the dining table.

'Hey everyone,' Zarish said.

'Welcome home. Come and have dinner with us,' Zia said.

'Dad, I'm full. I had dinner with friends. You guys carry on. I'm going to bed.'

'It's too early to go to bed, Zarish,' Zahaan interrupted.

'I'm tired. See you guys tomorrow!' She rushed upstairs.

Zia and Zarina exchanged a quick glance.

'She's always with her friends, isn't she?' Zahaan said, stuffing his mouth with spaghetti.

'She loves socializing, and yes there is a limit to everything. But I don't think it's a bad thing,' Zarina responded.

'It's not about good or bad, Mom. She is always avoiding her family and hanging out with her so-called friends.'

'This is the only time she has. Let her enjoy. Let her live her life, son,' Zia said. 'Her life will take a 360-degree turn after she gets married.'

'Should we talk to Haroon's parents?' Zarina inquired.

'Looks like we have to now,' he said.

Ahmar was watching a baseball match on the flat screen when a message popped up on his cell phone. It was from Zarish.

I have reached home safely. Take care of yourself.

Ahmar could not hide his smile. He replied instantly:

I will be fine. Don't worry about me. Have a good night. ☺

Muraad, seated beside him, saw the smile on his son's face.

'Ahem.' Muraad cleared his throat to catch his son's attention. Ahmar turned to look at his father.

'I really, really like this girl,' Muraad said.

'Which girl?' Ahmar asked, flipping through TV channels.

'You know who I am talking about. Don't act innocent.' Muraad turned towards him.

Ahmar looked at him and then lowered his gaze.

'What is cooking between the two of you?' Muraad asked teasingly.

'Dad! Are you kidding me?' Though Ahmar tried to sound surprised in front of his father, he knew deep down that it was not really a surprise for him. He had started liking Zarish and in spite of trying hard to stay away from her, he had failed. It was not easy to ignore her.

'Don't act innocent in front of me. I am your father and you cannot fool me.'

Ahmar's lips stretched into a shy smile.

'Hey . . . there you go. Now tell me what is going on between you and her?' he asked, patting him on his shoulder.

'I don't know, Dad.' He folded his arms. 'There's nothing more than friendship. I guess she's better off as my student.'

'Why are you saying that?'

Ahmar shrugged.

'I don't believe it's just friendship. She seems to be very fond of you.'

'What do you mean?' Ahmar asked.

'The way she barged into my office and asked about you; the worried expression on her face. I mean, no one else has really taken that sort of interest in you. At least not in front of me. And then how she looked at you at the dining table. A student would never look at her professor like that unless she has feelings for him. Do you understand what I am trying to say? She really likes you.' Muraad took a deep breath.

'Are you sleepy?' Ahmar said, trying to change the subject.

'Won't you say anything about this?'

'I really don't know how to respond, Dad,' he said nervously.

'Do you feel the same for her?'

'I am not sure of her feelings.' Ahmar sighed.

'Are you dumb? This girl is madly in love with you. Her eyes say everything.'

'But . . .' Ahmar's voice trailed off.

'What do you feel about her?'

Ahmar looked into his father's eyes.

'Son, I am asking you something.'

Ahmar remained quiet and lowered his gaze.

'I think there can't be a better girl for you. She loves you selflessly,' Muraad said finally.

'And why do you say that?'

'I have seen how she looks at you. Your mother used to look at me like that.'

Ahmar nodded.

'Give yourself some time and think about it.'

'It is difficult, Dad. Nobody is going to accept our relationship. She's my student and everybody knows that.'

'That means you've already thought this through. Haven't you?'

Ahmar remained quiet. His father knew how he felt.

Zarish thought of Ahmar as she undressed in front of the mirror. She reminisced about the moments she spent with him that afternoon. She remembered how she ran into his arms and how he held her firmly. The memory seemed so fresh, so real, like it was happening all over again.

'Do you really hate me, Miss Zarish?' he had asked her.

She remembered how he looked at her; his eyes full of love.

Her body shivered when she remembered his blazing stare. Standing half-naked in front of the mirror, she observed herself closely.

She hugged herself firmly and shut her eyes so that she could feel him around. It was dark in her room; only a dim light glowed in the corner. When she opened her eyes, she found *him* standing behind her. She knew she was hallucinating. He looked at her reflection admiringly. She lowered her gaze and smiled. He untied her hair and let it hang loose over her neck and shoulders. He then moved it to one side and brought his lips closer to her nape. She felt a chill run down her spine as he pressed his lips against her neck and slowly put his arms around her waist.

Zarish turned around to face him. She looked at him with love and his eyes returned the stare with equal passion.

Her breath was becoming uneven now. She couldn't hold herself any longer and hugged him tightly.

'I don't want to let you go. Not now. Not ever. I love you, Ahmar.'

It was around 5 a.m. when she slowly opened her eyes and checked the time on her bedside clock. Zarish wrapped the quilt tightly around her body. She felt a sudden chill and realized that her limbs were stiff and ached badly.

She noticed that she was still almost naked and had slept like that. She pulled the quilt closer to her body. She felt queasy, and her head throbbed with pain. Though it was not very cold, she shivered.

'Damn,' she whispered to herself.

Still wrapped in the quilt, she slowly put one leg on the floor.

She felt unsteady, but held on to the bedside table. She picked up her clothes from the floor and quickly put them on.

Later, she joined Zahaan and her mother at the dining table for breakfast.

'How are you, beta?' Zarina asked her.

'I think I have a fever,' she answered in a nonchalant way.

Zarina placed her hand on her forehead to check her body temperature.

'You're quite warm. Do you want me to call the doctor?'

'I don't think I need to see him. I'll be fine.'

'You'd better call the doctor, Mom. Don't listen to her,' Zahaan said, eating his toast.

'No. I'm fine. Don't worry,' Zarish told him.

'Your dad and I are going to Karachi this weekend,' her mother said.

'Why?' she asked, chewing her breakfast.

'We're going to meet your aunt as she's not well. Your dad also has a business meeting in Karachi.'

'When are you leaving?'

'We'll be leaving on Friday, day after tomorrow.'

'That's great. Zahaan and I will have the whole house to ourselves. Cool.' She winked at her brother.

'Will you be able to manage on your own?' Zarina asked them.

'Don't worry about us.' Zarish squeezed her mother's hand.

'Okay, honey. Do you need any medicine? I'm worried about your health.'

'Mom, I said I'm fine,' she reassured her and checked her cell phone. There were five missed calls: two from Saleha and three from Ahmar. Her inbox was flooded with messages. She choked on a piece of bread after reading Ahmar's message.

'What happened?' Zarina asked.

'Uh nothing,' she replied. Her heart raced as she opened his message.

Are you at the university? I need to talk to you.

'Damn. I'm late.' She checked the time; it was 11.30 a.m.

'What's wrong?' Zarina inquired.

'I'm late for my class. I better leave,' she said and rushed upstairs to get ready.

'Skip your classes today. You are not well,' Zarina called after her, but it was too late.

'She never listens to anybody,' Zahaan said, shaking his head.

'Zahaan, make sure you look after her while we're away,' Zarina said.

'She is not a kid, Mom. She doesn't need any protection.'

'For us she is. You'd better keep an eye on her. I don't want her to stay out late with her friends.'

'And what if she's with Haroon?' Zahaan raised a brow.

'Not even with him.'

Zahaan nodded.

'You can let her go out with Haroon,' Zia said as he sat down at the dining table.

'But Zia Sahib . . .' Zarina protested.

'It's okay, Zarina.' Zia cut her in the middle of the sentence. 'You should learn to trust Haroon.'

'What does he want to talk about? Damn . . . I am shivering. Why did he come to the university if he is still not properly healed from the accident? His arm is injured and he needs rest,' Zarish thought.

Zarish wanted to tell him but he was acting immature and stubborn.

'I feel like I am his teacher and he my naughty student. Naughty but handsome. Yes, I love him and he is mine,' she thought.

She asked the chauffeur to drive her to the university. Ahmar dominated her thoughts on the way.

'He had never sent a text message like this one earlier. Had he read my eyes? Does he know what I feel for him? Is this the result of what happened yesterday?' Zarish thought and blushed at the memory of his embrace.

She wondered if Ahmar would be able to read her mind. She felt embarrassed to face him but resolved to keep a poker face.

Zarish decided to surprise Ahmar in his office so she did not reply to his messages.

Once at the university, Zarish walked swiftly towards Ahmar's cabin but saw through the glass door that he was not at his seat. She asked a peon about Ahmar's whereabouts who replied that he was delivering a lecture to a class and would be teaching her batch next.

She felt uncomfortable while entering Ahmar's class that day. He was busy trying to attach his laptop to the projector when a group of concerned students crowded around him, asking about the accident. Ahmar assured the students that he had recovered from it. Some of the girls in the class, including Maha, Zoya and Fariha, had brought bouquets of flowers and get-well-soon cards for him. Ahmar accepted the gifts and thanked each of them.

Zarish felt pangs of both jealousy and guilt. The jealousy came from seeing him engage with the other girls and guilt because she had not thought of bringing him a gift or even a card on his safe return to the university.

'What is the difference between me and the rest of them?' Zarish thought. She had to exceed whatever they did; she would welcome him in a special way.

'Thank you for the lovely flowers once again,' Ahmar told the class from where he stood near the lectern.

The whole class cheered for their teacher. Ahmar's eyes travelled around the class, noticed Zarish and smiled at her. Zarish smiled back at him.

Once the students had taken their seats, Ahmar greeted them.

'Good afternoon everybody,' he said.

Zarish was busy thinking how handsome he was. His arm was still in plaster and whenever Zarish's eyes stole over it, her body cringed. Saleha poked her elbow slightly to tease her but Zarish ignored it. Her eyes were transfixed on Ahmar.

'I am really sorry that my injury has taken a toll on the course. I promise that I will try to cover anything that has been missed out from the syllabus,' he said.

The class returned to normality and Ahmar began his lecture on 'projected cash flows'. He made the boring topic interesting enough so that the students understood it. He also conducted a short surprise quiz to assess their to-date performance.

Zarish suddenly realized that Haroon was missing.

'Where's Haroon?' she turned back to Sherry and asked.

'He's your friend. You should know,' Sherry retorted with a sarcastic grin.

Zarish made a face at him.

While attempting the quiz, Zarish was distracted and intermittently kept stealing glances at Ahmar. From the corner of her eye, she could understand that his eyes were fixed on her. Whenever she looked in his direction, he shifted his eyes abruptly in another direction.

After playing this game for a while, there was a singular moment when their eyes locked at the same time. She blushed and looked away. Ahmar did not shift his gaze. With his elbows on the lectern, he was leaning forward to rest his chin on his upturned palms. He stood in this position, staring at her.

This distracted Zarish and she could not focus on the quiz.

She quickly circled the answers that seemed the most appropriate. When she lifted her head from the test, she found that Ahmar was still staring at her in the same posture. She swallowed and looked down again. She fished out her cell phone from her handbag and typed a message for him.

Stop staring at me or I will fail this quiz.

Zarish sent the message and looked up at his face to try and read his reaction to the message. His cell phone buzzed in his trousers and he took it out.

Ahmar read her message and smiled. Zarish smiled too.

'So, this is how he reacts when he reads my messages,' she thought. He quickly typed a reply. The text message from Ahmar lit up her phone's screen.

You'd better not fail in my quiz. Good luck.
P.S. Do not leave without meeting me. I need to talk to you.

With a surprised expression, Zarish raised her head to look at him. Finally, he was looking away, at the papers before him. This was the first time that he had said that he wanted to talk to her about something. It had usually been the other way around. She replied:

I'll see you in your office after this session. Are you angry with me?

Ahmar did not respond to the question, which she thought meant that he was annoyed with her. A tense Zarish bit her lower lip.

Again, they shared quick glances and she was just about to read his expression when Fariha exclaimed that she'd finished the quiz.

Zarish also went up to surrender her answer sheet and took her time in placing the paper on the lectern. She was about to say something to Ahmar but Fariha interrupted.

'Sir,' Fariha said.

The interruption made Zarish flinch in irritation.

Ahmar looked up at Fariha.

'May I have your phone number please?' Fariha requested. 'In case I have trouble with a question, I can consult you.'

Zarish overheard the exchange and it angered her. She turned to look at Ahmar, waiting to hear his response to Fariha's request. Ahmar wanted to avoid responding in front of Zarish because he could understand that it would upset her, but he could not break the classroom norms.

'Yes, sure. You can find my phone number on the back of your course,' he replied, glancing sideways at Zarish, who returned a cold stare.

'But Sir, I think that number is not valid,' Fariha complained.

'No, it is,' he said abruptly, looking back at Fariha. 'You can keep my card in case that phone number doesn't work.'

Zarish stared at him with fuming eyes when he handed over his visiting card to Fariha.

'Is it okay if I call or send you a text at any time?' Fariha asked, hesitatingly.

'Anytime?' he asked with a brow raised in question and stole another sideways glance at Zarish. Zarish squinted her eyes at him with an expression of incredulity.

'Yes,' Fariha said.

'Sure, but I will only reply when I am free,' Ahmar responded.

'Thank you, Sir,' Fariha said with a warm smile and left.

Zarish could not believe what she had seen. She thought she was the only one with whom he exchanged text messages and calls.

'Why did he give his private number to another student?' she wondered.

To Ahmar's surprise, in a single motion, she held his arm, shoved her quiz paper in his hand and stormed out of the classroom.

Later, when the university was quite empty, she sat on a bench outside his office, waiting impatiently for him to return. Saleha and Sherry had bid her goodbye and left the campus together. Despite her own internal conflicts regarding Ahmar, Zarish felt really happy for her friends and wished that they'd be together forever.

A few minutes later, Zarish saw Ahmar walking towards her with someone she could not recognize. They were chatting about something on their way to Ahmar's office. Ahmar bid the other person goodbye and beckoned her to follow him, as he walked past her and into his office. She got up from the bench, swept her hand through her hair, took a deep breath and stepped into his office.

The office was calm and everything seemed still. All the lights were turned off except for a single lamp that lit up the part of Ahmar's cabin where his desk was stationed. The desk was clean and the papers on it had been stacked neatly into a pile.

'Take a seat,' he said coolly, turning on his laptop.

'No thanks. I'm fine,' Zarish replied.

'Are you sure?' he said, with an eyebrow cocked.

'Yes,' she murmured and nodded.

'Would you like some tea or coffee? I'm going to order one for myself,' he said as he settled into his chair.

'What did you want to talk to me about, Ahmar?' she asked.

'Answer my question first,' he said.

'I don't want anything. Thanks,' she replied curtly.

Ahmar picked up the telephone on his desk and asked someone to bring two cups of coffee to his office.

'Why are you so stubborn?' Zarish asked and crossed her arms.

'I'm just trying to be more like you,' Ahmar said, leaning forward.

It made Zarish uncomfortable and she fidgeted with her bag and twiddled her thumbs in nervousness.

'Sit down, Zarish. Relax,' Ahmar said.

She sat down.

A peon entered the office with two cups of coffee.

'Thank you,' Ahmar told the peon, who retreated from the office, shutting the door behind him.

'So, what's the deal?' she asked.

'Why do you think there would be a deal anyway?' he asked.

'You said you wanted to talk . . .' she began to say.

'Yeah, I did,' He cut her midway. 'Why are you behaving rudely of late? I should be the one acting indignantly right now.'

'Why? Is it because I did not reply on time or because I did not reply at all? Neither should be a problem because you treat me in the same way,' she retorted.

'No. I'm not immature enough to be angry for either of these reasons. In fact, I didn't even think about it,' he said and flinched at her tone.

'I didn't reply to your message deliberately. I wanted to meet you in person,' she said.

'Why?' he asked. The eyebrow cocked again.

'Ahmar, I . . .' she trailed off mid-sentence.

'What?' he asked.

'Didn't you call me here to talk to me about something?' Zarish asked.

Ahmar could feel the uneasiness mounting in her demeanour.

'Fine. Please calm down. I did not intend to hurt you. I was just teasing you. Please drink your coffee,' he clarified.

Zarish took a long sip and fell back on the chair.

'I didn't know you flirt with other girls as well,' she hissed.

'So, has it upset you?' he asked.

'No,' she said, her anger rising.

'Why do you get agitated and become hyperactive?' he asked her with surprise. 'Why can't you be more composed?'

'That's you, Sir. Not me,' she said. It was the truth.

Ahmar inhaled slowly and then exhaled. He took a sip of coffee from his cup.

'That is the problem. You can't be like me,' he said briskly.

'No. The problem is that you want me to become like you but you see yourself failing miserably in this. I am nothing like you and you cannot swallow defeat. I have my own personality. Why should I be like you?' she responded.

He could not believe what she was saying.

'This is the problem, Sir. You do not accept me the way I am,' she spoke again, this time adding some more sarcasm in her tone.

'Don't overreact,' he said and fumbled with the papers on his table. 'Let me finish checking these papers. I have to submit them to the controller of examinations by tomorrow. It is important,' he said, ignoring all she had just said.

Zarish was amazed. 'How can he act as if nothing has happened?' she thought.

'In the meanwhile, you can finish your coffee,' he said, pointing at her cup without meeting her eyes.

'I don't want anything and I am certainly not overreacting,' she said aggressively, sliding the cup of coffee away from her with some force.

The cup rattled on the table, teetered for a bit and fell on its side, spilling the coffee across the table, staining the papers too. It was an accident, she had not intended it. She jumped up from her seat as the small pool of brown liquid swelled around the papers he had begun to correct.

'Oh!' she gasped. 'I'm sorry.'

'What the hell have you done?' he shouted, jumping off his seat.

It made her tremble a little in fear.

'Do you not realize how important these papers are?' he yelled.

Zarish had never seen Ahmar like this and it shocked her.

'You know what? You were right. You are not at all close to being like me,' he said.

His words sent another tremor through her; this time through her entire body. She started to tremble again.

'It's because you are an emotional fool!' he snapped.

Ahmar noticed that her eyes started to well with tears but it seemed to aggravate him more.

'Damn!' he said and ran his fingers through his hair.

Zarish stood still in front of him, wiping the tears that were now streaming down her face.

Zarish expected Ahmar to say these things because she knew the intensity of his anger. But ever since she had fallen in love with him, and since she assumed that he too was in love with her, it had become difficult to absorb the disappointment. Things were not the same as before.

Zarish had entwined hope and expectations with this relationship. Though she had not declared her feelings to Ahmar, Zarish had already told Saleha about it and believed it herself as well. She no longer needed to confirm or test what she felt for Ahmar. His harsh words did have an emotional impact on her earlier, but now they started to affect her physically as well. She felt her forehead pulse in pain when she heard him call her 'an emotional fool'.

'Yes. I am an emotional fool,' she muttered finally. It seemed as if she had spoken in a state of semi-consciousness.

Ahmar did not believe what she had just said. He thought that perhaps he had heard her wrong.

'I was a fool to fall in love with you,' she declared at last.

He was stunned on hearing this untimed, unexpected confession. Zarish too could never have imagined that she would declare her feelings to him in such a situation, a moment of crisis or that she would be the first to say it, before he did.

'A big fool,' she sniffed, as a fat teardrop rolled down her cheek.

'What did you say?' Ahmar asked, the incredulity and shock mounting on his face.

'Yes, Mr Ahmar . . . that's right. I am in love with you,' she said, wiping away the tears.

Ahmar did not know how to respond to her sudden confession and ran his fingers through his hair anxiously.

'Zarish . . . just listen to me,' he said, trying to calm her down.

She raised her hand, gesturing him not to say anything.

'Zarish . . .' Before he could say anything, she dashed out of his office, hiding her tears. He remained motionless, feeling guilty and disappointed.

'Damn. Damn. Damn!' He banged his fists angrily against the table. He sat back and held his head in his hands. Her last words echoed repeatedly in his ears.

'I was a fool to fall in love with you.'

'Yes, Mr Ahmar . . . that's right. I am in love with you.'

All of a sudden, he remembered his father's words: 'Are you dumb? This girl is madly in love with you. Her eyes say everything. Never let her go.'

'No, no, no. I cannot let her walk away. I have to talk to her,' Ahmar said to himself.

He was out of the door in a flash. But the pain of disappointment stabbed him in his chest when he saw her in Haroon's arms. Perhaps Haroon was only comforting her.

'Does he know she loves me? What would he think?' Ahmar wondered. Without looking for answers to his questions, he stepped back and left. He drove the car recklessly, his mind still imagining Zarish in Haroon's arms. He took out a pack of cigarettes from the dashboard and lit one quickly. He knew she was not like him. In fact, she was the exact opposite of him: stubborn, aggressive and proud. She was a girl who cried on scoring low marks; she was shallow, overemotional and weak. She was not a book person like him. They had contrasting personalities. However, she had a good side to her. She was caring, supportive, motivating and at times funny too. Above all, she knew how to love, and this quality of hers overshadowed everything else. She was not like other girls; there was something unusual about her. He had not been attracted to anyone for a while. In fact, he had dumped his feelings in a dead corner of his heart. But Zarish had managed to pull him out from that state of mind. She had taught him to love again.

Ahmar hoped to live a normal life with the one he loved. Would that be Zarish? This question startled him. She had confessed her love for him. Instead of reciprocating, he had let her walk away.

He soon reached home. But instead of going inside, he sat outside on the porch. When Muraad came home, he found his son sitting alone, brooding over something. Ahmar was completely oblivious to his father's presence. His body did not move an inch. A shadow crossed Muraad's face when he found his son in this state.

'Ahmar?' He patted him on his thigh lightly, startling him.

'Dad?' Ahmar turned around to look at his father.

'Yes son. Are you okay?' Muraad asked, firmly holding his hand.

'Yes. I am all right,' he said with a sigh.

'But you don't look fine. You might be physically present here, but your mind is wandering somewhere else. Tell me what is bothering you? See, I am your father and you cannot hide anything from me.'

Ahmar looked at him but didn't say anything.

'What is bothering you?' Muraad asked again.

They sat in complete silence for a while.

'Zarish,' Ahmar whispered after a while.

His father was the only person with whom he could share his feelings.

'What about her?'

'I don't think I deserve her. I am not good enough for her.'

'Why? You are the perfect man for her. What's wrong with you?'

Muraad narrowed his brows in confusion.

'We are very different from each other. We have contrasting views and personalities. I don't think I am the right person for her. She deserves better,' Ahmar explained.

'Why are you underestimating yourself, Ahmar? This makes you sound like a loser,' Muraad replied in a disgruntled manner.

'I'm not a loser, Dad.' Ahmar sighed again. 'We have very different perspectives. We want different things from life. There will always be a conflict between us. I do not think we are made for each other. And I cannot have a relationship with my student. I should not even think about it. It seems so unscrupulous and immoral. What will my students think of me? They will despise me!'

'Nothing is immoral, son. Love can never be immoral,' Muraad said, adding, 'see, it is very simple. There is an old saying that opposites attract. She likes you because she found something unusual in you and that is why she was keen on knowing you. On the other hand, you fancy her because she evoked your innermost desires. Love is like a magnet. Despite having nothing in common, you get attracted towards each other. Nature compels you to do so.'

Ahmar listened to his father intently.

'Your mother and I were also poles apart yet we fell in love,' Muraad continued, adding, 'son, love has no boundaries. It is free from all discriminations; it is limitless. You have your entire life to discover her and vice versa. I am sure your love will only grow with time. So, do not give up. Be a man and go and propose to her before it's too late.'

Muraad patted him on his thigh, and added, 'And do not bother about what the world will say about you.'

Ahmar shut his eyes and thought about what had happened in his office. He felt like killing himself for treating her like that. Despite being called an emotional fool, she had still confessed her feelings to him. 'How courageous of her,' he thought.

'I know you love her. Admit it to yourself first and then confess it to her,' Muraad said.

A guilt-stricken Ahmar uncovered his eyes to look at his father.

'Even if she loves you, you can't expect her to say it first. She is a woman and she expects you to tell her how you feel,' Muraad said.

After listening to his father's advice, Ahmar felt guiltier. He knew what he had done could not be forgiven. He was supposed to tell her how he felt but the opposite had happened.

'There might be a problem, Dad,' Ahmar said.

'What?'

'I spoke to her rudely again. I don't know if she would want to talk to me now. God. I'm so pathetic,' Ahmar said, sighing.

'Don't overthink. Just go and talk to her,' Muraad suggested.

Zarish and Haroon were sitting in his car in utter silence. All this while, she had not spoken a single word. Though Zarish was stubborn, she was not emotional. Haroon knew this about her.

'Will you say something now?' He broke the silence.

She sniffed and rubbed her nose with her forefinger. She wanted to tell him everything. After all, he was her best friend and would understand her. However, she decided to stay silent. What was the point when Ahmar was not even interested in her. Saleha's warnings whirled in her mind.

'Zarish?' he asked again.

'I'm fine. I was . . . I was just missing you,' she lied.

'Really?'

'Hmm.' She nodded and wiped her tears.

'Surprisingly, you have never reacted like this before, no matter how much you've missed me. At least, don't lie to me. I don't expect that from you.'

'Don't you trust me, Haroon?' she asked.

He suddenly placed his hand on her wrist and squeezed it.

'Hey, I didn't mean that,' he clarified. 'I am just saying if there is any other issue, you can share it with me. I am your best friend, and I will understand.'

'I know, Haroon. I am really glad to have you beside me, but for now, I am okay.' She held his hand tightly.

He smiled at her, his eyes brimming with love. For her, he was just a friend, but for Haroon she was his entire world. He hit on other girls for fun, but deep inside his heart desired Zarish. However, she was clueless about his feelings. Haroon had always wanted to tell her how he felt, but something or the other had stopped him. It was mostly fear; the fear of losing her. What if Zarish didn't love him the way he loved her? What if she considered him only a dear friend? He could lose her forever. But he also knew that there was no other man in her life and that she would eventually marry him.

That night Zarish did not eat properly. She could not. Zarina and Zia cajoled her, but she refused.

'Is she having some problems with Haroon these days?' Zia asked Zarina.

'I don't know. She never tells me anything,' Zarina replied.

Later that night, as she lay curled up in her bed, she made a promise to herself. She decided not to talk to Ahmar about it ever again. Love and self-respect were important aspects of her life. She could not let one take over and crush the other. She needed to create a balance between the two. Though she loved him passionately, she could not sacrifice or lose her dignity. She did not fear his reaction any more and was ready to face him at the university without any guilt or embarrassment.

The next day, she woke up determined to ignore Ahmar as much as possible. He was nothing more than a teacher. If he believed that they could not be together because they were different, now was the time to prove him right. She would become the person he wanted her to be: unemotional, cold.

On the other hand, Ahmar was feeling the exact opposite. Following his father's advice, he had decided to tell her how he actually felt. But he first had to apologize.

Now that he knew how she felt, it was quite easy to convince her. It had taken him a great deal of time to realize and accept the truth—that she loved him. His father's words had changed his viewpoint. He had made him realize that it was not too difficult to fall in love again.

He was in a good mood, happy at the prospect of seeing her. He had thought of sending her a message but then had decided against it. He knew she was angry with him. He stopped at a florist and bought flowers, white and red roses, to pacify her.

On his way to the class, he met Saleha and Maha.

'Hello,' he greeted them with a warm smile.

They exchanged a quick glance and seemed a bit uncomfortable in his company. They also noticed the bouquet in his hands.

'Good morning, Sir. How are you?' Saleha replied.

'I'm good. How about you?' he asked eagerly.

'We're doing great,' Maha replied.

'Great. I don't see your third companion with you. Is she here yet?' he asked, hinting at Zarish.

Saleha could see the eagerness in his eyes; the eagerness to see Zarish.

'Zarish was right. He does fancy her,' Saleha wondered.

'Zarish?' Maha asked.

He nodded.

'She is here. I think I saw her near the library,' Maha said.

'All right. See you in class. Have a good day.'

'First, I need to apologize to her. Make her understand that what I said yesterday meant nothing. And then tell her what I actually feel for her,' he told himself as he walked purposefully towards the library.

His eyes scanned the entire area and at last he found her sitting alone in the corner. She seemed busy reading a book. But when he looked closely, he realized that she was lost in thought; her eyes distant. Ahmar stood near her table and watched her silently.

After a few seconds, Zarish felt someone's eyes on her and turned around. She was shocked to see Ahmar.

'Hello. Good morning,' he greeted her in a husky voice and then cleared his throat.

She did not answer. In fact, she pretended to read, ignoring him altogether. Ahmar raised his brow and smiled as he had expected a cold response. He did not feel bad at all.

'What, no reaction?' he asked, teasing her.

She remained quiet.

'I know you are hurt, and you have every right to treat me in the same manner. You can abuse me, shout at me or even hit me, do whatever you like but please say something. I can't stand your silence, Zarish. I can't,' he said.

She did not look at him; her eyes fixed on the book in her hands. 'Zarish?' he repeated her name. 'Won't you say anything?'

She stood up and turned around to face him.

'We have a class with you today. Let's not be late,' she said coldly and walked away.

He stood there astounded, the bouquet still in his hands.

During the lecture, Zarish did not look at him even once. Ahmar tried hard to attract her attention but his attempts were futile.

'Are you okay?' Saleha asked after observing her glum expression.

'I'm fine,' she reassured her.

Ahmar caught them talking and tried to listen to their conversation.

'Did you talk to him?' Saleha asked.

'I have the house to myself tomorrow night. Mom and Dad are going to Karachi to visit my aunt,' Zarish said, ignoring her question.

'Oh, is Zahaan going too?'

'No. He will probably go out with his friends. I'll be home with the maids.'

'Oh,' Saleha responded.

'You can come over if you want. We can have a slumber party together,' Zarish said, smiling weakly.

'Great. I'll let you know.'

Before Zarish could say anything more, Ahmar's voice interrupted their conversation.

'Miss Zarish and Miss Saleha,' he announced.

Both of them suddenly looked at him.

'Is your conversation more important than my lecture?' he asked.

Zarish did not say anything. She waited for Saleha to respond.

'Err. Not really, Sir,' Saleha said sheepishly.

'Really?' he asked, folding his arms. 'So, what were you two discussing? Please share it with us too.'

Zarish gave him a stern look but he ignored her.

'Miss Saleha and Miss Zarish, please leave the class. I can't tolerate this kind of indiscipline.'

'Sir Ahmar is right. We are creating a nuisance here. Let's go out,' Zarish said in a mocking tone, glaring at him resentfully.

She took Saleha's hand and swiftly pulled her out. The classroom buzzed with murmurs. This irritated Ahmar even more.

Saleha broke free of her grasp as soon as they came out in the corridor.

'What the hell are you doing, Zarish?' she snapped. 'What is wrong with you?'

Zarish tried to control her anger as she clenched her fists.

'Tell me? Did you talk to Sir Ahmar? What did he say?'

'I'll tell you later. I'm going home. See you tomorrow.' Saleha went back to the class gingerly.

'Where is Zarish?' Ahmar asked her in a cold voice.

'Sir . . . she . . . left,' she replied.

'Where did she go?'

'You may find her in the parking lot,' Saleha answered.

Without giving a response, he rushed towards the parking lot.

Ahmar looked around frantically. After a few moments, he saw her standing near her car.

As he came close, he realized she was crying.

'Zarish?' he stood near her.

She wiped her tears quickly and opened the door of the car, pretending to get in. He held her arm and did not let her go.

'Talk to me,' he said. She did not respond. 'Please stop hurting yourself. Trust me, I am hurting too.'

She turned around to face him.

'Sir Ahmar, I don't want to talk to you. Please, let me go,' she said in a firm voice.

'Apart from your personal life, you are also letting your studies get affected. Do you understand that?' he said.

She tried to free herself from his hold.

'Please, Zarish. Try to understand.'

She jerked his grip off her arm, got into her car and drove off, leaving him standing alone.

It was clear that Zarish was not interested in talking to him. But he was not ready to give up. Ahmar had overheard her and Saleha's conversation in the classroom, and he knew her parents were out of town. He decided to go to her house to ask for forgiveness.

The next day, Zarish deliberately did not go to the university and decided to miss all of the lectures. The day passed slowly for Ahmar at the university. He noticed Zarish's absence in the class and felt it too. He had to talk to her. Before leaving for her place, he called her and even sent her a few text messages, but there was no response. Fortunately, he knew her address as he had dropped her home a few times.

The weather suddenly changed and it started raining as he made his way to her place. He parked his car outside her house and sat there in silence for a while. The only sound around him was that of raindrops splattering against the windshield. He rubbed his hands together to warm them up and then ran his fingers through his hair. He fished out his cell phone from his pocket and dialled her number.

Zarish, unaware of his presence, lay on her bed. She had avoided his calls all day. Her cell phone started to buzz again. She knew it was *him* and ignored it. He called her again; he was not going to give up so easily. She got irritated when her phone buzzed again. She decided to pick it up and tell him never to call her again.

'Hello, Zarish?' he said.

She did not say anything.

'I know you're listening. Please say something.'

'Why are you constantly calling me?' she asked.

'I . . . I need to talk to you,' he replied, pressing his lips together.

'As I said earlier, I do not want to talk to you about anything. My answer will not change, no matter how many times you call me,' she said curtly.

'Even if I tell you that I am in a lot of pain?' he asked in a low, husky voice.

Her heart melted; it was hard to resist his deep, throaty voice. She wanted to forget everything she'd said to him earlier and talk to him nicely.

'No,' she said instead.

'Zarish, I cannot let go of this matter so easily. I need to explain . . .'

'You don't have to explain anything, Sir Ahmar,' she said, cutting him mid-sentence. 'I should be the one explaining because you are my teacher and I am your student. This is how it is supposed to be. I already got your answer that evening,' she said.

'How can you just presume my answer when I have not even said anything yet?'

Zarish did not put much thought into what he said nor was she interested to know.

'Ahmar, please. Stop worrying about me because I am fine. All right? Just let it go,' she said.

'Okay. Just come and talk to me once,' he said eagerly.

'What? How can a sane man like you talk such nonsense? How can I come to your house right now?' she asked, looking at her watch. It was 10.30 p.m.

'I'm right outside your house.'

'What?' she gasped and then ran to her window to see if his car was parked outside.

It was raining heavily now. She slid open the window to get a better view. Ahmar was right. She could see him sitting in his car, which was parked right outside the main gate. He was still holding the cell phone, his head cocked to one side.

'Why are you here? I told you I don't want talk to you,' she said, looking into his eyes.

'I am waiting for you, Zarish,' he said.

'My parents are not at home, and I do not want to take this risk. My brother will be home any minute.'

'I know that. I wouldn't have come here otherwise. Just come here for five minutes,' he requested her.

She was shocked to hear this.

'How did he know that my parents and brother were not at home?' she wondered.

'Whatever. I'm not coming. No means no,' she said brusquely.

'Is this your final answer?'

'Yes,' she hissed.

He sighed heavily and said, 'Fine. I will wait for you and stand here till it stops raining.'

'What?' she asked, startled. 'I didn't know you were this stupid.'

'You think you are stubborn? I will show you what it actually means to be stubborn. So just wait and watch.'

'Ahmar please! You are not in a movie,' she told him.

'This is indeed a movie. My life's story.'

'You are insane,' she hissed.

'Yes, I am,' he said and hung up, his eyes still on her.

'Huh? Damn it!' she said as she shut the window. She sat on her bed feeling disgusted. She constantly looked at her cell phone to see if he was calling again. But nothing happened. She did not have the courage to open the window again and see what he was doing out there.

'What if he is actually standing in the rain? Damn. He might catch a cold and fall sick,' she shuddered at the thought.

After a few minutes, Zarish got up from her bed and walked to the window. She moved the curtain and peered outside, her breath fogging the glass. To her surprise, she saw Ahmar standing in the rain, right next to his car. The indicators of his car were still on and the headlights blinked continuously. She could see that he had tightly hugged himself as his entire body shivered; he was completely soaked.

'Ahmar!' she screamed.

He looked up at her, but didn't say anything.

'Get inside the car! Now!' she ordered.

He remained adamant and paid no heed to her order. He simply shook his head.

'I hate you,' she said, clenching her teeth.

Fearing that he would get pneumonia, she took out her red umbrella from the closet and rushed down the stairs. One of the maids was busy in the kitchen while the other was in the servants' quarters. Taking advantage of their absence, she quickly opened the front door and ran out.

The rain was lashing down ferociously. She looked around for the guard but he was not there on his seat. Ahmar was still standing near his car when she came out of her house. He smiled weakly when he saw her heading towards him.

'What the hell is this, Ahmar? Why are you behaving like a child? Cover yourself or you'll get sick!' she said, opening her umbrella.

Ignoring her remark, he glanced at her umbrella that only sheltered her from the rain. She followed his gaze but did not extend it in his direction, as she was already very irritated.

'I am saying something!' she yelled, to which he smiled.

She was tired of repeating the same thing again and again and did not want to argue any more.

'Why are you doing this to me?' she said in a defeated, weak voice.

'Can you please bring the umbrella a little closer? I am shivering to death,' he said innocently.

'No. If you don't listen to me, then I won't either.'

'Do you want me to get sick?' he asked innocently.

'Yes! What's the point of behaving so immaturely?'

'I want to talk to you once,' he said feebly, hugging himself tighter.

'Okay, fine! I am standing right here in front of you! Speak up before I . . .'

'I'm in love with you, Miss Zarish Munawwar,' he interrupted her.

For a second, her world turned upside down. She could not feel the ground beneath her feet. She could not feel her legs. They were numb. In fact, her entire body was numb. Her arms prickled with goosebumps, and she skipped a heartbeat.

'You . . . what?' she mumbled.

'I am sorry,' he whispered. 'I love you and I mean it.'

His words made her euphoric. She could not believe her ears and stared at him with a dumbfounded look on her face. This was certainly a dream. Everything seemed surreal to her. This could not be really happening.

How could he fall in love with her? Was he joking with her or playing with her feelings? The entire scene seemed right out of a fairy tale.

'I know this is not the right time to ask something like this but could you please share your umbrella with me?' he said, still shivering.

Zarish's silence spoke a thousand words. Ahmar knew how sensitive she was. She could never stay angry for long. He knew her heart would melt. He was right.

'I will get sick, yaar,' he said, shivering.

Without arguing further, she put the red umbrella over his head. He stepped forward to stand under it. They stood close together; their eyes locked. Suddenly, time stopped. The rain, the darkness, the night, nothing mattered to them any more. They were just two souls looking into each other's eyes with profound love.

Later, they sat in silence in his car. He had turned off the headlights and they were enveloped in darkness. There was no sound except the pitter-patter of the rain. Zarish was speechless after Ahmar professed his love. She had never thought this moment would come in her life. It was unexpected. He looked at her fixedly and noticed how she fidgeted with her fingers nervously. He wanted to hold her hand.

'You have not said anything since I . . . uh . . . professed my love,' he said, looking at her.

She timidly glanced sidelong at him.

'You'll get a cold. I'll get you some clothes from inside,' she said, interrupting the intimate moment. She was about to leave when he held her hand.

'No . . . please. Just stay. I like being here with you,' he said.

Her hand was warmer than his and he found it comforting. He squeezed it affectionately. This made her blush and she lowered her gaze.

'Ahmar . . .'

'Yes?' he asked, caressing her hand.

'Is this for real or are you just . . . playing with my feelings?'

'Do you really think I would play with your feelings, and mine?'

She shook her head and looked at his hand that held hers firmly.

'You know, I mostly listen to my mind. There have been very few instances when I have followed my heart,' he said.

She lifted her head to look at him.

'I tried to stay away from you and keep my feelings hidden, but I guess some things are not in your control. The more I resisted, the more attached I got. That is why they say, love is not bound to anything, whether it is your thinking or a custom. It is free,' he said, adding, 'I fell in love with you the night I accidentally cut my finger. Do you remember?'

She nodded, amused at the memory.

'And then I fell head over heels when I saw you at the masquerade ball.'

So Zarish's assumptions were correct that night. Both of them glanced at each. She squeezed his hand gently.

His hand was getting warmer.

'Why didn't you say anything then?' she asked. She had regained her confidence and was not shy to ask questions.

'Fear,' he replied.

'Of what?'

'I was scared of what people might think. Fear of putting our lives at risk. Fear of ruining our reputation. Fear of beginning a new relationship with you when everybody knows I am your teacher. Fear of . . . losing you and never having you again in my life.'

'I love you, Ahmar, and I would never leave you. Ever.'

'Don't make any promises. You don't know if you will be able to keep them. The circumstances might change.'

'My love is not dependent on the circumstances. I love you, Ahmar, and I will love you till the end of time,' she said.

Ahmar wanted to believe everything she said as he had found happiness after a long time.

'Let's not make any promises. Let's live in this moment. Now will you please let me look into your eyes?' he said, leaning a bit closer.

'Ahmar,' she said.

'Hmm?' He put his elbow on the steering wheel, rested his head on it and gazed at her. They were still holding hands.

'Stop looking at me like that,' she said, pretending to be irritated, but in reality, she loved every bit of it.

He smiled, knowing how she actually felt.

'Why are you smiling?' she asked.

'I'd never imagined I would fall in love with you.'

She blushed.

'It feels so . . . different and good.'

'Everything is destiny,' she said.

He looked at her deeply.

'I am sitting right next to you. We're close. We're together. Don't you think it's destiny?' she asked.

'Yes. Maybe.'

She smiled.

'Hey, your brother will be home any minute. You'd better leave now,' he said, looking at his watch.

'Oh,' she muttered, 'I forgot about him completely.'

'You shouldn't,' he said and chuckled.

'By the way, how did you know my parents were out of town?'

'Let it remain a mystery.'

'Tell me. Please.'

'Well, I sort of . . . eavesdropped when you were discussing it with Saleha in class,' he said awkwardly.

'What? Really?'

He nodded.

'I cannot believe you, Ahmar. I thought you were not like me,' she taunted him.

He smiled.

'Change your clothes as soon as you reach home. I do not want you to catch a cold. Okay?'

He nodded, adding, 'Anything else?'

'I'll see you at the university tomorrow.'

'Yeah. Right,' he said, smiling. 'Now go back home before anyone sees us.'

'I cannot go,' she murmured.

'Why not?'

'Because you are holding my hand.'

It was the best night of Zarish's life. She had never felt so happy and content before. Ahmar had finally professed his love for her. His undying affinity was no longer a secret. Her world was complete now.

When she came back to her room, she felt like a completely new person. Zarish stared at her hands for a long time, remembering the touch of his cold fingers against her warm skin. She loved him unconditionally and was ready to surrender herself to him.

Ahmar reacted a bit differently. He was madly in love with her, but he did not want the world to know. However, he forgot he could not keep secrets from his father. When Muraad saw his son's wet clothes, he unleashed a volley of questions. Ahmar sat him down and told him the whole story.

'Nothing would make me happier than your wedding,' Muraad said with a smile.

Ahmar was happy to get a positive response from his father. After changing his clothes, Ahmar sat on the bed and picked up his cell phone. By now, he had memorized her number by heart. He dialled it quickly and tucked the phone under his ear.

'Hello?' she answered.

'I don't think I will be able to sleep tonight,' he declared in a soft whisper.

She knew he was smiling.

'Why?' she said, sitting on her bed.

'You won't let me sleep.'

'As if I am with you right now,' she said, trembling at the thought of being close to him.

'I wish you were here, actually.'

She remained quiet, her cheeks reddening.

'And . . . you are blushing again. Aren't you?' he asked.

'No. I am not.'

'If you think I don't know you by now, then you are really stupid,' he said in a low whisper.

'Do you know how sexy you sound on the phone?' she thought but didn't say it to him.

'What?' he asked.

'What, what?'

'Did you say something?'

'No. I didn't,' she said, smiling to herself.

'Hmm. I get to know about many of my qualities from you. Is there anything else you like about me?'

'Everything. I love everything about you,' she thought but kept quiet.

'Hello?' he said when he did not get a reply.

'Yes?'

'Are you thinking about something else?' he asked.

'How can I think about something else when I am talking to you?' she asked.

'Hey, by the way, you forgot your umbrella in my car.'

'Oh. Did I? Never mind. I will take it from you later.'

'You did not answer my question.'

'Which question?'

'What else do you like about me?' he said, changing the subject.

'If you think I will answer this question, you're wrong. I won't tell you.'

'Why not?' he asked, resting his head on the pillow.

'Because I don't want to.'

'Do you love me?'

This question startled her. Her heartbeat quickened.

'Answer me, Zarish. Do you love me?'

Just then, she heard her brother's voice in the hallway.

'Hey, I'm going to hang up now,' she said nervously.

'Why, what happened?'

'Zahaan is here. I will talk to you tomorrow.'

'Hey, hey listen to me.'

'What?'

'Can we go out tomorrow after your classes?'

'Tomorrow? But why?' she asked. She could hear Zahaan's footsteps on the stairs. He was probably coming to check on her.

'Well, actually tomorrow is . . .'

'Ahmar, I have to go. See you tomorrow. Bye,' she said and hung up.

The next day was special for Zarish as it was the beginning of a new relationship; the beginning of a new life. She chose a special black salwar kameez and paired it with matching sandals.

Ahmar was already at the university, busy with his lectures.

Zarish told Saleha the whole story as soon as she reached the university. She couldn't hide anything from her best friend. Saleha was rather surprised.

After having a quick chat with Saleha, Zarish decided to go meet Ahmar.

'Hello. Good morning,' he said as she walked up to him.

She greeted him with her eyes. She noticed he was dressed exceptionally well. He wore a black leather jacket with a pair of denims. He looked sexy, she had to admit.

'Do you remember we have to go out in the evening?' he asked.

She nodded and looked into his eyes.

'See you then,' he said and turned away to leave.

'Won't we meet in the class before that?' she asked.

'Yes.' He turned to look at her. 'I have a request.'

She narrowed her brows and shrugged.

He came closer and brought his lips next to her ear. Zarish was a little shocked by this act of intimacy at the university.

'Please don't tell anyone about us. Please. Not yet,' he whispered and walked away.

As soon as the lecture ended, Ahmar rushed out of the class and Zarish followed him. He was waiting for her in the parking lot. She noticed he had parked his car slightly away from the rest of the cars; it was hidden behind a bamboo tree. Certainly, he did not want anyone to know about his secret plan.

'Hello,' he greeted her with a naughty smile, which brought colour to her cheeks.

'It feels so weird to run away like this.' She shrugged.

'Have you heard of the famous saying . . .?' He stepped closer and whispered in her ear, 'Everything is fair in love and war?' He began to laugh softly. 'Don't feel scared. I am with you,' he assured her. This made her heart flutter. 'And you look beautiful,' he said.

'This is the first time he has appreciated my good looks,' she reflected.

'Ahmar,' she said, stepping back.

Her voice broke his trance and he stood up straight.

'What happened?' he asked, looking around.

'Nothing,' she said, smiling. 'Where are we headed?' she asked, folding her arms.

'That's a surprise.'

This was their first official date. He had not told her where he was taking her. It was only 9.30 p.m. but it seemed as if it was quite late. On their way, both of them looked at each other from time to time but mostly remained silent.

'When are your parents coming back?' he finally asked.

'They will be back tomorrow evening.'

'Great. So, we have the entire night to ourselves,' he said, giving her one of his rare lopsided grins.

'The entire night?' Zarish gasped.

'Why, what's wrong with that?' he asked, raising his brow.

'I didn't know you had other plans,' she said teasingly.

'I intend to drop you home quite late.'

'May I know the reason?'

'Not now.'

She heaved a sigh.

'Please, Ahmar.'

'Shh. Stay quiet. Let me focus on the road.' In the meantime, she sent a message to her brother, telling him that she would come home late as she was going to Saleha's place. It was a pure lie. She didn't have a choice, she had to come up with something.

Ahmar had taken a longer route that seemed never-ending. She sat quietly. Her wristwatch showed it was 10.30 p.m. After an hour, Ahmar stopped his car in the middle of a dirt road.

'Why has he brought me here?' she wondered.

He stepped out of the car and opened her door like a true gentleman.

'You really don't have to do all this.' She tried to chuckle, feeling shy.

'Of course I have to. C'mon.'

They walked hand in hand. As they crossed the muddy path, a beautiful bridge came into view. A river gleamed under it, burbling as it flowed. He held her hand gently and stood in the centre of the bridge. It was a cloudy night; the moon peeped from behind the clouds occasionally. The moonlight shone through the clouds, lighting up the bridge. Her skin glowed in the sudden burst of light. Ahmar looked at her shamelessly. She felt a little uncomfortable when she caught him looking at her like that.

'Ahmar,' she whispered.

He nodded in response.

'Why are we here?'

'Is it 12 a.m. yet?' He checked his wristwatch to make sure it was midnight.

'Yeah, it is 12.03 a.m.,' she told him.

'I did not want to celebrate my birthday alone.'

She gasped.

'That is why I brought you here.'

'What? Wow. Uh . . . happy birthday . . . Sir . . . uh . . . Ahmar. I don't know what to say!' she stammered.

'You should have reacted this way when I told you I was in love with you,' he said with a laugh.

'Damn. He has a beautiful laugh,' she thought.

'So . . . uh . . . you wanted to celebrate your birthday with me?'

'Hmm.' He leaned against the railings, deep in thought.

'What?' she asked.

'I won't be alone on my birthdays from now on,' he whispered, gazing at her.

She flushed.

'Dad is not in town but he will be back soon,' he told her.

'What a coincidence. Both our parents are out of town at the same time.'

He nodded.

'You should have told me about your birthday. I feel bad for not buying you a present,' she said, making a face.

'Doesn't matter. You are here with me. That is all I want. Trust me.'

Both of them stared at each other for a while, but then she moved away.

'This place looks heavenly,' she said, looking at the moon.

'My family used to visit this resort quite often when I was a kid,' he said with a sad smile. 'My mother used to bring me to this bridge and we used to stand here for hours,' he went on, 'and when my dad would join us, we would throw pebbles into the flowing river.' He flinched at the memory.

'Good times, right?' she asked to lighten the mood.

He nodded.

'I know you miss your mother. A lot.'

He nodded and turned around to look the other way. A small tear rolled down his cheek, but he instantly wiped it off.

'Hey,' Zarish said, putting a hand on his shoulder. 'Look at me.'

He did not look at her. The sweet yet saddening childhood memory had made him unhappy.

Zarish could not imagine a person like him becoming weak and sentimental. She could not see *her* Ahmar sad. She put her arms around his shoulders and embraced him from behind.

He was surprised at her gesture.

'You don't have to be sad as long as I am here by your side and I intend to stay with you forever. I promise,' she assured him.

'Zarish?'

'I love you so much,' she told him and closed her eyes.

She wanted to savour every moment of being close to him. She did not want to let go; she wanted to hold him in her arms forever. Zarish felt every inch of his body against hers. She felt the warmth that radiated from his body.

Ahmar too could not hold back. He turned around, making her face him, and held her shoulders. She opened her eyes and blushed as their gaze met. Ahmar held her shoulders firmly and brought her closer to him. He held her chin and tilted her head.

'Zarish?' he whispered. It was so cold that they could see their breath.

'Hmm?' she mumbled, closing her eyes.

'I love you,' he said, taking her in his arms.

She passionately hugged him back. They stood like that for a long time: their bodies touching, their eyes closed, their skin bathed in moonlight.

After a while, they drove back to the city. He picked up dinner from a local restaurant on the way. Soon he reached her house and parked his car in front of the back gate.

'Time to go,' he announced in a low whisper.

'I hope this is not a dream, Ahmar,' she said looking at him lovingly. 'I do not want to lose you.'

He glanced at her, and then looked at the road ahead.

'I am not going anywhere. I am here as long as you want.'

'I want you . . .'

'Forever,' he completed her line with a smile on his lips.

She was still holding his hand, she realized. He brought her hand closer to his mouth and kissed it. Her heart skipped a beat and she blushed.

She heaved a sigh of relief when she realized that Zahaan was still not home. It was around 2 a.m. when she came back. Zarish had never stayed out this late before.

She sat on her bed and hugged herself tightly. Now she had only one purpose in life: to love Ahmar; to love him selflessly.

On the other hand, Ahmar had totally lost control over his emotions. He was not the sort of person who would fall in love with one of his students, take her out for a date and then eventually end up with her. Perhaps she was so irresistible that he could not stop himself from falling head over heels. He had changed. Zarish had transformed him into another person. It was so easy to fall in love with her. He wanted to spend his entire life with her.

'Are you hiding something from me?' Saleha asked Zarish the next day at the university.

'No, I am not,' Zarish said, munching potato chips.

'Hiding is one thing, but you've started lying too. I am really disappointed,' Saleha said with a grimace.

'What do you mean?' Zarish asked.

'Last evening, I saw you leaving the university with Sir Ahmar.'

'Yeah. He took me out to celebrate his birthday. He wanted to spend it with me,' Zarish said, accepting the truth.

'Oh. That is great. Sounds so romantic. Why didn't you tell me earlier?' Saleha asked excitedly, forgetting her anger.

'He loves me, Saleha. He doesn't want the world to know about it. Not yet.'

'Oh my god! Really?' Saleha gasped.

Zarish gave a triumphant smile, nodding.

'Sir Ahmar is in love with you. Wow!' Saleha said excitedly and started tapping on the table.

'Hey, stop!' Zarish held her hand. 'Please be quiet.'

'Okay. Okay.' Saleha took a deep breath.

'Today is his birthday, and I want to do something special for him,' Zarish said.

'Like what?'

'We will all go to his office and surprise him with a birthday cake.'

211

'Sounds great. Where is the cake?'

'I have already asked Sherry to bring it,' Zarish replied, flashing a wide smile.

Zarish invited all her batchmates and faculty members to Ahmar's office for cutting the cake. Ahmar, who was busy with work, looked up in surprise as everyone stepped in. Zarish placed the cake on his table and asked him to blow out the candles.

'C'mon, man. Go for it,' Jamal said.

Ahmar did not know how to react. He was touched by the gesture. He glanced at Zarish who gave him an encouraging nod. As he blew out the candles, everyone clapped. He carefully cut the cake and offered the first piece to Maleeha as she was standing right beside him. Zarish felt bad but she did not express it. She knew it would have looked inappropriate if he had offered her the cake first. After Maleeha, he offered the cake to Jamal and Wahab.

'Everyone please get back to your class. Celebrations can continue later,' Maleeha announced.

Zarish did not want to leave his office; she wanted to stay with *her* Ahmar. The students wished him and left. Zarish felt bad and left without even wishing him. It wasn't just her, Ahmar felt bad too. He noticed how disappointed she looked when Maleeha asked them to leave. After the students had left, Maleeha and Jamal sat down with Ahmar. They told him that the wedding was fixed for the upcoming week.

'You have to take care of everything. After all, you are our friend,' Maleeha told Ahmar.

'I am always here to help.'

'Ahmar, we also have a surprise for you at our wedding,' Jamal said, winking at Maleeha. She just chuckled softly.

'What surprise?' Ahmar asked.

'You'll know at the wedding,' Maleeha answered with a playful smile.

After her classes, Zarish sat alone on the stairs outside the library, waiting for her driver. All her friends had left early. She felt a pang of disappointment when she thought about Ahmar.

She was lost in deep thought when someone came and stood next to her. She quickly stood up and saw Ahmar standing in front of her, grinning as usual. She looked away, her face glum.

'What are you doing here?' he asked.

She chose to remain silent.

'It is too cold here. Come, let's go inside my office. Come,' he offered.

'My driver will be here any minute,' she answered without looking at him.

'Do as I say,' he ordered.

She glanced at him with a puzzled look.

'Come with me, Zarish. I need to talk to you.'

The desk was piled with papers and files, in addition to birthday cards and presents.

To her surprise, a soft English number played on his laptop. A lamp glowed in the corner, making the room snug and warm. A clicking sound distracted her. She turned around and found Ahmar standing near the door with his hand on the doorknob. He pulled the door shut and locked it. They were locked in his office. This thought scared her.

'Why d-d-did you l-l-lock the door?' she stammered.

'I am still waiting for my birthday present.' He stepped closer as he spoke.

'Perhaps he has taken the previous night's intimacy too seriously and now wants to take our relationship to the next level,' she thought.

'I am sorry I could not spend any time with you today,' he said. 'But that doesn't really matter, right? Because each and every second of my life belongs to you.'

She looked into his gleaming eyes.

'I belong to you. I may not be with you all the time, but my heart is always with you.' He held her hand gently and placed it on his chest. His words made her emotional.

'I want to stay in your heart forever,' he whispered, inhaling her fragrance.

'You're already here,' she said, placing his hand on her chest. A tear rolled down her cheek as she spoke.

He wiped it off and held her face gently.

'No tears tonight, okay?' he said.

She nodded.

'Now where is my birthday gift?' he said, chuckling.

'I do not know if you will like it or not but . . .'

'I will love it, Miss Zarish.'

'Sure?'

He nodded.

'Then close your eyes first,' she said.

'Hmm. Sounds very typical.'

'Please.'

'Okay. Here I go.' He did as he was told and shut his eyes. She observed his beautiful face for a moment. She touched his face gently, examining and feeling every feature.

'God has sculpted him beautifully,' she thought.

He was relishing the touch of her fingers and seemed totally lost in the moment. She then stepped on his shoes, making him squeal.

'Ah,' he gasped.

'You'll be fine,' she promised.

The tips of their cold noses touched, making her body tremble.

He inhaled her fresh, sweet breath. Her heart skipped a beat when his hand moved down to her waist. He wrapped it around her waist, pulling her closer. A tear escaped his eyes when she looked at him. She wiped it off with the tip of her finger. Ahmar held her hand instantly and kissed her finger, making her blush.

'You're not supposed to touch me,' she warned him in a low whisper.

However, he did not let go of her hand. He kissed the same finger once again. Zarish looked at him tenderly. With every kiss, she melted.

She held his face in her hands and looked at it affectionately. And then she planted a kiss on his cheek. Ahmar was dazed. He opened his eyes and pushed her back instantly, which somewhat perplexed her. He could not believe she had really kissed him.

'You shouldn't have done that,' he said. His eyes were burning with desire. A jolt of lust hit him. He pushed her against the wall, making her squeal, and held both her hands, not letting them go.

'Ahmar, please,' she said in a pleading tone, trying to free her hands.

'Do you trust me?' he whispered.

She nodded.

He brought his face close to hers, and lightly kissed her on her lips.

The kiss numbed her senses. She could not feel anything else other than his soft lips. She loved his lips on hers. She could not deny the fact that she had thought

about this kiss often and had longed for it. Ahmar opened
his eyes and looked at her.

'Thank you for the beautiful birthday gift,' he said,
smiling.

'Ahmar . . .' she said slowly.

'Hmm?'

'Was this right?' She had tears in her eyes.

'There is nothing right or wrong in love, where there is
love, there is nothing else, only love,' he said, wiping away
her tears.

By now, everybody had come to know about the upcoming
wedding. The couple had booked an open-air venue for
the celebrations. They had invited all their students.

'What? Are you serious?' Muraad said over the phone
when Ahmar told him that he was going to ask Zarish to
marry him.

Ahmar laughed at his father's reaction.

'It's not a joke. I'm quite serious,' Ahmar said in a
clear voice.

'I am very happy for you. I am coming back tomorrow,'
Muraad said. 'But when are you going to propose?'

'Soon,' Ahmar said.

'The sooner the better,' Muraad ordered.

'I miss you, Dad. Come home soon. You cannot miss
Maleeha and Jamal's wedding. The ceremonies will start
from today,' he said.

'I will be there on time,' Muraad promised.

Zarish couldn't decide what to wear for the wedding. She and Saleha spent hours at the shopping mall and then at the beauty salon to get the perfect look. She thought about Ahmar as she got dressed and blushed. The thought of having him by her side made her heart flutter.

Ahmar helped Jamal arrange everything. He and Wahab did not leave his side even once.

'This is a very special occasion for Jamal. He is getting married to the woman he loves,' Wahab said, looking at Ahmar.

'That's right,' Ahmar answered in a low whisper, thinking of Zarish.

Before the wedding ceremony, Maleeha and Jamal had organized a sangeet night for the students. Everyone showed up including Zarish and her friends.

Haroon stood next to Zarish and Saleha.

'Hey,' he whispered in her ear.

She responded with a quick nod.

'Will you dance with me?'

'I don't feel like dancing,' she said.

'Yeah, but . . .'

'What?' she asked.

'Uh. Nothing. Never mind,' he grumbled.

He could feel that their relationship had changed. They were not as close as they used to be.

Ahmar, from the other corner of the hall, glared at both of them. For obvious reasons, he did not like them interacting. He envied Haroon at times because he was her only male friend. He knew everything about her.

Right then, Maleeha came and stood next to Ahmar.

'Hello, handsome. What's up?' she asked, interrupting his thoughts.

'Hey,' he answered.

'It seems like you are waiting for someone impatiently,' she said in a teasing tone.

He looked at her with a confused expression. His heart sank. Had she caught him staring at Zarish; did she know about their affair? His mind whirled with these thoughts.

'What do you mean?' he asked.

'Do you remember the surprise I was talking about earlier?'

He nodded.

'That surprise will be here soon,' she said, smiling.

'It's your wedding, Maleeha. I am supposed to give you a surprise,' he said.

'Sure. You are welcome to do that, but you need this one badly. Trust me,' she said and winked.

'Let's see.' He smiled half-heartedly.

He had no idea what Maleeha was talking about. Either she had come to know about his and Zarish's secret love affair or she was just teasing him as she always did.

Muraad reached the venue on time. The dean of the university, Faris Ahmed, accompanied him.

'I can't believe they invited him,' Haroon said, looking at Faris.

Zarish and Saleha burst out laughing.

'He is the dean, Haroon. Why wouldn't they invite him?' Saleha replied.

'Let's hit the dance floor. What do you say, girls? Shall we?' Haroon asked both of them.

'Yeah, after you,' Saleha replied.

Haroon left, expecting the girls to follow.

Saleha grasped Zarish by the wrist to take her to the stage.

'Wait, Saleha!' Zarish said.

'Why?' Saleha asked.

'I want to dance with Ahmar,' Zarish said.

'What? How can you dance with a professor on the stage?' Saleha gasped.

'He is not my professor. He is Ahmar. My Ahmar,' she said.

'Fine. Whatever.' Saleha rolled her eyes and followed Haroon.

When Ahmar observed Zarish standing alone in the corner, he went and stood next to her.

'You are not going to dance?' he whispered in her ear, startling her.

'I don't want to dance,' she said sulkily.

'Why?' He almost frowned.

'Because I want *you* to dance with me but at the same time I know it is not possible. I can only dream about it,' she said solemnly.

'What? Do you dream about us dancing together?'

'Yes,' she said, looking at him.

'I didn't know that. I am quite surprised actually,' he said, grinning.

Just then, Saleha walked up to them.

'Let's go dance,' she said, grabbing Zarish's arm but Ahmar held her other hand.

'I'm coming, Saleha,' she said, freeing her arm.

'Don't leave me, please,' Ahmar whispered.

Zarish looked around in panic.

'Let go of my hand, Ahmar. This is not the right place or time for this,' she warned him.

'I'm not afraid of anyone now,' he told her.

His response made her angry.

'If he was not afraid of anyone, then why did he stop me from telling anyone?' she wondered.

'I think you're not in your senses. I have to go.' She freed her hand and ran away with Saleha.

After the party, Zarish found Ahmar standing alone. She walked towards him with a smile.

'Ready to leave?' he asked.

'With you? No way.' She rolled her eyes.

'Why?' he asked.

'I didn't expect you to behave like that. Why did you hold my hand in front of so many people?'

'Did anyone notice it?'

'Thankfully no one did,' she said.

'Then what is the problem?'

'You keep telling me not to tell anyone but then go ahead and hold my hand in front of everyone.'

'Look, I'm sorry. I know it was a stupid thing to do. I will be more careful next time.'

Zarish could see the regret in his eyes.

'Hey, don't apologize. It's fine,' she said, giving him a weak smile.

'I was not able to control myself,' he whispered.

'Why?' she asked, looking into his eyes.

'Nothing. Get into the car. I'll drop you home.' He quickly shifted his gaze and opened the car for her.

Neither of them spoke on the way back. When they had almost reached her house, she asked him the same question again.

'Why couldn't you control yourself, Ahmar?'

'Hmm,' he mumbled.

'Are you hiding something from me or you don't want to tell me?'

'There is nothing to hide or tell, Zarish,' he answered, his eyes fixed on the road.

'I've never seen you getting possessive like this.'

He looked at her and smiled.

'Why, you don't like it?' he asked.

'Of course, I do, but not like this.'

'Zarish . . . I have to tell you something.' He sighed heavily.

'Yes, sure, go ahead.'

'I don't like your closeness with Haroon. It bothers me. Though I understand you are his best friend, I still doubt his feelings for you. Please maintain some distance from him.'

Zarish became quiet for a moment and tried to compose herself. She knew he had problems with Haroon since the beginning of their relationship. Ahmar misunderstood her silence. He regretted saying anything.

'All right. Never mind. Just forget what I said,' he said.

'No. I understand. I think I should tell Haroon everything. That is the only solution.'

He sighed again.

'Okay?' she asked but he didn't reply.

'Ahmar? Please say something.' She held his hand.

'Zarish, I cannot even imagine losing you. Ever. I cannot go through the suffering again.'

'Again?' she asked.

'Yes. Again.'

'What does he mean by again? Am I his second love?' Zarish thought bitterly.

'I don't really understand what you're saying,' she whispered.

'I have already lost my mother, Zarish. I cannot lose you now.'

'I am not going to leave you ever. Always remember that,' she said, hugging him. She was relieved to know that there was no other woman.

'I love you,' he whispered, smiling.

'I love you more,' she replied. 'I don't feel like going home. I wish I could stay with you forever,' she said, stroking his neck.

'Great idea. Let's elope,' he said.

'What? Are you serious?' she exclaimed with a smile on her face.

He nodded.

'Let's go then,' she said.

'But where?' he asked.

'Somewhere we can be alone. Far away from this world,' she said, tugging at his sleeve.

'We don't have to elope, Zarish. We will be together and the whole world will acknowledge it.'

'You think so?' She raised her head to look into his eyes.

'I believe so,' he murmured, planting a quick kiss on her forehead.

She grabbed the side of his face and tried to kiss his cheek.

'Zarish, let me drive,' he said.

'No, I won't!' she said, laughing.

'Don't do this here. We're almost outside your house.'

'Please, Ahmar. One kiss is all I'm asking for,' she pleaded and then giggled at her own request.

He stopped the car on the side of the road, and turned around to look at her.

'What?' she asked, her heart pounding.

He came closer and slowly kissed her lips, taking her by surprise.

The kiss left Zarish breathless.

'You were right. I'm not letting you go home right now,' he said, starting the engine again.

When Zarish did not return home on time, Zarina started worrying. She nervously paced the living room.

'Relax, Zarina. She will be back soon,' Zia said, flipping through a magazine.

'Zia Sahib, she is not picking up her phone. We should be worried,' Zarina said.

'What was the need to attend this stupid wedding function?'

'I don't know. She is not even with Haroon. I asked him. He told me she left the function an hour ago.'

'Did you ask her other friends? She is not with them?'

'I don't know.'

'Don't worry. She will be back soon. She's a responsible girl,' he assured her.

'I know she is, but I don't know what she is up to these days. She is always out with friends. It's not good to socialize so much.'

'You're right. Do you have any idea where she spends her time? Who does she hang out with?'

She shook her head.

'Is she seeing someone?' Zia asked.

'No. I don't think so. She is always with Haroon. But you never know.'

'I will ask her tonight. Don't worry,' Zia said.

Zarish did not know where they were going. But she didn't ask him. She trusted him.

He stopped the car in a meadow. The dark silhouettes of trees stood out against the moonlit sky. All they could hear was the chirping of the crickets and their own breathing. Her heart pounded.

'Ahmar . . .' Zarish said, reaching for his hand.

He turned to face her, his eyes burning with passion.

'Are you scared?' he asked.

'No, I'm not.'

She held his hand tightly and looked into his eyes.

'Don't look at me like that. I won't be able to stop myself,' he said.

'It does not matter. I know how much you want me,' she said, clutching his collar and pulling him closer.

She then unbuttoned his black kurta and reached for his warm neck.

'I want you too,' she whispered.

The strong smell of citrus and wood hit her nostrils, making her want him more. She inhaled it for a second and then started kissing his neck softly. The moment her lips grazed his skin, he wrapped his arms around her

waist, burying his face into her soft hair. He held her face
and rubbed his nose against hers.

Caressing her cheek with his thumb, he slowly kissed
her lips. She kissed him back, a deep, long, never-ending
kiss.

The minute Zarina heard the sound of a car, she hurried
towards the window to see if Zarish had returned. Zarish
slowly got out of the car and waved at Ahmar. Zarina
could not see the driver's face properly, but she was sure
that it was not Haroon.

Zarish came in and saw her father sitting in the living
room all alone. Her heart skipped a beat.

'Dad?' she said.

'Hey. You're back.'

'Why are you sitting here alone?' she asked and sat
beside him on the couch. She knew her father was upset.

'I was waiting for you,' he said, looking at her.

'I'm sorry I kept you waiting. I had to go and visit
someone.' She did not know if she could tell her father
about Ahmar. She did not know how he would react.

'Who?' Zia inquired.

'Err . . . a friend from the university,' she lied.

'Hmm. We checked with Haroon and he said you
weren't with him.'

Zarish's face turned pale.

'Where are Mom and Zahaan?' she asked, changing
the subject.

'They're upstairs.'

'I should go and meet them,' she said getting up.

'Zarru.' He held her hand.

She turned around to look at him.

'My question still remains unanswered.'

'Dad . . .' she said with a sigh. She didn't know what else to say. She couldn't tell him she was with Ahmar.

'Who were you with?' he asked her again.

'A friend, like I said earlier,' she maintained.

'Which friend? May I know his name?'

'Her,' Zarish corrected him. 'Her name is Saleha and she's my classmate.' She felt pathetic about lying to her father.

'So, you were with her?'

'Yeah.'

'Weren't you at the wedding party? Why did you go to her place after the function?'

'Yes, I was at the party before, but then Saleha took me to her place. She needed some help with an assignment.'

'Zarish, this shouldn't happen again!' Zia bellowed.

'But Dad, I was just helping her out,' she tried to explain.

'I don't want you to get into any kind of trouble.' Zarish narrowed her brows. She did not know what he meant by this.

'There is no trouble, Dad. What made you say that?' she asked.

'Just listen to what I am saying. Stop arguing.' He seemed annoyed.

'Dad, what's wrong with you?' She quickly sat beside him and held his hand. 'Why are you saying this?'

'Zarish,' he said, softening a bit, 'I am your father, and I have every right to feel worried. Like I have always told you, it is not safe to roam around with friends late at night. You should respect the freedom we have given you.'

'Dad, I can't even image hurting you or anyone else in this family.'

'I know that. I am just asking you to be cautious. Stay away from the wrong people because the universe is full of such beasts. You should always remember our family's values and traditions before making any mistake. Do not forget that there are certain limits that should never be crossed.'

'I know, Dad,' she said, feeling embarrassed. 'I promise I will never let you down.'

Her mind whirled with the intimate moments she had shared with Ahmar in his car. She felt guilty.

Zarina was folding Zahaan's shirts when she saw Zarish walking towards her room.

'Zarru,' she called out, 'I want to talk to you.'

'What happened?' Zarish asked.

'Where are you coming from?' Zarina asked in a cold voice.

'I . . . I told you I was going to Sir Jamal's party. Didn't I?'

'Yes, you did. But why didn't you pick up my calls? Do you know the time? Don't you realize how late you've come back?'

'Saleha asked me to help her with an assignment. So, I went to her place after the function. I'm sorry,' Zarish replied, looking down.

'Who dropped you home?' Zarina asked, folding her arms.

'What?' Zarish was stunned.

'Who dropped you home, Zarish?'

'Mom . . . it was . . . a friend.'

'Which friend?'

'He is my classmate. You don't know him,' Zarish lied.

'Since when have you started hanging out with other guys other than Haroon?'

'That's normal, Mom. I have other friends too. My life is not limited to Haroon.'

'What?' Zarina was shocked to hear her reply.

'Yes.'

'Are you involved with someone?'

The question drained the blood from her face. Was it the right time to tell her mother about Ahmar? Would she understand her daughter's feelings?

'Zarish? Answer me!' Zarina yelled.

She stood in front of her mother like a statue.

'I saw you come home with a guy. Tell me, who is he? Tell me before I tell your father about it.'

Zarish wanted to escape. She wanted the floor to swallow her. She had never thought it would become this serious. She had to tell her mother everything. It was the only way out.

'Mom. Please don't overreact. Yeah,' she paused. 'I'm in a relationship with someone.'

Zarina was shocked to hear this.

'With whom?' Zarina asked frantically.

'Ahmar Muraad, my FSA teacher. I love him,' Zarish declared.

It was a big day for Maleeha and Jamal. Everybody seemed excited for their wedding. Maleeha was getting ready in the salon along with her friends.

'Damn. Damn. Damn. Why are you not picking up my phone?' Maleeha said impatiently.

'Calm down, Maleeha. It's your wedding. Stop stressing out. You'll ruin your make-up,' her friend told her.

'I know, but just look at her. She has not picked up my calls since morning. I hope she turns up at the wedding,' she said, looking at her reflection in the mirror. She looked stunning in a beautiful red lehnga.

'She'll be here on time. Don't worry,' her friend reassured her.

Zarish had hardly slept after last night's conversation with her parents. Her mother hadn't spoken a word since she told her about Ahmar. She was scared her mother would tell her father everything. She wanted to talk to Ahmar about it before the situation got out of hand.

Maleeha and Jamal stood on the stage, beaming at the guests. They looked beautiful together. Ahmar, Wahab and a few other faculty members stood next to Jamal. Ahmar spotted Zarish in the crowd, her face clouded with worry.

'Is she upset about the intimate moment we shared last night?' he thought.

Zarish stood silently beside Saleha, her gaze lowered the entire time. Ahmar could not take his eyes off her. 'Something is bothering her,' he thought. 'Something is not right.'

'Don't be upset, Zarish. It's good that you told your mother about him. Everything will be fine. We will sort it out,' Saleha comforted Zarish. She was the first one to know the whole story.

Zarish nodded lightly.

'Talk to Ahmar about it,' Saleha suggested.

'I will. I am just waiting for this ceremony to end,' Zarish murmured.

Soon, a beautiful trolley with the wedding cake was wheeled in.

'This looks beautiful,' Maleeha said.

'C'mon. Let's cut the cake together,' Jamal said, nudging her playfully.

Maleeha hesitated.

'What happened?' Jamal asked her.

'Jamal. She hasn't come yet. Shouldn't we wait for her?'

'Don't worry. She can join in later,' Jamal assured her.

Ahmar and Wahab exchanged a confused look. In fact, everybody wondered who Maleeha was waiting for. Saleha also nudged Zarish but she did not respond. She stood still like a statue, witnessing the scene expressionlessly.

As Maleeha and Jamal stepped forward to cut the cake, a woman's voice distracted them.

'How can you cut your wedding cake without me?' she said.

'Amber!' Maleeha cried out in joy.

Ahmar felt a pang of shock when he saw Amber. He couldn't believe his eyes. He was seeing her after so many years. Amber Khalid, his college batchmate, was standing across the room. Dressed in a turquoise saree, she looked exactly how she used to. He watched in amazement as Amber ran into Maleeha's arms.

'I can't believe you made it!' Maleeha said cheerfully.

'It's my best friend's wedding. How could I miss it?' Amber said and smiled.

'Amber, I want you to meet someone. Come with me.' Maleeha grabbed her arm and brought her face-to-face with Ahmar.

'Amber, see who is here,' Maleeha said, looking at Ahmar.

'Hello, Ahmar. It is nice to see you after so long,' she said.

'Same here,' he whispered.

'So, Ahmar, this was the surprise I was talking about,' Maleeha said, grinning.

He gave her a nonchalant shrug. He had never thought this surprise would upset him.

'Aren't you happy to see her?' Maleeha whispered into Ahmar's ear.

He did not know what to say.

'I'm sure you are.' Maleeha smiled.

The crowd slowly dispersed as the ceremony came to an end. Zarish looked for Ahmar but couldn't find him anywhere.

'Where is he?' she whispered to herself. She tried his number, but it was unreachable.

'How could he leave without meeting me?' she thought.

Ahmar went home without informing anyone.

He took off his shoes and lay down on the couch, putting his arm over his forehead.

'Why has Amber come back after all these years?' he thought.

The next day, Ahmar went to Maleeha's office to inquire about Amber.

'Hey, may I come in?' he asked.

'Sure. Come in,' Maleeha said.

He took a seat opposite her.

'No break after the wedding?' he asked.

'I'll take one soon,' she said.

'When are you going for your honeymoon?'

'Probably next week. Jamal is taking me to Europe,' she said, looking up at him.

'That's great. Europe is a great place for honeymooners.'

She nodded animatedly.

'Yeah. . .' his voice trailed off.

'Ahmar.'

'Yes?'

'Stop beating around the bush and ask about Amber!' she said, raising her arms.

'No . . . actually . . .' Ahmar hesitated, his cheeks reddening.

'I know you've come to ask about her,' she said.

He did not know what to say.

'She's not here right now. She will come in a while.'

'Why is she here, Maleeha?' Ahmar finally asked.

'Well, she needed a change.'

'Change?'

Before Maleeha could answer, Amber knocked on the door.

'May I come in?' she asked.

Ahmar instantly recognized her voice and turned around to look at her.

'Sure. Come in, darling,' Maleeha said gleefully.

Amber became a bit hesitant when she saw Ahmar.

'Hey,' Ahmar said.

'Hello,' she replied in a low voice.

'Come and join us. Let me order coffee for you guys,' Maleeha said. For the next twenty minutes, Maleeha babbled about her wedding and both of them intently listened to her. Every now and then, Ahmar looked at Amber.

She was still the same. She had the same innocence on her face. Only her hair had grown in length. Earlier she used to dress up in Western clothes, but now she wore more traditional attire.

'The coffee is here,' Maleeha announced.

'Thanks for the coffee, Maleeha,' Amber said. 'So Ahmar . . .' She turned to look at him. 'What made you come back to Pakistan?'

Ahmar looked at her, firmly holding the cup in his hands.

'Dad was alone here. He was getting old and lonely, so he called me back,' Ahmar said and chuckled, trying to lighten the mood.

Both Maleeha and Amber laughed.

'Jokes apart, I felt he needed me. I had been away for too long,' he said.

'Hmm,' Maleeha said, savouring her coffee.

'And how's Samira?' Amber asked.

'She's doing pretty well with her husband and daughter in the States.' He smiled.

'Oh, she has a daughter?' she asked, surprised.

'Yes. A three-year-old daughter.'

'How sweet!' Amber said.

'In fact, I have her picture in my phone. Let me show you,' Ahmar said, taking out his phone from his pocket.

'She's adorable!' Amber said after seeing the picture. 'Just like her mother.'

'Agreed. Amber, she reminds me of your daughter, Pari. Where is she?' Maleeha asked all of a sudden.

Ahmar was shocked to hear that Amber had a daughter.

'Oh, she's at home,' Amber told her.

'Bring her here sometime. Anyway, you both carry on. I have a class. See you later,' Maleeha said, giving Amber a peck on her cheek. Ahmar and Amber sat alone in her cabin.

'Uh . . . care for a walk?' Ahmar asked.

They went for a walk on the university grounds. He remembered the old days when both of them were students in the same university.

'So, how has life been treating you?' Amber asked him.

'It's not good. It's not bad. It's the same I guess.' Ahmar shrugged.

They walked on the damp grass for a while.

'Why did you come back?' he asked, looking at her.

'I missed Pakistan and . . . Pari wanted to meet her grandparents. That's why I'm here.'

'Have you come alone or . . . has your husband come with you? Oh, I forgot his name. Omer, right?' he asked.

Amber stopped midway, looking at him in silence.

'What happened?' he asked.

'I don't want to talk about him,' she said, walking past him.

Ahmar was amazed.

'But why?' he called after her.

Amber stopped again.

'He is not in my life any more. He left me.'

Ahmar's heart shattered into pieces. He stood there in bewilderment and could not believe what Amber had just said.

Ahmar couldn't sleep that night. His mind kept going back to Amber and what she had told him about her marriage. All his past memories came flooding back.

She was his first love but he had never told her how he felt. By the time he had mustered up the courage, it had been too late. She was already getting married to someone else. He had accepted the reality and moved on. And now she was back in his life. The girl he had once loved was all alone now. The thought made him uneasy. He rose from his bed and walked to the kitchen to get a glass of water.

He found Muraad sleeping on the sofa in the living room. Not wanting to wake him up, he put a cushion under his head and covered him with a quilt. Just then, Muraad woke up, rubbing his eyes.

'You're here,' he said.

Ahmar nodded.

'Are you okay, son?' He stroked Ahmar's back.

'Dad . . . Amber is back.'

'I know. Rumour has it that her husband left her and she also has a daughter.'

'Yes.'

'May god give her the strength to forget her pain.'

Ahmar was lost in thought when his phone started to ring. Muraad looked at the screen. It was Zarish. Ahmar ignored it.

'You're getting a call, son.'

'I know.' Ahmar sighed.

'It's Zarish. Talk to her.'

'What should I tell her?' Ahmar replied. 'I haven't told her anything about Amber.'

'Ahmar, wasn't Amber a good friend to you?'

'Yes, she was,' Ahmar whispered.

'Then why are you scared? It's not like you were involved with her. She has nothing to do with your past. You never told her you were in love with her.'

'Dad . . .' Ahmar said. 'I feel . . . I feel Amber needs me now. She has been through a lot already. I want to help her get her life back on track.'

'You can sympathize with her and support her. She needs you as a friend.'

Ahmar nodded.

'Go and talk to Zarish. Don't blame yourself. Everything is okay.'

'Okay, Dad.' Ahmar sighed.

He went back to his room and lay on his bed. Soon his mind wandered off, bringing back buried memories.

'So, you're leaving tomorrow?' Amber stood opposite Ahmar in the library.

He nodded as he looked for a magazine.

'Is it necessary to leave?' she asked, folding her arms.

'Yes. It is,' Ahmar replied.

'You can complete your higher studies from here too. Why go so far, Ahmar?' she asked.

'It won't be the same here, Amber. I want to work in the US too. That's what I've always dreamt of. Don't you support my decision?' he asked.

'I support you, but not if you have to leave your friends here.' She looked down at her hands.

He turned to face her.

'You need to understand that I am not doing this only for myself,' he whispered.

She looked into his eyes.

'What do you mean?'

'I will tell you when the time is right.'

'Ahmar. Please. Tell me.'

'Not now.'

'Okay, whatever. Can you do me a favour then, please?'

'What?'

'I want you to delay your flight by a week.'

'Why?'

'Because I am getting married next week,' she said, smiling shyly.

This is how she had broken the news to him. He still remembered her face when she had said it. The news had left him heartbroken. He wanted to tell her about his feelings but had decided against it. He did not want her to have second thoughts about her marriage. He would have known if she had felt the same for him. She considered him a good friend, nothing more.

Ahmar's phone buzzed again, bringing him back to reality. It was Zarish.

'Hello,' he said.

'Ahmar!' Zarish cried. 'Where are you? You've been ignoring me since yesterday.'

'No. I have not. I'm sorry if you felt like that.'

'Ahmar ... I ... I want to talk to you about something very important.'

'Me too, Zarish.'

'Are you okay?' she asked in a concerned voice.

'I'm never okay when you are not with me,' he whispered.

'Where were you? I didn't see you at the university. You didn't even meet me before leaving the wedding venue.'

'I'm sorry. I'll tell you everything when we meet tomorrow,' he promised.

Zarina had not been at peace ever since her daughter had told her that she was in love with her finance professor. She was not at all happy with her daughter's decision. She thought Ahmar was too old for her. It was becoming impossible to keep this secret from her husband. She had to tell him what their daughter had planned for her future. She did not want Zarish to ruin her life.

'What the hell are you talking about?' Zia screamed at his wife when she told him what Zarish had been up to all this while.

'It's true, Zia Sahib. Our daughter is involved with that professor. She herself told me,' Zarina said.

'I will not spare that guy! Who is this professor?'

'The guy we met at the PTM. Ahmar Muraad.'

'Ahmar Muraad? Muraad Hussain's son?' Zia asked, narrowing his brows.

'Yes, I think so.'

'I won't let him take advantage of my daughter. He thinks it is so easy to woo my daughter and take her away. I won't spare him!' Zia said angrily.

The next day, Zarish brought flowers for Maleeha and Jamal. However, she was surprised to find another woman sitting in Maleeha's office.

'Hello,' Zarish said, clearing her throat.

'Oh hi. Come in,' the woman invited her in.

'I brought these flowers for Ma'am,' Zarish said hesitantly.

'They're beautiful. Come, have a seat. Maleeha has just stepped out for some work. She will be back any minute.'

'Are you friends? I saw you at the wedding,' Zarish said as she sat down.

'Yeah. I am Amber. We were together in college. Maleeha, Jamal, Ahmar and I.'

This was news for Zarish. Ahmar and the rest of the faculty members had studied together in the same college. Surprisingly, Ahmar had never told her this.

'So, how is it meeting them after so many years?' Zarish asked.

'It feels great, but I won't be staying here. My family is in Islamabad. I will leave in a few days.'

'Oh. I thought you came here to join the university,' Zarish said.

'No, I will be leaving.'

Just then, a cute little girl, around five years old, came running in and hugged Amber.

'Mama, see what I got.' She showed Amber her hand which was full of candies.

Zarish looked at them with a shocked expression. Amber looked really young to be a mother of a five-year-old.

'You'll get a cavity if you keep eating these sweets, Pari. Okay, c'mon. Say hello to her,' Amber said, pointing at Zarish.

'Who is she?' Pari asked.

'She is a student,' Amber told her.

'Hello,' Zarish said, extending her hand.

Pari shook hands with her and then ran back to her mother.

'Your daughter is adorable. I can't believe you have one. You look so young,' Zarish said.

Amber smiled, hugging Pari tightly.

Just then Maleeha entered the cabin.

'Oh, hello, Zarish,' Maleeha said.

'Hello, Ma'am. I brought these flowers for you,' she said, giving her the bouquet.

'Oh, these are lovely. Thank you.'

'You're welcome. I should leave now,' Zarish said, getting up.

'Sure. Good luck,' Amber said.

As Zarish walked out of the office, her scarf got stuck in the doorknob. She turned around to free it, but stopped when she heard Ahmar's name. She crept closer to hear what they were talking about.

'Who got you these candies?' Amber asked her daughter.

'Ahmar,' Pari replied.

'What? How do you know him?' Amber asked.

'She must have met him outside,' Maleeha interjected.

'You guys are really spoiling her,' Amber complained.

'It's all right, Amby. Come on. She is just a kid. Pari, why don't you go outside and play for a bit?' Maleeha said.

'Okay sure!' Pari said, leaving the room.

Zarish made sure the girl did not see her.

'She is such a beautiful child. Didn't that bastard think about his daughter when he decided to leave you?' Maleeha said angrily.

'Forget about it, Maleeha. I am glad he did. He didn't deserve me or my daughter.'

Maleeha nodded.

'His parents don't talk to him any more, but they have remained in touch with me. That's why I came back to Pakistan. They had been telling me to come back for quite some time. Pari should know her grandparents.'

'I wish your parents were alive,' Maleeha said with a sigh.

'They're in a better place. Trust me,' Amber said, squeezing her hand.

Zarish, who was still eavesdropping, felt bad for Amber and her daughter.

'I know how hard it is to survive in this world all alone,' Amber said. 'But I have learnt to manage my life. I have Pari with me. She is all I want.'

'Amby,' Maleeha said, leaning forward, 'for how long are you going to stay alone? Have you ever thought of remarrying?'

'No. I don't want anyone in my life. I'm happy the way my life is right now.'

'What if someone wants to see you happy?'

'Who?' Amber asked.

'Ahmar.'

Zarish became a bit more alert when she heard Ahmar's name.

'What are you talking about?' Amber asked casually.

'Oh, you don't know, right?' Maleeha asked.

'Know what?'

'Ahmar has always loved you, Amby. He has had feelings for you since college,' Maleeha said.

For a moment, the world turned topsy-turvy for Zarish.

'What? Is this true?' Zarish thought, a sob escaping her throat.

'What are you saying, Maleeha?' Amber seemed shocked.

Maleeha nodded in response.

'I don't believe this. He never told me anything,' Amber said.

'Because he was too shy at that time. Everybody knew he had feelings for you. Everybody except you,' Maleeha said, adding, 'when he finally mustered up the courage to tell you, you told him you were getting married. So he decided to keep quiet.'

'Maleeha! Why are you telling me this now? None of these things matter to me any more.'

'Amby, I want you to think about him now. Think of marrying him. I'm sure he still loves you,' Maleeha said.

'Stop it, Maleeha. Please. I have a daughter and I am happy with her.'

'He will accept her and give her the love she needs. Trust me. Ahmar is a good person,' Maleeha told her. 'Think about it.'

Maleeha's voice slowly faded away as Zarish stood there in a state of shock. It seemed like a bad dream to her.

'All this time, he kept a secret from me,' she thought, fighting back her tears. 'He never told me about his past. He never told me he had loved someone else. Why? Why? Why? What is he going to do now that she has returned? Is he thinking of going back to Amber? Oh no. What am I going to do without him? I cannot imagine my life without him. Oh god, please help me. I'd rather die than lose him,' Zarish cried.

The teachers were having a meeting with the dean. Faris Ahmed told them about the new undergraduate programmes they were planning to launch next year. Everyone listened quietly except Ahmar. He was still thinking about Amber. 'How quickly her life has changed,' he thought.

Then his thoughts turned to Zarish and he remembered her childish nature, her innocence, her ability to love easily. It was true he had loved Amber at one point. But now he felt completely different.

He had to tell Zarish everything: about Amber, about the feelings he once had for her, about their relationship. He had to tell her that Amber had remained oblivious to his feelings. They had been friends, nothing more.

'So, what do you think about this proposal, Ahmar?' Faris asked him, interrupting his thoughts.

Ahmar came out of his reverie all of a sudden. He looked around at everyone present in the seminar room.

'Uh. I think it is a great idea. We should go ahead with it,' he said without even knowing the question.

'Take me to Model Town,' Zia ordered his driver and lit a cigarette.

He had been infuriated after learning about Zarish's affair with Ahmar. After thinking for hours, he had finally decided to pay Muraad Hussain, his old business nemesis, a visit. Zia had played an important role in the development of the university. He had made large donations for its upkeep.

Zia told his driver to park the car outside and go and inquire if Muraad was at home.

'Yes?' Muraad asked, lowering his spectacles.

'Mr Zia has come to meet you.'

'Zia Munawwar?' he asked, a bit surprised.

The driver nodded.

'Please call him in,' he said.

They had been rivals at some point, but now things had changed. Zia was still in the same business, but Muraad had shifted to something else.

Both of them shook hands firmly, without looking at each other.

'I was not expecting you, Zia, but I am glad you came,' Muraad said with a forced smile.

'How are you, Muraad?' Zia asked curtly.

'I'm fine.'

'Seems like you are settled in your life now,' Zia said.

Muraad nodded.

'You might have forgotten the past, but I haven't. Tell your son to stay away from my daughter,' Zia said coldly.

'What are you talking about?' Muraad asked, his face reddening with embarrassment.

'Your son is playing with my daughter's life. If he doesn't stop, then I am afraid I will have to take some serious action against him,' Zia said.

Muraad felt helpless for a moment. His son had found happiness after a long time. But it seemed he would have to fight for it.

'Zia . . . If they like each other then what's the problem?' Muraad asked, trying to calm him down.

'That cannot happen!' Zia suddenly became furious. 'This is nothing but a mere trap. I have understood your plan, Muraad. When you could not destroy me by taking over my business, you thought why not take revenge by spoiling my daughter's life. I will never let this happen.'

'I don't have any such intentions, Zia. I just want our kids to be happy.'

'My daughter will never be happy with that professor. I know she's immature and is making a mistake. But I am her father. I will never let you and your son take advantage of her innocence.'

'But . . .' Muraad tried to speak, but words failed him.

'You and your son can never achieve what I have in life. Do you get that? Ask your son to get out of my daughter's life or he will pay heavily for this!' he said, storming out.

Muraad stood there speechless.

On the way back to his cabin, Ahmar saw Zarish walking down the corridor. He rushed towards her, calling out her name.

When she heard his voice, she quickened her pace. She did not even turn to look at him.

'Zarish, wait!' he called again.

When he realized she was ignoring him, he ran to catch up with her.

'I want to talk to you,' Ahmar said, holding her arm. 'Why didn't you stop?'

She didn't meet his eyes.

'What's wrong?' he asked.

'Sir, I am going home. I cannot talk to you right now,' she said.

Ahmar knew there was something wrong. She had addressed him as 'Sir' and not 'Ahmar'.

'What? Are you okay? Are you angry with me?' he asked.

'I have no right to be angry with you,' she said, looking away.

'Why? You have every right to be angry with me, Zarish. I'm sorry I couldn't answer your calls. I was really upset over something.'

'Upset? You should be happy,' she said sarcastically.

'What are you talking about?'

'Nothing. Just let me go. I have to leave now.' She walked past him, but he grabbed her arm once again.

'You wanted to talk to me about something. What was it?' he asked her, searching her face.

'Zarish?' he asked again.

She buried her face in her hands and burst out crying.

'Zarish?' Ahmar asked. 'What's wrong? Please tell me.'

'I cannot lose you, Ahmar. I just can't,' she whispered between sobs.

'I'm not going anywhere, okay? I'm here. Right here with you.' He held her hands firmly. 'Just calm down and tell me what's wrong.'

'Amber,' she said at last.

'Amber? What about her?' he asked.

'Why didn't you tell me about her? Why didn't you tell me you loved her?'

Ahmar heaved a sigh.

'I heard Ma'am Maleeha and Amber talking about you. All your friends want you two to get married,' she sniffed.

Ahmar remained silent.

'Why, Ahmar?' she asked, looking at him accusingly.

'Okay . . . Now that you know about her, listen to me carefully. Amber is nothing but my past. I used to like her during my college days but now things have changed. She means nothing to me. You are my present and my future,' he said, looking into her eyes.

'Why didn't you tell me about her earlier?' she asked.

'Because I didn't think it was important,' he shrugged.

'She was a part of your life once and now she is nothing?' she asked, surprised.

He heaved a sigh and looked away.

'One day even I won't hold any importance in your life. Are you that selfish?' she asked, wiping her tears.

'Zarish, please.' He grasped her shoulders again.

'Tomorrow when someone will ask about me, will you give them the same answer?'

'No, Zarish. Listen to me. Try to understand. Amber was a part of my life once, but now we have both moved on. She has a daughter. She has not come here for me. Please. In fact, she never loved me.'

Zarish looked away restlessly.

'She taught me how to love, but the truth is, you taught me how to live.'

'Perhaps she needs you more than me, Ahmar,' Zarish cried, fresh tears streaming down her face.

'What?' He was amazed.

'Her daughter needs a father. They need you.'

'Who put these weird notions in your mind?' he asked. 'There is nothing between us. Please stop crying. She doesn't have any such intentions, neither do I. All I know is that I love you. Nobody else. Please trust me,' he said.

'Ahmar . . .' she whispered.

'What,' he asked, looking into her eyes.

'There is something else I need to tell you. Mom knows about us . . . probably Dad too and I . . .'

'Zarish, it's all right. I will sort out everything. They will agree.'

'But . . .'

'I said, I'll take care of everything. You trust me, right?'

She nodded.

'Then don't worry,' he said, stroking her cheek with his thumb.

'Ahmar . . .' she said.

'Yes?'

'Will you always love me? Will you remain by my side?' she asked.

'Always and forever. I don't want this life without you.'

She managed a smile.

'I love you,' he said, wiping her tears.

'I love you too.'

On returning home, Ahmar found Muraad pacing the living room.

'Dad. Is everything okay?' Ahmar asked.

'Mr Zia came here in the morning,' Muraad said.

'What did he say?' Ahmar asked.

'Ahmar . . . he knows about you and Zarish,' Muraad told him.

'Zarish's mother must have told him everything,' Ahmar said, looking away.

'He wants you to back out of the relationship,' Muraad said.

Ahmar smirked.

'He thinks this is our plan to seek revenge.'

'Revenge?' Ahmar asked. 'What revenge?'

'For the differences we had in the past.'

'I can't believe he is so stupid,' Ahmar said.

'Son. All I want from you is to . . .'

'No, Dad. Please. Do not ask me to step back. It's too late now. I won't leave Zarish.' Ahmar shook his head.

'No, son. Listen to me,' Muraad said.

Ahmar looked at his father.

'I want you to fight for your relationship. Do not give up. Do not be afraid of his threats.'

'Threats? Dad, did he threaten you?'

'Not really. Nobody can threaten your father, son. He just said in case you don't back out, we will have to face some serious consequences.'

'I am ready to face anything,' Ahmar said.

When Zarish reached home, she found Haroon's family sitting in the living room, chit-chatting with her parents.

'Hey!' Haroon said. 'Where have you been? We have been waiting for you.'

She greeted Haroon's parents and exchanged an awkward glance with her parents.

'I was at the university,' she told him, looking at her parents.

'Oh, right,' Haroon said, nodding happily.

'I'll be right back, excuse me,' Zarish said and left the room.

'Is she okay, Zarina?' Haroon's mother inquired.

'Yes,' Zarina hesitated. 'She just came back from the university. Must be tired.'

'It's okay. We can wait,' Haroon's mother said.

'I'm glad Haroon has finally agreed to marry my daughter,' Zia said, patting Haroon's shoulder.

'Thank you for accepting our son's proposal, Zia Sahib,' Haroon's father joined in.

Soon Haroon and his family got busy talking to Zia. Zarina thought this was the right moment to go and talk to Zarish. She excused herself and went to look for her daughter.

'Zarish. I need to talk to you,' Zarina said, entering her room.

'Yes?' Zarish said.

'Where were you?' Zarina asked, shutting the door behind her.

'I was at the university, Mom. You know that,' Zarish told her.

'Zarish, I don't want any nonsensical answers. Do you get me? I sent the driver to pick you up but you didn't come with him. Who dropped you home?' Zarina asked in a stern voice.

'If you already know the answer, then what's the point of asking me?' Zarish replied curtly.

'Did you come with that professor?'

Zarish heaved a sigh.

'Tell me!' Zarina shouted.

'Yes! I did!'

'Why? I told you not to see him again.'

'That is not in my control, Mom. I can't fall out of love just because you said so. Why can't you understand my feelings?' Zarish asked, feeling helpless.

'You have no future with him, Zarish! He is not good enough for you! Your father took over his dad's business years ago. Now they have nothing,' Zarina said.

'Mom . . . please . . . money doesn't matter to me at all. I only want to be with him. I will be happy with him. He is a good person. Trust me!' she said, holding her mother's hand.

When Zarina didn't return to the living room, Zia excused himself and went looking for her. He heard them talking and stood outside his daughter's room. He did not want to go in and interrupt the heated conversation.

'Mom, I love him,' Zarish said.

Zarina sighed hopelessly.

'Please. I beg you. I want to marry and live with Ahmar. Please,' she said as tears trickled down her cheeks.

'Zarish,' Zarina said, cupping her daughter's face, 'we want you to get married to Haroon.'

Zarish could not believe her ears.

'What?' she asked, shaking her head disbelievingly.

'Yes. This is what we want for you. There cannot be a better match than Haroon,' Zarina told her.

'No!' she said, freeing herself from Zarina's hold.

Zarina didn't know what to say.

'I have already told you my decision. I love Ahmar, and I will only marry him. Nobody else,' she said and burst out crying.

Zia could not take it any longer and stormed into the room.

'What's happening here?' he asked in a low voice.

Zarina looked at her husband nervously.

'Dad . . .' Zarish said, wiping her tears.

'Zarish . . . what are you saying?' he asked in a stern voice.

'Uh . . . Dad . . .' she said, looking at her mother, who looked away. She could not find the courage to talk to her father.

'Are you in love with someone?' he asked her.

She looked at him in bewilderment.

'Tell me!'

'Dad . . . I . . .' she stammered.

'Haroon and his parents are downstairs. They have come with a marriage proposal. What am I supposed to tell them?' he asked in an agitated tone.

'I can't marry Haroon, Dad. I can't marry . . . marry anyone except . . .' she blurted.

He looked at her with disappointment; his eyes red with anger.

'I know you will not like it when I tell you the truth but I can't help it. This is the reality of my life,' she said, lowering her gaze. 'I love Ahmar. Ahmar Muraad. And I want to marry him.'

Zia froze with shock.

'Dad . . .' Zarish said. 'Dad . . . please . . . don't let my feelings get hurt. Try to understand. It is about my happiness. I won't be happy with anyone except Ahmar,' she said. 'Please.'

He looked at her as tears rolled down her cheeks. He wiped them off with his thumb.

'Stop crying,' he said. 'I cannot see you crying. Just stop it.'

She sniffed and looked at him with affection.

'If this is what you want, then okay. We just want to see you happy.'

'Really?' she gasped.

He nodded.

'Oh! I love you, Dad!' she said, hugging him. 'I love you so much!'

'Ask Ahmar Muraad to come and meet me,' Zia said.

'I will, Dad . . .' she said excitedly. 'I will.'

Zarina watched them in bewilderment. Zia looked at Zarina and signalled her to keep calm.

Zarish still could not believe that her father had agreed. She could not wait to break the news to Ahmar.

Zia and Zarina went downstairs to attend to their guests. But they didn't look happy; they had forced smiles on their faces and exchanged worried glances. Haroon guessed something was wrong. He decided to talk to Zarish about their marriage.

'Hey,' he said, knocking on Zarish's bedroom door.

'Haroon! Please come in,' she said. 'There is something I need to tell you,' she said.

'What?' He narrowed his brows. She took a deep breath.

'What is it, Zarish?'

'I know I have hidden this from you all this while. You should have been the first person to know.'

He looked at her with curiosity.

'Haroon. I need to tell you about someone. You already know him. He is loved and respected by everyone at our university. And I love him.'

'What?' he murmured his eyes wide with shock; he was caught off guard.

'Yes, Haroon. I am . . . I am in love with Ahmar. I love him and . . . he loves me too,' she declared.

Haroon felt as if someone had slapped him hard. He could feel his heart pounding with fury and jealousy. The girl with whom he had spent his entire childhood, his adulthood, now loved someone else. He blamed himself for not understanding Zarish's feelings.

'Zarish . . . what are you talking about? You are in love with that stupid professor?'

'He is not stupid! Mind your words, please!' she snapped.

'Then you have lost your mind,' he retorted.

'Haroon, please try to understand. I don't know when I lost my heart to him but it is true. I love him and it is not going to change.'

'Your parents will never agree.'

'They have already agreed.'

'What?' he asked, shocked.

She nodded happily.

'I can't believe this. You're making a mistake, Zarish.'

'Haroon . . .' she said, holding his hand. 'You are my best friend. I expect you to understand and respect my decision,' she said, looking into his eyes. 'I cannot live without him,' she added.

'Is that how much you love him?' he asked, his expression softening.

'Yes. Even more than that.'

He drew back his hands. It was then he realized that he had lost his childhood sweetheart to someone else.

The next day, after his usual lectures, Ahmar retired to his office and ordered tea. He was thinking of ways to convince Zarish's parents, when Maleeha walked in.

'Hey,' she said, taking a seat.

'Hi. What's up?' he asked, leaning forward.

'I've come here to talk to you,' she said. 'Did you meet Amber recently?'

'No. I did not,' he replied.

'Why not? I want you to talk to her, Ahmar. She is our friend. We have to help her in every possible way.'

'How can we help her? Marrying some guy arranged by her parents was her choice. Not ours,' he said harshly.

Maleeha seemed shocked by the sudden change in his behaviour.

'All right.' He sighed. 'How can we help her, Maleeha?' he asked.

'Ahmar . . . she needs us. She needs you.'

'Fine. I'll talk to her,' he promised.

'She's staying with me. You can meet her at my place,' Maleeha replied.

He decided to put an end to this matter. It was time to dump his past and move on with his life. He drove over to Maleeha's place. On his way, he bought Amber's favourite flowers and some presents for Pari.

He walked up to the front door and rang the bell. After a few seconds, Pari opened the door.

'Hello, princess,' he said, handing her the present.

'Hi. Is this for me?' she asked.

'Yes. These gifts are for you,' he said, stroking her cheek.

'Who is there, Pari?' Amber called out from the kitchen.

'Mama. Ahmar got me a new doll,' Pari said cheerfully.

'Hello, Amber,' Ahmar greeted her with a warm smile. 'I got flowers for you.'

'Please come in,' Amber said, taking the bouquet from his hand. Pari got busy with the new toy, and Amber went into the kitchen to make coffee for Ahmar. He soon joined her.

'So, why are you here, Ahmar?' Amber asked as she handed him the coffee mug.

'To catch up with an old friend,' he replied instantly, smiling.

'Ahmar. I know why you're here.' She sighed. He glanced at her intently.

'Has Maleeha asked you to talk to me?' she asked.

Ahmar looked away, avoiding her eyes.

'She just called me and told me that you wanted to talk to me,' she said.

'Yeah but Maleeha has nothing to do with it. I wanted to talk to you.'

'Okay . . . what do you want to talk about?' she asked.

'I am here to confess something.'

She looked at him with a puzzled expression.

'I used to like you when we were in college together . . .' he paused, adding, 'in fact, I was in love with you.'

Amber didn't know how to respond; she looked away nervously.

'But I knew you didn't like me the way I liked you, so I never told you,' he said.

'Why are you telling me this now?'

'I was too shy to say it then. I thought I might ruin our friendship. But when I finally decided to tell you, you broke the news of your wedding,' he said, smiling.

She looked down.

'Ahmar. We shouldn't talk about it now. It's too late,' she murmured.

'I know, but my conscience wouldn't have allowed me to move on if I hadn't told you about my feelings.'

'I understand.'

'Amber . . . I'm really sorry I said all this . . . I shouldn't have . . .' he said, suddenly feeling embarrassed.

'Ahmar, please! Don't be sorry about anything. I am happy the way I am. I am a mother. I can manage on my own. I have all of you around me. I don't need anyone else,' she said with a smile.

'If you ever need anything, I'll always be there for you. I promise,' he said.

She gave him a reassuring smile.

He was on his way back home when Zarish called him. She asked him to meet her at a cafe near the university.

'Why did you call me here? Is everything okay?' he asked, taking a seat.

'Ahmar . . . I spoke to my dad last night.'

'What?' He was taken aback. 'What . . . what did he say?'

'He wants to meet you.'

Ahmar took some time to absorb the news.

'He wants you to meet him and ask for my hand in marriage,' she added.

He leaned back in his chair and looked at her thoughtfully. It was difficult to believe what she was saying.

'What happened?' she asked, trying to understand his reaction. 'Are you nervous?'

'Nervous? Of course not. I'm . . . I'm just a bit surprised,' he said.

'Are you happy?'

'I'm really happy, Zarish,' he said, squeezing her hand. 'I just hope everything works out.'

'Everything will be fine, trust me,' she said to which he nodded.

'When are you meeting Dad?' she asked, leaning forward.

'Today,' he said.

It was late afternoon when Ahmar reached Zarish's house. She did not accompany him because Zia wanted to meet him alone. It would be wrong to say that Ahmar was not nervous. This was the first time he was going to ask for a girl's hand in marriage. The fact that he loved this girl made the situation even more difficult. Their fathers had been business rivals, so this was not going to be easy. He recalled how coldly Zia had spoken to Muraad when he had come to their house.

Ignoring the thought, he walked to the door and knocked gently. A servant opened the door and welcomed him inside. Zarish's house was quite different from his own. It was bigger, more spacious and decorated with expensive knick-knacks. The servant led him to the living room which was done up classily. To his surprise, Zia was already seated on one of the Victorian-style couches, smoking a cigar.

'Good afternoon, Sir,' Ahmar said, extending his hand.

'Good afternoon,' Zia said as they shook hands. 'Have a seat.'

'Thank you,' Ahmar said.

'So, Ahmar Muraad, right?' Zia asked, puffing on his cigar.

'Yes, Sir.' Ahmar nodded.

'We both know why you are here,' Zia said slowly.

Ahmar looked at him in silence.

'What made you think I'll let you marry my daughter?'

'Sir . . . I . . .' Ahmar cleared his throat.

'Wait! Let me complete!' he ordered.

Ahmar look at him blankly.

'How could you even think I'd let my daughter marry a person like you? A mere finance professor? Huh! Do you think my daughter deserves a partner like you?' Zia said, turning red with anger.

Ahmar was on his feet now, completely perplexed. The drastic change in Zia's behaviour was unexpected. However, Ahmar did not lose his cool.

'Mr Zia Munawwar, I love your daughter. Isn't that enough for you?' Ahmar asked.

'Love? What nonsense!' Zia rose from the couch, his face distorted with anger. 'Don't you dare say those words in front of me! Don't you and your father have any self-respect? Do you want me to repeat what I told your father the other day?'

Ahmar's jawline hardened as he tightly clenched his fists. Had he known Zia's intentions, he would have never come here.

'If you've any shame or self-respect, then walk out of my daughter's life and never look back. She's going to marry Haroon because she has always loved him. You were nothing but a little crush of hers.'

These words hit Ahmar like a thousand bullets. He did not have the strength to hear this crap any more.

'Mark my words, my daughter can never stay happy with you because you can't give her what Haroon can.'

'Mr Zia Munawwar,' Ahmar folded his arms, 'I'm really sorry but these threats can't make me change my mind. I cannot leave Zarish because she's become an important part of my life. In fact, she is my life and leaving her would mean killing myself. I'm sorry but I will not back out. I can't.'

'You probably don't understand the consequences of your decision.'

'I pity you, Mr Zia,' Ahmar said.

'What?' Zia hissed.

'I can see that your plan has failed miserably,' Ahmar said with a smirk.

Zia cringed.

'Before telling me anything, ask your daughter to forget me or back out. Can you do that? If she agrees, I'll never speak to her again,' Ahmar said.

'Oh, shut up,' Zia retorted. 'She'll forget you as soon as she gets married to Haroon. Now get the hell out of here, or I'll be forced to ask my guards to throw you out.'

Ahmar's heart pounded hard in his chest and his face burnt with rage. His cell phone buzzed as he made his way out. It was Zarish. He did not know what to do. He was still holding the phone in his hand, thinking what to do, when he came face to face with Zarina. She looked at him helplessly. He gave her a weak smile and walked out.

Just outside the front gate, he bumped into Haroon.

'What are you doing here?' Haroon asked agitatedly.

'Nothing,' Ahmar replied as he opened the car door. He certainly did not want to talk to Haroon at this point.

'Hey, you! Listen to me,' Haroon said, grabbing Ahmar's arm. 'You don't deserve Zarish as she is too good for you,' Haroon said.

Anger clouded Ahmar's face as he tried to free his arm from Haroon's grip.

'Haroon,' he said, 'I'm in no mood to argue with you. It's my private matter so please stay out of it.'

'Zarish is mine. She's always been mine. Everyone knows it. How could you remain oblivious to our relationship?' Haroon asked, flaring up.

Ahmar shot him a cold look.

'She has always loved me. Always. What she shares with you is momentary and unimportant. So get out of my Zarish's life.'

'I said I'm in no mood to talk to you. Get out of my way and let me go,' Ahmar said, pushing Haroon.

'You bloody professor!' Haroon said as he shoved Ahmar against the bonnet.

'Stop it, Haroon!' Ahmar screamed.

'You should be ashamed of yourself for getting involved with a student. You piece of shit!' Haroon said and punched him in his face. Ahmar lost consciousness and fell flat on his face. Blood oozed out from his nose. Haroon picked him up, put him in his car and asked his driver to take him to the hospital.

Haroon told Zia the whole story of how he had beaten up Ahmar. However, Zia was still not satisfied. He knew Ahmar was stubborn and wouldn't give up so easily. He discussed his next plan with Haroon.

Zarina didn't know Zia had invited Ahmar to their house. After Haroon left, she went to talk to her husband in the living room.

'What happened?' Zia asked, lighting a cigarette.

'Why was Ahmar Muraad here? Did you call him?' she asked.

'Yes, I did,' he said, blowing a cloud of smoke.

'Have you agreed to their relationship?' she asked.

'What do you think?' he asked, looking at her.

'Zia Sahib, you have given your consent to Zarish.'

'Are you happy with my decision?' he asked.

'I want my daughter to be happy,' she said. 'He seems like a fine gentleman. He really loves our daughter. I could see that in his eyes.'

'Oh, shut up, Zarina! What's wrong with you? Do you think she will be happy him? His father lost everything to me. They have nothing,' he said.

Just then, Zarish reached home.

'Answer me, Zarina?' Zia asked.

Her father's urgent and worried voice made Zarish stop. She leaned closer to the door to hear what they were discussing.

'Ahmar doesn't deserve her. They will do everything to make her life miserable,' Zia said.

'You think I want to spoil my own daughter's life?' Zia asked again.

Zarish stood near the door, puzzled.

'What do you mean?' Zarina inquired.

'I will never agree to this!'

'Then why did you lie to her?' she asked.

'Just to calm her down for some time.'

Then Zia recounted his meeting with Ahmar, and how he had insulted him and thrown him out of the house. Zarish couldn't believe her own father had tricked her, betrayed her. She sat down near the door and burst out crying.

'So, this is the reason why Ahmar was not answering my calls,' she thought.

'Oh god, where are you, Ahmar?'

Z ia took out his cell phone from his pocket and dialled a number.

'Hello, Faris Ahmed Sahib! How are you?' Zia asked. 'I need a favour from you.'

'I want you to fire Ahmar Muraad from the university. Make sure he doesn't get a job anywhere else. Slap a case on him and throw him out. I want his career and life to be ruined!'

'But Zia Sahib, I cannot fire Ahmar without speaking to Muraad. Also, we were planning to send him to Canada,' Faris said.

'Just make sure he leaves the country. I hope you won't disappoint me,' Zia said.

'I'll see what I can do, Zia Sahib.'

'Thanks,' Zia said.

Zarish, who was still standing near the door, let out a blood-curdling scream when she heard her father speaking to Faris.

Zarina ran out to see what had happened. Zarish was about to faint but her mother broke her fall. Zia immediately hung up and came out to see what was wrong.

'Zarru . . . Zarru beta . . . are you all right?' Zarina asked with concern, holding her daughter's arm.

'What happened to her?' Zia asked.

'She has fainted. Please call the doctor!' Zarina said.

Faris had no choice but to follow Zia's orders as he donated a lot of money to the university. He called Muraad and told him that Ahmar was being sacked and his Canada posting had also been cancelled.

Muraad tried to ask Faris the reason for the decision but Faris didn't say much. Muraad was not a fool; he knew Zia was behind this. He didn't tell Ahmar as he was still in the hospital. Instead he decided to call Zarish.

She gained consciousness, but was advised complete rest by the doctor. Everything seemed like a vague dream to her. She could not believe that her father had played such a dirty game with her. Just then her phone beeped.

'Hello?' she answered.

'Zarish?' Muraad said.

'Sir Muraad . . . how are you?' she asked, sitting up.

'Zarish . . . I'm sorry I'm calling you at this hour but it's urgent.'

'What . . . what happened, Sir?' Zarish asked.

'Ahmar is in the hospital, and I believe Mr Zia Munawwar is responsible for his current state.'

'What?' Zarish cried.

'Your father has also asked the dean to sack Ahmar and cancel his posting to Canada.'

Tears filled her eyes. She leaned back and covered her face with her hand.

'Zarish, will you do me a favour?'

Zarish remained quiet. She was still in shock.

'Zarish . . . I've nothing left except my son. I don't want to lose him. I can't live without him. Only you can save his life. Just walk out of his life and marry the person your father has selected for you. Please. This is my first and last request to you.'

Zarish was speechless, numb and heartbroken. The thought of Ahmar lying lifeless on a hospital bed scared the hell out of her. She hung up the phone and, without wasting any time, ran downstairs. Her parents were sitting at the dining table, involved in a deep conversation. They looked up when they saw Zarish.

'How could you do this to me, Dad? I trusted you more than anyone else!' she screamed.

Zarina lowered her gaze but Zia looked straight at his daughter.

'You know how much I love him! You know what he means to me!' she cried. 'He means the world to me, Dad! I cannot live without him! You knew that! Still you brutally beat him up and asked the dean to throw him out of the university.'

'Yes. If you still don't agree to marry Haroon, I will ruin his career!' he said.

'Dad? Please! No . . .' she pleaded.

'I trusted you, Zarish. I thought you would never do anything that would hurt your parents. But you broke our trust. All of a sudden, that professor means the world to you. What about us? What about your parents who brought you up and looked after you all your life?'

She looked away with tears streaming down her cheeks.

'Do we mean nothing to you?' he asked.

She looked at him tearfully.

'Dad?' she walked up to him and held his hands.

'Do we mean nothing to you, Zarish?' he asked again, his eyes moist.

She had never seen her father cry before. He was a man of dignity, power and honour. How could a person like him cry in front of his daughter?

'Stop it, Dad! Please stop it!' Zarish said, gathering her wits.

'Zia Sahib . . . please,' Zarina said, wiped his tears.

'Dad . . . please don't cry. I cannot see you or Mom in pain. I would rather die than see you both like this,' she said.

'Zarru . . .' Zarina said.

'Mom, please,' Zarish said, 'I'm sorry for hurting you and Dad. I promise I will do as you say.'

'Marry Haroon,' Zia said abruptly.

She glanced at him, surprised.

'Yes, marry Haroon,' he said.

Without uttering another word, Zia walked to his room. Zarina followed her husband, leaving her daughter behind. Zarish fell on the floor; her father's words had numbed her senses. She was on the verge of losing her love, her world, her life. She was about to do the most selfless thing ever. She was going to sacrifice herself to save the one she loved. She sat on the floor with a blank expression on her face. There were no more tears.

She got up and walked to her parents' bedroom.

'I will marry Haroon,' she announced, leaning against the door. 'But on one condition.'

Zia and Zarina exchanged a quick, nervous glance.

'Promise me you won't get Ahmar fired from the university or put his life in danger. Promise me, Dad, please,' she said sternly. 'I will never speak to him again, but please don't ruin his life.'

'I promise,' Zia said.

She went back to her room absent-mindedly and stood near the window, staring out blankly. She picked up her cell phone lying on the floor and dialled a number.

'Hello, Zarish? You okay?' Haroon asked.

'Haroon. I am ready to marry you,' she said with a heavy heart. Haroon did not ask any more questions. He felt a twinge of guilt. He didn't know how he would face Zarish after what he had done to Ahmar.

After a week in the hospital, Ahmar felt better. Amber, Maleeha, Jamal and Muraad were with him throughout. But Ahmar remained restless. He missed Zarish. He missed her face, voice and everything about her.

He tried to contact her but the doctors didn't let him use his cell phone. He tried to ask his father but he gave him vague answers.

He was eager to go back to the university; back to his world; back to Zarish. Muraad wanted him to rest for a few more days but Ahmar didn't agree.

It was a difficult day for Zarish, as she had to meet Ahmar and tell him that she was marrying Haroon. She texted Saleha as soon as she reached the university cafeteria. Since Saleha was still on her way, she sat there alone and rehearsed the words that she had to say to Ahmar; the words that would shatter their world.

'How will he react? Will he understand if I tell him the truth?' she thought.

Someone tapped her on her shoulder, breaking her reverie.

'Hey,' Saleha said, 'all okay?'

Zarish nodded with a half-hearted smile.

'Saleha . . . I have decided to marry Haroon,' she suddenly said.

Saleha's jaw dropped. She opened her mouth to speak but the words froze in her throat.

'Please don't give me that look. But yes, this is what I've decided for myself,' she said casually.

Obviously, Saleha had a million questions. Zarish answered every single one but did not tell her the exact story. She did not tell her how her father had forced her to marry Haroon. She did not tell her what Muraad had asked her to do.

Saleha understood her reasons and was completely satisfied by her answers. It was difficult to go against your parents' wishes. Zarish had done the right thing.

After his lecture, Ahmar stood near the lectern. He ran his fingers through his hair and rested his head on the desk.

Just then, his cell phone vibrated. It was a message from Zarish.

Need to talk. Urgent. I am waiting for you in the parking lot.

He quickly packed his bag and rushed out. As he walked towards her, she noticed he had a slight limp. Zarish felt a pang of guilt because she knew she was the reason for his condition.

'Hey,' he murmured, folding his arms. 'It's pretty cold, yeah?' he tried to initiate a normal conversation.

She did not respond and kept her gaze lowered.

'Are you okay?' he asked.

She looked up. He looked into her eyes and noticed the puffiness around them. It seemed she had been crying.

'Hey.' He reached for her arm, but she pushed him away. 'Is everything all right?' he asked in a concerned tone, 'did you talk to your parents again?'

She did not reply. She did not know where to begin. She did not want to hurt him, but she was left with no other option. She had to break his heart.

'I know what you're worried about. Your dad insulted me at your place the other day, but don't worry, Zarish,' he said, adding, 'I have not lost hope. Your father is wrong if he thinks he can scare me by threatening and beating me. I won't give up so easily. I have sorted out everything. I'll come to your place again and try and reason with him. I'm sure your parents will understand and give their consent. Even if they don't, we will think of another plan. There has to be a way out of this. I am confident about myself but, trust me, I have more confidence in our love.'

Zarish looked at him steadily. There was sincerity in his eyes. She had to tell him before her heart melted. She had to remain strong. She could not appear weak or he would know she was lying.

'No matter what happens, I will always stand by your side and never break my promise. Okay?' he asked.

She remained quiet.

'We will try and work it out. Don't worry,' he said, caressing her shoulder.

'Ahmar! Please stop', she said, pulling her hand away.

He was shocked by her reaction, but tried to remain calm.

'Okay. I'm sorry. I should have let you speak first. I know why you're angry. I couldn't call you while I was at the hospital because I wasn't allowed to use my cell phone. And I know why you didn't come to visit me . . .' he said, adding, 'your father must have stopped you. I know that.'

She stood still like a statue, motionless. Her silence made him nervous.

'Anyway, everything is going to be fine now. You wanted to talk to me about something important, right? So, what is it, Miss Zarish?' he said with a weak smile. Just then a white-coloured envelope in her hand caught his attention.

'What's this?' he asked casually.

Now was the time to break the news, she thought. She slowly handed him the envelope. He gently took it from her and opened it.

It was an invitation card.

Mr Zia and Zarina Munawwar invite you to the engagement party of their daughter, Zarish, with Haroon on 19 December 2013, 7 p.m. onwards at Royal Palm Club, Lahore.

'Is this a joke?' he asked after reading the card.

'This is not a joke,' she replied curtly.

'Look at me and speak!' He grabbed her by her shoulder and made her face him. 'Zarish, please tell me this is nothing but a joke! Isn't it?' he asked.

'No, Ahmar!' she said, pushing him back. He was shocked.

'It is not a joke. I'm really getting engaged to Haroon this Thursday,' she said.

Shock was writ large on his face.

'You were right about me and Haroon. There was something more than just friendship. It is my fault that I realized it so late,' she lied. She had to. There was no other option.

He looked at her furiously and his hands trembled.

'How can I love someone else when I already have Haroon in my life?' she told him. 'And we love each other a lot. If you hadn't come into my life, I would have never realized my actual feelings for Haroon. I want to thank you for that, *Sir* Ahmar.'

He shook his head in disbelief.

'So . . . I guess that's about it. I have to leave now. If possible, do attend my engagement ceremony.' She turned to leave but Ahmar held her hand.

'I know why you're doing this. Your father has forced you to say all this. Right?'

She did not look at him.

'Zarish, you don't have to be scared of anyone as long as I'm with you. I said I'll sort things out. You don't have to lie to me.'

'I'm not lying to you, Sir Ahmar!' she retorted. 'Now let me go.'

'You had promised you would never leave me,' he mumbled, still holding her hand.

A tear threatened to escape but she quickly wiped it away before he could notice.

'You promised!' Ahmar continued.

'Ahmar! I did not mean any of it,' she lied again. 'It was merely an infatuation. I am sorry if you misunderstood my feelings.'

'Don't do this to me,' he said tearfully. 'I won't be able to survive this. I need you, Zarish. Do you have any idea how much I love you?' he asked.

She pushed his hand away. 'I'm sorry, Sir Ahmar. I have to go.' She walked past him and did not look back.

That entire night Ahmar called her but she did not answer.

She finally switched off her phone with a heavy heart. He finally sent her an e-mail:

Zarish,
Why are you doing this to me? Are you hiding something? I hope you realize that this lie will destroy our lives. I can still talk to your parents and make them understand. Do not make any decision under their pressure. I assure you that I can convince them. You know I love you and can go to any extent to prove it. I am waiting for your response. Please talk to me.
Yours,
Ahmar

An entire week went by but she did not talk to him. All his attempts to get in touch with her were futile. Exams were coming up so there were no lectures as well. Zarish decided not to sit the exams. As it is, she was getting engaged to Haroon on Thursday and there was no time to study.

She lay on the bed, lost in thought. She had let go of her love too easily. She had suppressed her conscience all these days but now it had started to prick her, asking her questions. She could not marry Haroon, she thought.

He was involved in her father's evil plans. He was also responsible for ruining Ahmar's life.

'I have to escape from this situation,' she told herself and wiped her tears.

The next day, Muraad walked into Ahmar's room. It was in a total mess as clothes were scattered everywhere. Two suitcases lay open on the floor. Ahmar was sitting on the bed, sorting out his things.

'Ahmar,' Muraad said.

'Dad please,' Ahmar said, raising his hands. 'Don't try to stop me.'

Muraad had tried to dissuade him from leaving, but it seemed it was all in vain. He had asked his son to continue leading his life as he was before he met Zarish. But Ahmar hadn't agreed. He couldn't live in the same city as her. So he had decided to move back to the US. He could not go back to the university either as that would mean seeing Zarish and Haroon together as an engaged couple all the time. He was flying out a day before Zarish's engagement ceremony.

'I've not come here to stop you,' Muraad said.

'Then?' Ahmar asked without looking at his father.

'Someone is here to meet you.'

'Who?' Ahmar's heart missed a beat. 'Zarish?'

'No. Someone else.'

Amber was waiting for him in the living room. When she saw Ahmar coming down the stairs, she stood up and gave him a warm smile.

'I heard you're leaving,' she said.

'Yeah,' he said.

'Uncle won't be accompanying you?' she asked.

'Not right now. I'll call him as soon as I settle down.'

'Oh okay,' she mumbled.

'Anyway, you tell me? How are you? How's Pari? You didn't bring her along?'

'She had to complete her homework.'

He nodded.

'Uh . . . Ahmar,' she said.

'Yeah?'

She looked at him longingly.

'Do you want to say something?' he asked.

'Do you really have to leave?'

'What do you mean, Amber?'

'Can't you stay here?' she asked.

He sighed again.

'I can't stay here. There are better opportunities abroad. I have to go for the sake of my career.'

'That's good.'

'Now is the time to take things seriously. I don't know where to begin but I know there is a long way to go,' he said, 'I know it's going to be a tiring journey but I'm left with no other option.'

'And you intend to take this journey alone?' she asked.

He looked at her and then narrowed his brows.

'Ahmar . . . I need to tell you something. Will you help me?' she asked.

He stared at her with his mouth slightly open in bewilderment.

'Please?' she murmured.

Back to Present
Lahore, Pakistan

Ahmar Muraad had immigrated to Washington DC three years ago. Though he had moved with his father and daughter, the family had not sold their house in Lahore. Muraad divided his time between the two countries, and a few weeks ago had arrived in Pakistan on one of his business visits. Ahmar had not visited Lahore since he shifted to the US. He was teaching finance at a university since completing his PhD, and it was difficult to take leave.

Ahmar seemed satisfied with his life: he had a fantastic job, a beautiful daughter, great friends, colleagues and his father was with him. Life was extraordinary in the US, yet very different from the one he had had in Pakistan—a life whose memories Ahmar had carefully buried when he left the country.

Sometimes a stray reminder would unleash a flood of memories. Ahmar would build back the barrage that held them out, each time making the wall stronger. It had helped him settle in his new life, besides he had lived in the US before.

Ahmar had not felt the need to get married. He had promised Amber that he would give Pari the life she deserved and he ensured that the child had proper care, attention and love.

Just before Ahmar had left for the US, Amber had reached out to him for help. He had been shocked to learn that she had been diagnosed with a brain tumour and her doctors had lost all hope of her recovery. He stuck around to support Amber, deciding not to leave her alone.

Ahmar took Amber and Pari to Islamabad to consult a renowned oncologist. The doctor had her admitted to a hospital where Ahmar spent close to a month with them. During this time, he grew very fond of Pari, rarely left her alone and started to take care of her almost as if he were her own father. A rigorous set of tests, scans, results and chemotherapy sessions followed. The oncologist finally declared that Amber could not be saved.

As her last wish, Amber asked Ahmar to take care of Pari. He promised her that he would never leave her side; that he would look after her as his own daughter. With her grandparents' permission, he legally adopted Pari before shifting to the US.

Ahmar was content with his new life. He did not want to move back to Pakistan ever. However, he had now stumbled to another crossroads in his life. Zarish's father had expired but she didn't come to visit her parental home. Zia Munawwar had wanted to talk to Ahmar before he died. What had he wanted? Ahmar felt emptiness when he thought about what had happened in Pakistan three years ago.

The questions still lingered and Ahmar wanted answers. Moreover, he wanted to see Zarish. He wanted to know if she was happy with her life or not.

Muraad's driver was waiting for Ahmar at the Allama Iqbal International Airport in Lahore. Everything had changed in the last three years; there were new roads, buildings, skyscrapers.

'Lahore has become more beautiful,' he thought.

Ahmar called his father as soon as he reached Zia's house. He got out of the car and looked around. The bitter memories of that fateful day sent a shiver down his spine. The house hadn't changed much; only its walls had aged a bit and the lawn seemed somewhat unkept.

Muraad came outside to receive him.

'Glad to see you, son,' Muraad said.

'Me too, Dad,' Ahmar murmured as they hugged.

'Okay . . . are you ready to go inside?' Muraad asked.

Ahmar nodded.

At first, Ahmar seemed a bit hesitant. Perhaps he was not ready to face her mother and other family members. Even though he knew she had not turned up for her father's funeral, he still felt nervous. What if she came right then? His heart fluttered at the thought. In reality, he was dying to meet her, to listen to her voice. He remembered the roundness of her face, those slightly chubby, pink cheeks, tender lips, the delicate arch of her eyebrows and beautiful almond eyes. Though she had cheated on him and broken his heart, he still felt something for her. Ahmar had not been able to forget her. He still loved her. It was the only truth of his life.

He saw many familiar faces as he stepped into the living room. Zarish's brothers, her mother and other family members stood huddled together in a corner. His face clouded over when he saw Haroon.

'How could I forget about him? Why didn't I think he would be here? If he is here then where is Zarish? Why has she not come?' he thought.

'They are probably married by now. Happily married. They might also have kids. Their own kids,' he flinched at this thought. However, Ahmar had to face the truth. So he braced himself and stepped forward to meet people he knew.

He exchanged glances with Haroon but did not approach him.

Muraad asked him to pay his condolences to Zia's wife, Zarina.

'Good afternoon, Mrs Munawwar,' he greeted her amiably. She was sitting on a couch, surrounded by elderly women.

Zarina seemed shocked to see Ahmar. She first gasped and then tears rolled down her cheeks.

'I am very sorry for your loss, Mrs Munawwar. May his soul rest in peace,' Ahmar said.

'Hmm. Thank you for coming,' she murmured, looking down at her fragile hands.

There was an awkward silence as neither of them knew what more to say. Ahmar smiled weakly and then turned to walk away.

His eyes searched for Zarish but she did not come. Soon the funeral ended and the crowd dispersed.

'Why did Haroon come alone? Why didn't Zarish accompany him? Was she okay? Why didn't she attend her own father's funeral?' he thought again on his way back home.

But there were others matters to be taken care of, and he forgot all about Zarish when he got a video call from Pari.

'Hey, my little princess, I hope you're not troubling your aunt too much,' Ahmar said, waving his hand in front of the webcam.

'No Daddy, I'm doing fine,' Pari said as Samira caressed her hair.

'She's a sweetheart, Ahmar. Don't worry, she's fine here,' Samira assured him.

'Thanks,' Ahmar whispered.

'How's Dad? Where is he? Let me talk to him.'

'He's sleeping.'

'How did the funeral go? Did you . . .' Samira hesitated a bit. 'Did you meet her?'

Ahmar heaved a sigh and then shook his head.

'Why?' she asked.

'Surprisingly, she wasn't there. I couldn't meet her,' he said.

'That's pretty strange. Why would a daughter miss her father's funeral?' Samira asked.

'I am wondering the same,' Ahmar said distractedly.

The next day, Ahmar decided to pay Zarina another visit. His father had told him that Zia had wanted to talk to him before he died.

The house was still filled with friends and relatives. He found Zarina sitting with Haroon and his family. 'Perhaps Zarish has come today,' he wondered. He cleared his throat and went to greet them.

'Hello, Mrs Munawwar. How are you?' he asked.

'I'm fine, thank you,' she said.

Haroon exchanged an uncomfortable glance with him.

'Ahmar,' Zarina suddenly said, looking at him.

'Yes?'

'Come with me. I need to talk to you.' She rose from the couch and slowly walked towards one of the bedrooms. He blinked his eyes in confusion and then followed her.

It was an enormous room with off-white walls. It was sparsely furnished with a king-sized bed, two bedside tables and a large dressing table. Zarina took out a white envelope and gave it to Ahmar.

'What's this?' he asked, taking the envelope from her.

'Zia Sahib wanted to tell you something, but unfortunately he didn't get the chance. He was waiting for you to return to Pakistan,' she said.

He narrowed his brows.

'Where is Zarish?' he suddenly asked. He was getting restless now and had to know why she wasn't here.

'The letter will answer all your questions,' she said and stepped on to the balcony. He looked around in confusion, a million questions on his lips.

'Why would Zia Munawwar leave me a letter? What was so important that he waited for me to return to Pakistan? Why didn't he contact me earlier? He could have called me or sent a letter,' he thought, as he opened the envelope.

Dear Ahmar,

I don't know where to begin. I am ashamed of what I have done to you and my own daughter. I am living the last days of my life miserably. I do not want to

die with guilt in my heart. I was solely responsible for
ruining your and Zarish's life. I forced her to leave you.
I threatened her with dire consequences. I told her that
I would ruin your career, and get you fired from the
university. On hearing this, she decided to back out.
I never wanted to hurt her feelings. I wanted happiness
for my daughter and strongly believed she would not
be happy with you. However, I was wrong, Ahmar. I
was completely wrong about you.
When you left for the US, she left us too. She left her
house and family. It has been three years since I have
seen her face. We do not know her whereabouts. We
have lost her, Ahmar. I have lived with this guilt long
enough, don't let me die with it too.
I request you to find my daughter and bring her home.
I know only you can bring her back. This is my last
wish. I want to see her once before I die.
If possible, please forgive me.
I am sorry, Ahmar. I am sorry for everything.

Regards,
Zia Munawwar

He had a look of utter shock on his face. He felt breathless
and couldn't feel his legs. He froze to the spot and the
letter fell from his hand. Zarina noticed his reaction and
came running in.

'Where is Zarish?' he asked her.

'She left us, Ahmar. We do not know where she is
now,' she said, her voice breaking.

'When did she leave exactly?' he asked.

'Right after you left. Right before the engagement
ceremony,' Zarina said.

Ahmar tightened his jaw muscles.

'We looked everywhere but could not find her. We first thought both of you had eloped,' she said.

'So . . . she never married Haroon?'

'No.'

He felt relieved for a moment. Zarish never married Haroon. She could not. She had proved her love for him but he had failed. Ahmar never understood the actual reason behind her decision. He had doubted her love. He had blamed her for nothing. It was now time to prove his love. He would bring her back. No matter where she was.

On his way out, he bumped into Haroon.

'Hey,' Haroon said, feeling a twinge of guilt.

'Hello,' Ahmar replied as both of them shook hands.

'How are you?' Haroon asked hesitantly.

'I'm fine, thank you. How are you?'

'I'm good; living life on my own terms,' Haroon said, smiling half-heartedly.

'That's good to know,' Ahmar said.

'I'm sorry. I'm sorry for everything. Please find her,' Haroon said unexpectedly.

Ahmar was taken aback. Haroon was actually pleading for something.

'I didn't look for her . . . I just couldn't. I got angry when she left me; I felt humiliated. By the time I realized my mistake, it was too late.'

'Do you have the slightest clue about her whereabouts?' Ahmar asked.

Haroon shook his head.

'Don't worry. I'll find her,' Ahmar said, patting him on his shoulder.

He decided to visit the university first to check with his former colleagues and friends. A few of his students had joined as professors. Ahmar felt glad to see them in respectable positions.

He went to the 'alumni department' to get Saleha's address and phone number. He knew he could get some clues from her. Zarish must have told someone before leaving and that someone could be Saleha.

The same day he visited Saleha's place but met her mother instead. She told him that Saleha was married and now lived in Rawalpindi. He requested her mother to give him Saleha's new address to which she agreed.

He came back home and told Muraad that he was leaving for Rawalpindi the next day with the driver.

He opened his suitcase to pack some stuff for the long journey ahead when his eyes were caught by a red umbrella tucked under the couch. He had a sudden flashback of the day he had proposed to her. It had been raining, and they had taken shelter under this very umbrella. He smiled as a tear rolled down his cheek.

'I'll bring you home, Zarish. That's my promise,' he said to himself.

The next morning, Ahmar left for Rawalpindi to meet Saleha. His driver was easily able to locate her house.

Since the front gate was open, he walked right in and rang the doorbell. To his luck, Saleha opened the door. She was shocked to see Ahmar standing in front of her.

'Sir . . . Ahmar? Is that you?' she gasped, looking at him from head to toe.

He nodded with a warm smile.

'I don't believe you're here,' she said, covering her mouth with her hands. 'It's . . . it's so good to see you after such a long time,' she said.

'Same here,' he replied.

'Please, please. Come in.' she said, letting him in.

'How did you find my address?' she asked.

'I got it from your mother.'

'You met her?' she asked.

'Yeah.'

'I'm glad you're happy,' he started. 'Perhaps you have already guessed why I'm here.'

She hesitated a bit.

'Please do not disappoint me,' he said in a solemn voice.

'What are you talking about?'

'Where is Zarish?' he asked finally.

She looked at him with a horrified expression.

'How would I know?' she blurted out.

'I know that you know something, Saleha. She must have told you before leaving.'

'How can you be so sure of that?' she asked, folding her arms.

'Listen, Saleha, I am sure you know her father passed away yesterday,' he said.

'Yes . . . I know that.'

'Good. I am sure you also understand that Zarish's family needs her,' he continued. 'So, without wasting my time, please tell me where she is.'

'I'm sorry, but I can't help you.' She looked away. Ahmar sensed that something was wrong. He noticed how Saleha was not looking into his eyes while talking to him. Perhaps she was hiding something from him.

'Please, Saleha. Tell me. I need to know. I want to help her.'

'What did you say? You want to help her?'

He nodded.

'Where were you when she left home? Where were you when she made this decision? You should not have left her. You should have tried to find out why she left you, why she took that decision,' she said.

'She left me with no damn choice! She did not give me a chance to explain! I tried to get in touch with her, wrote her so many emails but she never responded. She ignored me completely!' he exclaimed.

'How will you help her now?' Saleha asked.

'By bringing her back to her family, to where she belongs.'

'Sir Ahmar . . . please . . . please do not make me do this,' Saleha said, wiping the sweat off her brow.

'Tell me where she is. Please.'

'I cannot break my promise,' she said.

'What promise?' he asked, surprised.

'She asked me not to tell anyone about her whereabouts,' Saleha confessed. 'Even I don't want her to live away from home. I want her to stay with her family but she doesn't listen to me. Her family, Haroon, they all came to me once, but I did not tell them anything as she told me not to. I told her to go back but she does not listen to me. Maybe she will listen to you.'

'I will not disappoint you, Saleha. I will bring your friend back,' he promised.

'She is running an orphanage in Mansehra,' she told him.

'What?' He was stunned.

'Yes. She regretted leaving you and decided to run away before the engagement ceremony,' she said.

Ahmar looked at her fixedly.

'She wanted to come back to you. She even went to your house to meet you, but you had already left.'

Ahmar didn't know this.

'The security guard told her that you had left with Amber. Zarish tried to contact Sir Muraad but his phone was not reachable. So she thought you married Amber.'

'What? That's not true! I didn't marry her! I took her to Islamabad for her treatment,' he said, getting impatient.

'I don't know, but this is what the guard told her,' she said.

Ahmar ran his fingers through his hair.

'Zarish was heartbroken after that. She did not go back home. She did not tell me where she was going, but promised to call back later.'

'What's the address of the orphanage?' Ahmar asked her in a desperate tone.

'Wait,' she said and went to the adjoining room.

Ahmar smiled. He knew he would find her.

A hmar left for Mansehra, a city located in the Khyber Pakhtunkhwa province of Pakistan, the same day.

He fished out the note Saleha had given him and read the address again:

Help Children Grow Foundation, Terha Road, Bherkund, Khyber Pakhtunkhwa

Why did she go so far away from home? She could not even think of living poorly, then how did she manage all these years? The thought of her living in a strange city among strange people sent a shiver down Ahmar's spine. 'She must have changed a lot,' he thought

It was around 2 p.m. when they reached Mansehra. The city was blessed with natural beauty along with cultural diversity that, once upon a time, attracted international tourists. Recent security issues had taken a toll on foreign tourists to Mansehra.

After asking several locals for directions, they managed to reach Bherkund village, the third largest in Mansehra. Ahmar spotted several private clinics and schools in Bherkund.

It was a typical rural scene: children ran around playing while their mothers called out for them; villagers drew water from the well; some men were away toiling in the fields while some sat around with a hookah.

He asked one of the villagers about the organization. The Pashto-speaking villager could not understand Ahmar's Urdu. Ahmar could not make the villager understand as he did not know Pashto.

Thankfully his Khyber-Pakhtunkhwa-origin driver stepped in and inquired about the orphanage in their native Pashto. The villager responded by pointing at a red-brick building to their right. Ahmar walked towards the building. A signboard with the name of the organization indicated he had reached the right place.

Ahmar saw children of different ages, ranging from five to ten, running around happily. Some children sat on benches, reading storybooks. Since most of them spoke Pashto, he could not understand what they said as he strolled down the corridor. Children gawked at him with curious eyes and spoke in murmurs.

He came across an office where an elderly woman was sitting behind a desk. She was dressed in an Arabic-style gown and her head was covered with a scarf. He knocked on the door and stepped in.

She said something in Pashto, perhaps greeted him, but he did not understand.

'Hello. I am sorry but I don't understand Pashto,' he said embarrassedly. The woman smiled in response.

'It's okay. I understand. My name is Maryam. I'm in charge of this orphanage,' she said. 'How can I help you, young man?'

'I'm looking for someone,' he said.

'Who?'

'Zarish.'

A frown creased her brows.

'Zarish Munawwar?' she asked.

He nodded in response. 'Do you know her?'

'Are you Ahmar Muraad?' she asked.

This surprised him. 'How does she know my name?' he wondered.

'Yes,' he said instantly.

'Oh my god. I can't believe this. *Ya Allah tera karam* [Thank you, god, for being generous],' she said.

'Can you please tell me how you know me? Is she here? Is she all right?' he asked.

'Yes, yes. She is here.'

He heaved a sigh of relief.

'Can you please take me to her? I want to see her!' he said.

'Yes. Come with me, son,' she said.

He followed her down the corridor. He did not know where she was taking him. With every step, his heartbeat grew faster.

'How do you know me?' he asked her.

'She told me about you.'

'Really? What did she tell you?'

'You are the protagonist of all the fairy tales she makes up for the children,' she said.

Ahmar was awestruck. 'She still remembers me,' he wondered.

'She has told me everything about you,' the woman added.

They finally reached a room which smelt of medicines. The woman pointed at a girl dressed in a black salwar kameez and an off-white shawl. She was applying medicine and bandaging a child's wounded arm. He could not see her face properly since she had her back towards him. He rubbed his eyes to make sure it was her.

'There she is,' the woman whispered. 'Your Zarish.'

'My Zarish,' he whispered, smiling.

'How did she come here?' he asked.

'I met her at a bus stop in Lahore three years ago. She asked for my help. She said she wanted to help poor children because it made her happy. Since then, she has been helping them here.'

He could not believe that a girl who once lived a life of luxury was now living in a village, looking after poor children.

'She works for them selflessly. She reads them stories every night, cooks for them and even teaches them. Children have learnt how to speak English because of her,' the woman said.

'She is not known as Zarish Munawwar here. Children call her Zarri Bi. She means the world to them.'

'She never thought of going back?' he asked.

The woman heaved a sigh before speaking again, 'I told her to go back but she did not want to. She said she cannot live around those who give more importance to money than relationships,' she said.

'Maryam Apa, I've come to take her with me. Her family needs her,' Ahmar told her.

The woman became quiet for a moment.

'I need her,' he said.

'She needs you more than you need her,' she said after a long silence.

He glanced at the woman and then looked at Zarish.

'I have done whatever I could for her. Now it is your responsibility, son. You love her and she loves you. Take her with you and make her happy,' she said as tears streamed down her face.

'I will. I promise.'

'Thank you, Zarri Bi,' the child said after his wound had been dressed. Zarish smiled in return and he kissed her on her cheek.

'Okay, who's next?' she asked in a tired voice.

'Can you help me too? I have been suffering for years,' Ahmar said as he sat in front of her.

Her heart skipped a beat when she heard his voice. She recognized his voice instantly.

'No. It can't be him,' she said, shaking her head.

'Help me, please?' Ahmar said.

At last, she raised her head to look at him.

He had changed over the past three years. He now had a beard and his tired eyes looked at her through thick-rimmed glasses.

He felt the same when he looked at her face. It had changed drastically. Even though she was only twenty-five, she looked much older. There were dark circles and wrinkles around her eyes. Her skin appeared dull and lifeless. He noticed strands of white hair sticking out.

'What has she done to herself? Why didn't I ask her more questions back then? Why did I let her go so easily?' he thought bitterly.

'Ahmar . . .' she whispered, her lower lip quivering. She smiled mirthlessly as a tear rolled down her cheek.

'Zarish . . .' he said, holding back his tears.

'How did you find me?' she asked, adjusting her shawl nervously.

'That is a very stupid question to ask,' he said, grinning.

'Did Saleha tell you about this place?' she asked.

He nodded in response.

'Oh, Saleha,' she said as she clamped a hand over her mouth.

'Did you think it was so easy to run away from me?' he asked, folding his arms.

'Ahmar . . . you should not be here.'

'Zarish, I am here to take you home.'

'What?' she asked.

'Yes,' he replied firmly.

'*Na mumkin* [Impossible]!' she said in Pashto, ignoring his statement.

'Let's go back, Zarish. Please,' he requested.

'As I said earlier, na mumkin,' she said and left the room. He followed her outside. When she noticed that he was following her, she became a bit angry but tried to calm herself down.

'It is good to see you after all these years,' she said, quickening her pace.

'Likewise.' He looked at her and smiled.

'Now, please go back,' she said.

Ahmar could sense the sarcasm in her tone.

'No, I am not leaving without you,' he replied. She stopped midway.

'Why are you doing this to me, Ahmar?' she asked, looking at him.

'What have I done?'

She looked away helplessly.

'You are to blame, Miss Zarish. Only you!' he said, raising his finger.

'What?'

'Yes. You lied to me. You deceived me,' he said.

She looked down, her cheeks reddening.

'Just because your father threatened to ruin my career, you left me?'

'Don't talk like this about my father, Ahmar. Please,' she said as tears filled her eyes.

He took a deep breath and looked at her.

'Do you know about him?' he asked.

She nodded.

'I'm sorry for your loss.'

She didn't reply and continued walking. He stood in her way.

'Let me go, please,' she begged.

'You have to answer my questions first!'

'I can't. Please. I do not want to talk to you right now. I just can't face you.'

'You have to face me, Zarish. You have to.'

'Do you still want to know why I left you?' she asked, sobbing.

'I know. Your dad told me everything.'

'What? When did he tell you?' she asked.

'Read this letter. It will explain everything,' he said and gave her the letter.

She read it in silence, tears pouring down her cheeks.

'So now you know how much he regretted his decision,' Ahmar said.

She buried her face in her hands and bawled. He wanted to hold her but he couldn't as there were people around.

'He wanted you to come back home, Zarish. He wanted me to bring you back,' he explained.

'I know,' she whispered. 'But . . .'

'What?'

'I cannot leave this place. These children need me,' she said.

'But I've already talked to Maryam Apa, and she has agreed to let you go.'

'The purpose of my life has changed, Ahmar. My purpose is to help and serve these poor children. I cannot leave them,' she said and went back to her room.

Ahmar shook his head and followed her again.

He decided to leave for Lahore the next day along with Zarish. Though she did not agree to leave with him, he remained adamant.

That night, after serving dinner to the children, Zarish went back to her dorm. Ahmar did not follow her assuming that she needed some time alone. He kept himself busy with the children. When Zarish came back, she saw them playing ludo. Not wanting to interrupt, she went back in to make the beds and finish her chores. She then offered her evening prayer. It seemed she had completely devoted herself to religion. Soon the children went to sleep and Zarish served Ahmar dinner. After he was done, they went out for a walk. They found an abandoned bonfire and sat around it to keep themselves warm. She was wearing a beige-coloured salwar kameez with a maroon woollen shawl wrapped tightly around her shoulders. To Ahmar, she looked as beautiful as ever. They sat close together, their bodies almost touching.

'Are you cold?' he asked.

'I'm fine,' she replied as she slowly rubbed her hands together.

Though he wanted to reach for her hands and hold them, something held him back.

'Where is Amber? Did you marry her?' she asked out of nowhere; breaking the silence.

Ahmar sighed and told her the entire story. He told her how he took Amber and her daughter to Islamabad for Amber's treatment and how she died after a month. He also told her about Pari's adoption. Zarish burst into tears after hearing the tragic story. Ahmar put a comforting arm around her shoulder.

'Ahmar, a lot has happened since we last saw each other. We have lost people we loved,' she said.

'That's true.' He sighed. 'We've lost so much. Now I don't want to lose anything more.'

She buried her face in his shoulder and sobbed.

'Zarish, tell me one thing.'

She sat up and looked at him, her eyes moist.

'How did you manage all these years?'

'You taught me,' she answered.

'Me?' He raised a brow.

'Yes.'

'How?'

'Whenever I faced a problem, I asked myself what Ahmar would do if he was in my place, and accordingly took decisions.'

He pulled his eyebrows together in bewilderment.

'Zarish, you know what?' he asked.

She turned to look into his eyes.

'Everything is destiny's plan.'

She looked at him but did not say anything as she remembered those lines clearly. He looked back at her.

'I am sitting right next to you. We're close. We're together. Don't you think it's destiny?' He held her hand.

She pulled her hand away when she realized they were sitting too close together. He kept looking at her, amazed.

'Ahmar . . . I don't know what you expect from me, but I want you to know that I am not the same Zarish. I have changed,' she said.

'I like the new Zarish then.' He held her hand again. 'Change is good sometimes.' He smiled.

She lowered her gaze.

'For me, you're the same Zarish. Your heartbeat has the same rhythm. Your eyes have the same sparkle. Your hands have the same warmth. Your face has the same glow and still lights up when I am around. So nothing has changed and nothing ever will.'

She stood up, ignoring his words, and walked into the woods.

'Zarish . . . stop,' he called after her but she did not listen.

It started drizzling. She walked for a while until she noticed she had reached the deep part of the forest. She stopped and looked around, he was not behind her.

Suddenly someone touched her arm and she gasped. He stood in front of her, smiling. She coughed a little and then looked at him.

'Ahmar . . . you should go back. Now. Please. Don't make me weak,' she pleaded.

'I want to become your strength, Zarish,' he said, pulling her closer. 'I am here so that I can stand by you and become your support. I'm here for a reason, Zarish,' he said.

She shut her eyes as tears poured out. He wiped them with his thumb.

'If you don't want to leave, it's fine. I will stay here with you.'

'No . . . you can't!' she cried.

'Yes. I will if you do not come with me.'

She looked away helplessly.

'Your family needs you, Zarish. I need you.'

When she opened her eyes to look at him, he held her face gently.

'I need you more than you need me,' he murmured.

A sudden downpour made them look up. They were completely drenched.

'I love you, Zarish. I have always loved you, and I will always love you.' He brought his face closer to hers. 'I will never leave you. I was a fool to believe your lies. I should not have listened to you. I regret it. I know I cannot undo it. But now, I promise to always stay by your side,' he assured her.

'And forever?' she asked, finally.

'Yes,' he replied, smiling.

'Ahmar . . . I . . . I do not know what to say . . . I am sorry for ruining your life. I know I have hurt you a lot. And I . . . I do not deserve you . . .' He put a finger on her lips before she could complete the sentence.

'Don't say anything! You do not have to apologize for anything, Zarish. What is done is done. I just want to be with you. Let's start afresh. Okay?'

She didn't say anything.

'God . . . see what you've done to yourself!' he said, holding her face in his hands.

She nodded glumly. The rain was still pouring down.

'You deserve a better life. A happy and healthy life with me,' he whispered and smiled.

'Ahmar . . .' she murmured.

'Yeah?'

'I thought I had lost you forever,' she whispered.

'You haven't. I'm still with you.'

'I can't explain how glad I am to see you here. I have missed you so much,' she said as she kissed his hand.

'I'm here, Zarish. And I will always be,' he said.

'You're all wet,' she said.

'Yeah. It's all right.'

'I'm sorry,' she murmured.

'For what?' he asked.

'I wish I had an umbrella,' she said as her face lit up.

He knew what she was referring to and smiled too.

'Don't worry. It is still with me,' he said and pulled out her red umbrella from his jacket.

Zarish was shocked.

'You . . . you still have it?' she asked.

He nodded triumphantly.

She smiled as she held his other hand and brought it close to her cheek.

'I'm a bit surprised,' she whispered.

'Why?'

'I thought you had forgotten me.'

'I can never forget you, Zarish. Not in this lifetime at least. Do you know why?' he asked.

She looked into his eyes and realized they were standing too close to each other. She could almost hear his heartbeat and feel his cool breath.

'Why?' she asked.

'Remembering you is like breathing. If I cannot forget to breathe, then how can you expect me to forget you?'

She smiled and closed her eyes, feeling content.

Before leaving for Lahore the next day, Zarish promised to stay in touch with Maryam Apa and the kids. She also promised to send money no matter which part of the world she lived in.

They reached Lahore before dusk. She hesitantly stepped out of the car and looked at her house. She had come back after three years.

'Ready to meet your family?' Ahmar asked.

'I can't . . . go in,' she said.

'You have to. C'mon,' Ahmar said. 'They're waiting for you.'

Her entire family, including her brothers, stood on the porch to welcome her. Haroon and Muraad were there too. Zarish burst into tears when she saw her mother.

'Come,' Ahmar said, pushing her forward.

Zarina ran towards her daughter and hugged her. Tears rolled down her cheeks and they both held each other tightly. Her brothers came forward and hugged Ahmar, thanking him profusely. Haroon shook hands with him.

Zarina gave him a warm, happy smile and mouthed a silent 'thank you'. He nodded with a smile on his face. It was then she decided to get Zarish married to him.

Epilogue

A Few Months Later . . .

'Get off me, Ahmar!' Zarish said.

'No, I won't,' he said and wrapped his arms around her waist tightly.

'Let me make breakfast for you guys. I don't want Pari to be late for school,' she said, flipping the French toast in the pan.

He brought his face closer and stroked her big, round belly. She was eight and a half months pregnant.

'In fact, you will be late for work too,' she added.

'I don't care. I don't feel like leaving you right now,' he whispered in her ear and kissed it.

'Ahmar,' she said, trying to free herself from his hold.

'Stop fidgeting. Stand still,' he said, kissing her earlobe again.

'Pari will be here any minute,' she told him.

'Oops,' he said, stepping back.

'Thank you.' She put a chocolate chip in his mouth and pushed him away.

'Do you know how much you mean to me?' he said as he leaned against the refrigerator.

'I know,' she said, not paying attention.

'Do you know how much I love you?' he asked. 'Do you know how much I've waited for these moments?'

'I know,' she said without looking at him.

'Do you know how much I miss you at work?'

'I know everything, Ahmar,' she said as she put the plates on the table.

'Do you know how much I . . .'

She interrupted him by covering his mouth with her hand.

'Don't you get tired of repeating these lines over and over again?'

He shook his head.

'He is so handsome,' she thought.

'Why?' she asked, uncovering his mouth.

'Because my love is limitless,' he murmured. 'I can't and I won't live without you,' he said and smiled, making her blush.

'What?' he asked.

'I love you.'

'I love you more, Mrs Ahmar Muraad.'

Acknowledgements

I would like to thank the following people for inspiring me, for contributing towards my work and helping me write this book. My younger sister, Ayesha Naveed, helped me at every step of the writing process. I want to thank her for urging me on and giving me new brilliant ideas every time. She was the first person to read my book and also my first critic. I love you so much, Ashu!

I want to thank my family—my parents and my brother—for trusting me and my writing and helping me fulfil my dream of becoming a writer. Without their support and encouragement, I could not have completed this book.

I would like to thank my friends and readers for supporting and encouraging me.

A special thanks to the following people:

Thank you, Tarini Uppal, for seeing potential in my writing and giving me a chance to become a Penguin author. I owe it all to you!

Thank you, Rajni George, for forwarding my work to Tarini. You're the best!

Thank you, Meena Rajasekaran, for designing a beautiful cover for my book and giving it a brand-new look.

Thank you, Saloni Mital, for being the best copy editor and making the strenuous process of editing so easy.

Thank you, Peter Modoli, for listening to my queries and helping me out in the best possible way. You're the best publicist to work with.

Thank you, Zohaib Ahmed, for showing immeasurable support.

Thank you, Manaum Zain, for being one of my first editors and reviewers.

Thank you, Khalid Sahib, for helping me understand the nuances of writing better.

A big thank you to the amazing team at Penguin Random House India.

Lastly, I would like to express my gratitude to Fawad A. Khan for being my inspiration. I had the idea for my book for a few years but something was holding me back. He was a driving force in my life. I wrote *Undying Affinity* with him in mind. The character of Ahmar Muraad is highly inspired by Fawad—his way of speaking, body language, facial expressions, postures and movements, and even his dress sense.

I dedicate this book to you, Fawad. I deeply thank you for being the hero and centre of my story.

Last but not least, I want to thank Allah for giving me the ability and patience.